Guardian
of the
Dead

Karen Healey

LITTLE, BROWN AND COMPANY
New York   Boston

Little, Brown and Company

Hachette Book Group
237 Park Avenue, New York, NY 10017
Visit our website at www.lb-teens.com

Little, Brown and Company is a division of Hachette Book Group, Inc.
The Little, Brown name and logo are trademarks of Hachette Book Group, Inc.

The publisher is not responsible for websites (or their content) that are not
owned by the publisher.

First Paperback Edition: August 2011
First published in hardcover in April 2010 by Little, Brown and Company

Reading Group Guide prepared by Susan Geye

Library of Congress Cataloging-in-Publication Data

Healey, Karen.
Guardian of the dead / by Karen Healey. —1st ed.
p. cm.
Summary: Eighteen-year-old New Zealand boarding school student Ellie Spencer
must use her rusty tae kwon do skills and newfound magic to try to stop a fairy-like race
of creatures from Maori myth and legend that is plotting to kill millions of humans in
order to regain their lost immortality.
ISBN 978-0-316-04430-1 (hc) / ISBN 978-0-316-04438-7 (pb)
[1. Magic—Fiction. 2. Mythology, Maori—Fiction. 3. Boarding schools—Fiction.
4. Schools—Fiction. 5. Immortality—Fiction. 6. Maori (New Zealand people)—Fiction.
7. New Zealand—Fiction.] I. Title.

PZ7.H3438Gu 2010
[Fic]—dc22
2009017949

10 9 8 7 6 5 4 3 2 1

RRD-C

Printed in the United States of America

For Robyn, who has supported this
story from infancy, and for my parents,
who have done the same for me.

Part One

CHAPTER ONE

Southern Lights

I opened my eyes.

My legs were bound and my head ached. There was one dark moment of disorientation before the bad-dream fog abruptly lifted and I woke up all the way and rolled to smack the shrilling alarm. I was exactly where I was supposed to be: in my tiny room, lumpy pillow over my head and thick maroon comforter wrapped around my legs. I disentangled myself and kicked the comforter away. The muffled tinkling as it slithered off the foot of the bed reminded me that Kevin and I had stored the empty beer cans there.

Well, that explained the headache.

I could hear voices in the living room, where the other girls in our little dorm-cum-apartment were gathering. I huddled farther under the pillow, willing myself ten minutes more sleep and hangover recovery time. The wisp of a thought was drifting somewhere in the bottom of my mind, refusing to rise to the level of consciousness. Something I'd forgotten.

A truly incredible snore resounded from the boy sleeping on the floor.

I rolled out of bed so fast that I lost my balance and fell right on top of him, my full weight thumping against his impressive chest. He wheezed, his dark eyes popping open.

"Shut up!" I hissed, jamming my hands over his mouth. "It's morning!"

Kevin's eyes went from huge to enormous. The living room was horribly silent. I tensed as someone knocked on the door.

"Ellie? Are you okay?" Samia asked.

"I'm fine! I just fell!"

"Did you hurt yourself?" The doorknob rattled.

"I'm naked!" I yelped. Samia wore headscarves and long sleeves in public, but she often walked through our girls-only apartment in nothing but her underwear and for a moment I entertained the horrible vision of her ignoring my fictional nudity and coming in anyway. She'd find a boy *and* alcohol in my room, she'd tell Mrs. Chappell, I'd get expelled from boarding school, my parents would have to leave their once-in-a-lifetime dream trip around the world, and then, they would kill me.

On the other hand, being discovered lying on top of

Kevin Waldgrave would definitely improve my reputation at Mansfield for the short days I'd have remaining. I might even become someone vaguely acknowledged by the other students.

Tricky.

The doorknob stopped moving. "Oh!" she said. "See you in Geography."

"See you!" I cried weakly, and let out a sigh of relief as the noise from the living room became a shuffle of departure.

"Your breath smells like an alcoholic's ass," Kevin remarked.

I got to my feet, hauled him to his, and punched him on the shoulder, not nearly as hard as I could have. "You fell asleep!"

"So did you."

"It's *my* bedroom. And you have to get out of it before someone sees." I gave him a quick inspection, and made him zip his tracksuit up over the beer stain on his long-sleeved shirt. The light brown carpet lint I picked from the side of his face was almost the same shade as his skin, so I was lucky to catch it. His dense black hair was also a mess, but that was normal. "Okay. If you can make it to the road, you can say you went for a jog before breakfast."

"You're a genius." He grinned, then shot me an uncharacteristically shy look. "Um. And a real mate. I think I said some stuff?"

I couldn't face that conversation feeling this sick. "You have to go," I said, hating myself a little for the way he stiffened. "We'll talk later, though?"

Dark eyes looked down into mine. At six foot four, Kevin

3

was one of the few people I knew who was taller than me. He was gratifyingly wider too, though in his case it was mostly muscle. "Sure," he said. "We can talk on the way to rehearsal. Meet you at six?"

"Rehearsal for what?" I asked, and then that dream-foggy memory caught up with me. "Oh, *shit*."

"You promised," Kevin said.

"Because you got me drunk! I can't believe you!"

"Ellie, you get permission to get away from this place for a while, and all you have to do is teach the cast how to pretend to smack each other without actually smacking each other." He spread his hands, looking very reasonable.

I wasn't fooled. "I have a black belt in tae kwon do, not in...stagey fake fighting."

"You promised," he insisted. "And we really, really need you. Iris is getting pretty desperate."

Iris Tsang was a year older than us, stunningly pretty, permanently enthusiastic, and so nice it made my teeth itch. As far as I could tell, she'd also been in love with Kevin since kindergarten, completely undaunted by his lack of reciprocation. It was no wonder that she'd dragged him into her play when the original cast members had started deserting, even though all natural laws stated that first-year university students should forget all about people still at their old high schools.

This was what happened when I drank. It all seemed great at the time, and then it resulted in bad dreams and being dragged into situations where I'd have to talk to perverted egomaniacs who liked to prance around in tights, led by a woman who made me want to crawl into a total-body paper bag after ten minutes in her perfect presence.

4

"Fine," I growled. "But I'm never drinking again. Get the hell out."

"You're a real mate," he said again, and hugged me before he went out the window, which was fortunately large. The building backed onto Sheppard's celebrated gardens, and from there it was just a quick climb over the fence. I watched him jog cautiously between the trees, and then turned to the concerns of the morning.

Samia could walk around in her underwear because she was slender and had actual boobs and smooth coppery brown skin that never got pimples. *I*, burdened by skin that was less "creamy" and more "skim milk," and not at all blemish-free, avoided the mirror and peeled off my pajamas. I replaced them with my last clean long-sleeved blouse and the hideous maroon pleated skirt that stopped at mid-calf and made my legs look like tree stumps. My mustard-colored blazer was lying crumpled over my desk chair, so I grabbed the jersey instead. The scratchy wool cut into my upper arms and stretched awkwardly over my belly, leaving a bulging strip of white cotton exposed between skirt waist and jersey hem. I'd always been big, but after half a year with no exercise, living on the dining hall's stodgy vegetarian option, I'd gone up two sizes to something that I was afraid approached outright fat, without even the consolation of finally developing a decent rack. I put on knee-high gray socks—the girls were supposed to wear pantyhose, but no one ever did, just as we never wore the maroon trousers in winter instead of the stupid skirt—and slipped my feet into scuffed black shoes without untying the laces.

There. A proud representative of Mansfield College, New

Zealand's third-ranked coeducational high school, at her dubious best.

I hid the beer cans in the empty drawer under the bed and hit the communal bathroom to brush my teeth, throw freezing water on my face, and brush my hair back into a sleek ponytail. Then I hoisted my ragged backpack, pinched the bridge of my nose against the hangover headache, and stepped out into the morning mists.

The Anglican settlers, in their inspired wisdom, had established the city of Christchurch, jewel of New Zealand's South Island, in the middle of a swamp. Every leaden day of this winter I had longed for my hometown in the North Island, the clean lines of Napier's Art Deco buildings and the scattered sunlight on the sea, much brighter in my memory than it really was. In my head, I knew that I hadn't liked winter in Napier either, and that Christchurch had its fair share of crisp, bright days where the smog kept to a decent altitude. But on bad days, the musty-smelling fog seemed to rise out of the sodden ground and ooze along it, seeping into streets and buildings and my skin.

Every time I went past the drab stone mass of Sheppard Hall, I was glad I didn't have to live there with the younger girls. Sheppard had central heating and an impressively weighty tradition, but it also had lights-out times, hall patrols, and ground-floor windows that didn't open all the way. The Year Thirteen buildings were brand-new, meant to prepare us for independence at university next year, and conveniently free of most obstacles to rule-breaking late night visits.

When Mansfield had first gone coed, the board of trustees had spent some time debating where exactly the new boys' hall should go on the undeveloped land. Eventually, they'd paved Behn Street beside the girls' hall, and plunked down brand-new and well lit rugby fields on the far side of the new road. Pomare Hall, all steel and glass, and much nicer than Sheppard's drafty tower, sat smug and distant at the edge of the fields, as far from the girls' side of the boarding area as possible. The trustees hadn't been very trusting.

There were plenty of boys trudging along the path beside the fields, but no one tall enough to be Kevin. If he'd been caught, he wouldn't give me away. But if he was suspended or expelled, I'd suffer all the same. He was all I had here.

I wasn't quite sure how this had happened. I hadn't been really popular in Napier, but I'd had friends, even if I'd drifted from most of them during what I thought of as Mum's Cancer Year. When she'd recovered, she and Dad had decided to spend the remainder of the inheritance from my Granny Spencer on their lengthy trip around the world. Still suffused with relief at the recovery, I hadn't minded being left behind. I *had* minded Dad's response to my suggestion that I spend the year with my older sister in Melbourne. He was worried about her "influence," which neatly translated to: "But, Ellie, what if you also catch the gay?" And none of my remaining friends' parents had the room for me to stay.

"Boarding school," Mum had decreed. Sulking at losing my Melbourne dreams, and angry on Magda's behalf, I'd arbitrarily applied to Mansfield instead of to any of the North

Island Catholic high schools Dad would have preferred. To my own shock, I'd been accepted—at least, by the selection committee. The students had been less welcoming. They weren't really *mean;* just unwilling to open their tight social circles to a new girl. And, as I privately admitted when I wasn't too busy feeling really sorry for myself, I hadn't made much of an effort. Kevin had been a fortunate fluke—most of his friends had been in the year above. While plenty of people wanted to know him better, including most of the girls in our year, he'd settled on newcomer me.

In light of last night's confession, picking the one girl his age who wasn't eager to make kissy-face with him took on a more sinister dimension. But it had worked out well for both of us.

Unless, of course, he was expelled.

I waited at the pedestrian crossing with a cluster of younger Pomare boys, all of whom were happy to ignore me in favor of talking about the latest Eyeslasher murder.

"—heard that he keeps them around his waist like a belt."

"Yeah? My cousin said it's this cult, and the cops know who it is, but the Prime Minister's son is mixed up—"

"She doesn't have any kids, you dick!"

"—*secret* kids—"

I rolled my eyes and outpaced them when the light blinked green.

Busy mentally snorting at the appetites of fifteen-year-old boys for grisly conspiracy fantasies, I was going way too fast to stop when the girl in front of me halted abruptly at the gate. I tried to dodge sideways and ran straight into Mark

Nolan, day student, loner, and focus of more than a few of my Classics-period daydreams. Everyone but me had gotten used to him and his enigmas; as a newbie, I still had some curiosity left.

Embarrassing, then, to crash into him outside the school gates.

"Oof," he grunted, and tried to sidestep around me while I wobbled a few steps and bounced into the rough wall. He about-faced and grabbed my elbow. It was presumably to prop me up, but he didn't have the weight to support me. Caught off-balance, I staggered into him again, threatening to send us both to the ground. Giggles bubbled out of my throat, dancing on the dangerous edge between amusement and mild hysteria.

"This is no good," he said decisively, and braced himself against the wall while I put myself back on even keel. "Okay, I'm letting you go on three. One, two, three."

"Ow!" I protested, my head jerking down.

And a tingling shock ran down my spine and through my veins. It reverberated in my head, like a thunderclap exploding behind my eyes. It wasn't static electricity; it was nothing I'd ever felt before. Startled, I met Mark's eyes, and found no comfort there. The perfect planes of his pale face had rearranged themselves into something frightening. It was the same face—same high cheekbones, same arched, feathery eyebrows, same thatch of shaggy red hair—but frozen into unnatural and shocking stillness. He stared at me, inhaled sharply, and then, as I blinked and stuttered, made himself look almost ordinary again.

Mark lifted his hand, easing the sting in my scalp, and I saw the cause—a strand of my hair had come loose and wrapped itself around something silver shining on his wrist. In defiance of the uniform code, it wasn't a watch, but a bracelet made of links of hammered silver, small charms hanging off the heavy loops. The charms weren't like my childhood jewelry—no tiny ballerinas or rearing ponies—but a jumble of more ordinary things: a small key; a bottle cap; a broken sea shell; a tuft of white wool; a gray pebble with a hole in the center; a stick figure bent out of No. 8 wire. My hair was twisted around the bracelet itself, caught between a stylized plastic lightning bolt and a rusty screw.

I'd never seen the bracelet before, and that was odd because I'd shamelessly memorized every visible inch of Mark, right down to the greasy tips of his hair, which he didn't wash very often, and the way his maroon trousers were worn shiny at the knees. And those weird, compelling eyes; not blue-green or gray-green or brown-flecked hazel, but a uniform dark green, a color so pure and strong that it could (and often did) stop me dead from halfway across a room.

No one knew why anyone so good-looking seemed to make such an effort to disguise it. Rumor had it that he was super religious or a scholarship student, but the really religious kids tended to turn up well scrubbed, and the scholarships included uniforms. He took part in no school clubs, never had parents come for family days, and barely talked except in class. The only thing anyone knew for sure was that he'd been awarded the English and Latin cups every year at prizegiving, and never turned up to claim them. Samia thought he might be a communist. Kevin thought he had social anxiety. I thought he was far too pretty to be entirely real.

I'd never thought he could be *scary*.

He picked at the hair for a second, then met my eyes, now looking rueful and adorable. "Sorry, Spencer. Either I cut this loose, or we're stuck together forever." I hoped I didn't look too awestruck. Was I a giggling idiot, to be struck by lightning at my first physical contact? But then, he'd felt something too. And he knew my *name*.

"Option two is tempting, but…" I yanked at the wayward hair. It resisted, then snapped raggedly, leaving a blondish strand knotted in the bracelet. "Yuck. Sorry."

"No worries." He rubbed thoughtfully at the knot and smiled at me, a sudden flash of white, even teeth. My breath caught in my throat and I felt the blush burn in my cheeks. "I like your laugh," he said.

Apparently, that was a goodbye. He turned and strode through the school gate, head extended and fists clenched in his pockets to make bony wings, a heron stalking along a bank.

I stooped, fiddling with my shoelace until I felt my treacherous complexion was under control. That peculiar tingling sensation was still there, but it wasn't as strong as the rising wave of glee. Mark Nolan had noticed my laugh.

Mansfield's boarders' dining hall was happy to give us hot breakfasts and dinners, but school-day lunches were packed for us in the morning, and available for pick-up at the morning break. I sat huddled in my jersey at my usual bench in the covered area outside the Frances Alda music center and occupied myself in picking the bacon out of my cold BLT. No matter what I put on the order form, I never got my vegetarian options for lunch. The kitchen staff was notoriously bad at "special" diets, although Samia's sustained campaigning had finally got them to have halal beef and lamb sometimes. I was glad for her, but it didn't do me or my mood much good.

Despite my best efforts at making eye contact, Mark Nolan had sat in the back row of Classics, and resolutely ignored everyone but Professor Gribaldi all period. It was his modus operandi, but I'd been hoping for more. Some shared joke, about my clumsiness, or his bracelet, or *something*.

"Hey," Kevin said, and dropped onto the bench beside me, large and resplendent in his blazer.

I sat up straight. "Hey! Are we expelled?"

He took the piece of bacon from my fingers and dropped it into his mouth. "Yep. We'll have to run away into the woods and live on nuts and berries."

"I could eat bugs," I offered courageously. "When the hunger pangs get really bad."

He grinned. "Nah, we're good. Walked in the door, told the guys I'd gone running. Even found a fresh pair of socks. Hey, did you hear there's been another Eyeslasher murder?"

I grimaced. "Samia said in Geo. A phone psychic in Tauranga. God, I hope they catch the bastard soon."

"Me too. Murder's bad enough, but taking their eyes is sick."

"I think the murder probably matters more."

"Sure, but eyes are *tapu*, Ellie."

I blinked at him. Kevin's parents, on the two occasions

I'd met them for uncomfortable dinners, had been as stiffly Anglo-Saxon as posh New Zealanders came, but Kevin's light brown skin wasn't the result of a good tan. I knew that his great-grandmother had been Ngāi Tahu, and that he was one of the leading lights of Mansfield's *kapa haka* performance group, but I hadn't realized his desire to learn more about his roots had meant this much investment in Māori beliefs about the sacred.

"You're right. Sorry. Wait, don't you have kapa haka on Wednesdays?" I made vague hand gestures meant to invoke the poi twirling the girls did; Kevin rightly ignored me in favor of stealing my apple and holding it above my head.

"Give that back or I won't turn up to your play," I threatened. "And then there'll be no one to be the no-woman's-land between you and the admiring hordes."

I meant it as a joke, but he scowled and shoved the apple into my palms. I blinked at him, awaiting explanation.

"Iris keeps…" he said. "She keeps…looking. Like maybe I'll like her back if she can just be there enough."

"She's stalking you?"

"No!"

"You could tell her what you told me last night," I ventured. His scowl deepened.

I tried to smile, but the humor in my voice was too forced. "Come on, it can't be that hard. You just say, 'Hi. My name is Kevin. And I'm asexual.'"

Kevin stared at his big hands. "Great. You think it's like alcoholism."

"No!" I said, and tried to think of something not stupid to say. Nothing came to mind.

There was a pause while Kevin picked at his cuticles and I scraped my teeth down the apple. "Now that we're sober, just to clarify," I said at last, and let my voice trail off when my courage gave out. I couldn't stop myself from picking at scabs, either.

"I'm not gay."

"Okay," I mumbled.

Kevin's lips twisted. "People understand gay. Even if they think it's sick. But asexual . . . they don't understand someone who's not interested in sex at all."

"Really not at all?"

He flattened his hands on his thighs. "Really."

I thought about saying *Maybe you'll change your mind*, and then remembered Dad saying exactly that to Magda when she came out, and my sister's strained, white face as she fought back equal measures of fury and despair.

"Okay," I said instead, and covered one of his hands with mine. A smile appeared at the corners of his mouth and rested there a while.

"About Iris. She's my oldest friend."

I took my hand back. "I know."

"And you're my best friend," he said, matter-of-fact, as if it was something I should have already known. "I want my oldest friend and my best friend to get along, you know?"

I swallowed hard against the sudden dryness in my throat, and knew that I'd never ask if he'd only befriended me in the first place because I'd been too withdrawn to go all gooey over him. What did it matter? It was real now. "You're my best friend too."

"I'll tell her. In my time. Okay?"

"Like I should have any say in it," I said, exasperated and flattered. "Is that what you came to tell me?"

He nodded.

"Idiot. Go to kapa haka. Shout manly things."

He bumped my shoulder with his and strode away. I returned to the contemplation of my soggy sandwich. Maybe I could skip lunch too. No; that led to eating disorders and hunger headaches. I bit into the apple instead and caught a flicker of movement in my peripheral vision.

Mark Nolan was walking toward the music center, covering the ground with his stalky heron gait. His gaze was unerringly fixed on me. "Spencer."

I chewed and swallowed, little lumps of apple burning on the way down. "I do have another name." That was tarter than anything I'd rehearsed in my head while I waited for Classics, but there was no reason for him to scowl at me like that.

His frown deepened. "Eleanor?"

"Only if you're a teacher. Ellie."

"Ellie," he said. "Can I have a word? In private?"

I glanced around. Most of the older students preferred to eat in their common rooms on cold days, but there were a bunch of younger girls at a picnic table in the nearby quad, and a mixed group of Year Twelves flirting a little way beyond them.

"Sure," I said, and shouldered my backpack. We were actually the same height, I noticed; only Mark's slenderness and my slouching made him seem taller. "We can talk in the music center." I could feel an echo of that same tingling thrill, and tried to tamp it down. No need to get excited, just because someone who never spoke to anyone was talking to *me*.

He nodded shortly and led the way through the glass doors, going left at the foyer, toward the smaller practice rooms in the back. In his wake, I had little time to admire the center's blond wooden floors and atmosphere of peaceful light.

"Is something wrong?" I asked, wondering if I'd damaged the bracelet in our crash. He turned into the small corridor that led to the bathrooms. "Hey! Mark!"

He spun to face me, and I felt my breath catch at the angry tension in his face. "Did you know?" he asked, long fingers sliding over his bracelet's charms.

I stared at him, and he moved closer, bringing the blood to my cheeks. "Spencer. Do you know what you are? What you could be?"

"No," I said, dazed, knowing it was a strange question, but unable to work out why. I had no idea who I was or what I could be; wasn't that normal, for people my age? My skin felt vibrant, warm and loose, as if it might slip off and tap-dance up the walls. I giggled at the thought.

Mark ignored my laughter and muttered to himself, eyes darting around the hall. "Do you break curfew?" He was wearing that frightening face again, and his green, green eyes were intent on mine.

The euphoria vanished and I swayed back into the wall. My head was pounding. "Sometimes."

He stepped easily to the side as a skinny boy exited the bathroom, tugging at his belt. Mark's long, lean body was suddenly right next to mine, his voice clear and quiet in my ear. The hairs on the back of my neck raised. "Don't go out after dark alone," he ordered, his breath soft against my throat.

Something was *not right*. I struggled for a moment, shaking my head and shoving my palms hard against the wall, but Mark's hand clenched tight around his braceleted wrist and my resistance faded. "No," I said. "I won't."

The tension went out of his shoulders and his hands relaxed. "Okay, Spencer. I'll see you later." He hesitated a second. "Sorry," he added. "I had no idea." Then he brushed past me and vanished around the corner, back stiff against some invisible strain.

I walked into the bathroom, uncertain of why my cheeks were flushed, and unable to remember how I'd gotten there. I had the dimming notion of an odd conversation, but not of whom I'd spoken to or what had been said. When I tried to mentally retrace my steps, my scalp suddenly stung as if I'd been yanking out fistfuls of hair. The pain swallowed whatever had jolted my memory, and I splashed water onto my face and frowned in the mirror until the color in my cheeks faded.

"You," I said softly, "are never drinking again."

CHAPTER TWO
Suddenly Strange

Mrs. Chappell was the Sheppard Hall Dorm Officer, which was the new term for Matron. She had a bony face, a thin platinum bob, a rotating set of pastel cardigans, and, it was rumored, her husband's skeleton arranged neatly on his side of the bed, not that I could catch any glimpse of the alleged bones from my uncomfortable seat in her austerely decorated office.

I needed her permission to attend Iris Tsang's heavy rehearsal schedule, so I had taken the trouble to change into my nicest pair of jeans and my best-fitting pink wool sweater under my black winter coat, and the effort seemed to be paying off. My lack of school spirit had not endeared me to Mrs. Chappell, but when I explained I was trying to increase my participation in extra-curricular activities, she very nearly managed a smile.

"I must say, it's good to see you with some enthusiasm for something, Eleanor. Even if it is an out-of-school affair."

I beamed. "I'm very interested in stage production."

"My nephew is a costume designer, you know. He works in Wellington."

"How interesting!"

"He once helped in a rush at Weta Workshop with that Peter Jackson," she confided, and then straightened, hair swinging stiffly. "Now, as this is a non-Mansfield activity, I will need your parents' written permission."

I nodded gravely. "My mother said it was okay in this email from Florence." I was mildly proud of myself. I'd even looked up today's weather for Tuscany to give the forgery that extra-realistic touch.

Mrs. Chappell made a pretense of looking the printout over. "We would normally prefer a signature, but under the circumstances, I suppose that will be fine. How will you be traveling to and from the university?" She gave me a stare that was probably supposed to frighten details of non-approved debauchery out of me.

I smiled and looked straight back. "Kevin Waldgrave has car privileges and his full license. He'll be attending all the rehearsals I'm going to and he's offered to escort me."

Mentioning golden boy Kevin, scientific genius and— as far as the school knew—perfect boarder, neatly did the trick. "Excellent. We don't want you girls wandering around at night with that awful murderer on the loose."

I refrained from pointing out that all the Eyeslasher murders had been in the North Island, and that only one of the five victims had been female, and nodded obediently.

"All right. As with weekend and ordinary after school leave, you will sign out on leaving and in on returning, and be back in your building by ten p.m. This is, of course, conditional on your completing all your homework and class work to your usual standards. Having no official lights-out for the senior girls doesn't mean you can stay up until the wee hours completing rushed assignments."

"Thank you," I said, realizing that I would actually have to do this. Oh well. Kevin would be happy, anyway.

Mrs. Chappell pursed her lips. "Have you given any further consideration to what you might study at university next year, Eleanor?"

Typical Mansfield. Ambushing you with the grim prospect of Your Future every other time you turned around. "I thought a Bachelor of Teaching at Waikato. Like my mum."

"Professor Gribaldi has noted your good work in Classics."

"Really?" I blurted, then shut my mouth at her raised eyebrow. Classics was my favorite subject, and I'd always managed decent marks, but La Gribaldi had made me love class more than I'd have thought possible. She had her share of eccentricities—like insisting on *Professor* instead of Ms.—but she demanded nothing less than the best from her students, and I ended up giving it. If she'd complimented me to someone else, I must have been somehow nearing her astronomical standards. But Waikato didn't offer any Classics courses.

"Mmm." As if regretting the almost-warmth, Mrs. Chappell glanced at the golden watch swinging around her skinny wrist. "Well, I think you'd better get going, don't you? You don't want to be late for your first day."

I levered myself out of the chair, which was reluctant to release me. "Thank you, Mrs. Chappell."

"You're welcome, Eleanor. I will look forward to attending one of the performances."

Oh, excellent. I managed a sickly smile and edged my way out of the office.

Kevin was waiting on Behn Road, looking unreasonably good in a pair of dark jeans and a maroon school rugby jersey. "Yes?"

I rolled my eyes. "You sound nervous. 'It's a sure thing, Ellie. It's just a formality, Ellie.' You didn't mention 'You'll get thoroughly interrogated, Ellie.'"

His eyes went huge and round, but before he could panic I gave him the thumbs-up and crossed the road, heading toward the car park. "Of course it was a yes. I am a master."

His grin flashed. "Mistress, I think."

"Sexist," I scoffed. Kevin's ancient blue Volkswagen Beetle wasn't with the other boarder cars. "Where's Theodore?"

"Iris borrowed him yesterday. We'll have to walk."

"I *just* told Chappell—"

"Only this first time," he said. "Come on, it's not far."

I glanced at the gray sky. The dim reddish glow of the sun was settling on the mountains to the west of Canterbury's wide, flat plains. "It's getting pretty late," I said, scrubbing my gloved hands against my denim-clad thighs. In mid-winter, sunset came in the late afternoon. It would be nearly dark by the time we followed the creek to the university grounds.

Kevin snorted. "Since when does that bother you?"

There was a twisting pain in my scalp. "Since... I don't know." There was something I wasn't remembering, something important.

"You're Wonder Woman. I'm counting on you to protect me." He took a few steps down the path and then turned when I failed to follow, looking mystified, then concerned. "You're really worried about this?"

"I — I won't be alone."

Kevin touched my shoulder. "I'll be right here."

"I can't go out alone," I said, not entirely coherently, and managed to make my legs work. The prickling sensation in my head eased after a few steps, but I glanced nervously at the gathering fog. It was ridiculous, was what it was. "Bloody Chappell. She started in on the Eyeslasher and now she's got *me* scared."

"Oh," Kevin said, in tones of enlightenment. After a brief pause, he continued. "So, did you hear that Mr. Reweti nearly blew up the lab this afternoon?"

I let him go on about the interesting properties of potassium, the monologue washing over me as I settled into the freedom of being outside the school on a weekday. Most of the weekends were our own, provided we didn't drink or smoke (even if, like eighteen-year-old Kevin, we were legally allowed to) or violate curfew. And it wasn't hard to get permission for after-school leave. But I was used to a more complete freedom — I'd been able to roam Napier at will since I turned sixteen. My parents trusted me, and had relied on me during the Cancer Year; Mansfield's rulebook treated me like a stupid kid, and I found myself acting like one. Drinking in my room was a total moron move, and it hadn't been the first time.

Kevin's chatter trailed off after a while, and we walked in friendly silence. Even cold and smog and the thick smell of burning couldn't make the path completely unpleasant. Ducks floated serenely along the creek, occasionally passing on an important piece of duck-related news. The houses between Mansfield and the university were invariably owned by the wealthy, and lush lawns and well kept gardens showed in glimpses over red brick walls. Most of the gardens were populated with imported English varieties, but there were a couple of house owners who had made some effort with native New Zealand vegetation, and the dark greens and rich browns stood out among the bleak, bare branches of the non-native trees that seemed to claw at the gray air.

We followed the creek, which divided one of the university halls of residence from another, and cut into the sports fields that stretched all the way to the edge of the university proper. Wet grass and mud squelched under my sneakers. There were going to be boys in the play — possibly hot university boys — but choosing not to wear my decent boots in this muck had obviously been the right decision. Still some way distant, the tall column of the main library loomed up to dominate the skyline. Kevin picked up the pace; I pointedly checked my battered watch.

"Got to pee," he said. "I'll jog ahead."

"It's getting dark," I protested, but not too loudly. There were plenty of people around now, students lugging backpacks and making their way back to their halls for dinner. The important thing was that I not be alone.

"Sorry," Kevin said, not sounding very sorry, and took off at something close to a dead run.

"I can't take you anywhere!" I yelled after him, and continued at my own speed. I could have kept up, but only at the price of arriving sweaty and rumpled. Iris made me feel grubby even at my most polished and composed; there was no point in spotting her an advantage.

We were supposed to be meeting in the student union building. I was vaguely familiar with the university grounds — Mansfield students were allowed to use the library, which was much better stocked and stayed open later than ours — and the fastest way there would have been to turn south at the road and walk straight down the block to hit the student union parking lot.

But I was enjoying the walk, and I still owed Kevin for dragging me into this. It would serve him right if he had to wait for me. I carried straight on into the university. Out of my school uniform, I could pass for a first-year student, I thought. Maybe even a second-year. Studying Commerce, maybe, or Law, or Forestry. Or Classics — why not, in a daydream, even if it was useless for getting a job — a Classics honors student, soberly occupied with a translation of Euripides that would make her famous and admired the world over...

Caught up in the fantasy, I realized I was in danger of walking right through the campus. I dodged around two girls practicing Māori as they walked, turned southwest at the next path, and found myself in a strange spot I hadn't seen before.

The ground had been shaped into a semicircular hill—an amphitheater, really, sloping down to an outdoor concrete stage jutting out of the building behind it. The cherry trees that studded the top of the rise must have looked pretty in bloom, but now their black branches glinted sullenly in the heavy air and the feet of other shortcutters had churned a straight line of muck through the grass, up and over the slope. I avoided that sodden path as I crested the hill, more out of fear that my worn sneakers might skid than out of fastidiousness.

With a shiver of fear, I saw that the others had all vanished into school buildings or other paths.

I was alone, in the growing darkness, when the red-haired woman walked out of the fog.

I ducked my head nervously, but though she surveyed me from my sneakers to the collar of my coat, she didn't meet my eyes. I gained the impression that, my heavy body being of no interest, my face could hold nothing more, and flushed, half-furious, half-ashamed. Of her, I saw white skin, red hair, piled and pinned, and a tight, short-waisted jacket.

As she came closer, her beauty struck me, almost physically— a weird, ageless beauty that lifted the hairs on the back of my neck. I felt like an alley cat, bristling at the sudden appearance of a Siamese.

I pulled my hands out of my coat pockets. She was almost as tall as I was, but her wrists were delicate and the high sweep of her cheekbones almost painfully fragile. If it came to a fight, I could hit for her face, and run.

The rush of aggression subsided a little in the bloody horror of that image. My hands were in fists so tight they squeezed my bitten-down nails into my palms and I forced them flat against my thighs. They stiffened there, blades of bone and sinew.

But the gesture gained her attention. She tilted a glance at me as she passed, and I saw her eyes, undimmed by dusk and fog. They were strong and dark—like greenstone under water—but there was something wrong with them. It took me a long moment to realize that her face gave reason to my fears.

The woman had no pupils.

A shout stalled in my throat as she regarded me with that inhuman gaze for seconds my heart stammered out in double time. My throat was too dry for words, too tight for air; I felt breath whistle harshly out through my nose and a straining tightness in my chest.

Then she smiled slightly and stepped past me, precise and measured through the mud.

I managed a sound that was more a whimper than a cry and scrambled up the rest of the slope, bracing myself against a tree trunk before I dared to look after her. I half-expected her to have vanished, but I could still make out the straight line of her back through the fog. When she did disappear, it was into one of the university buildings, via a door held open by one of a group of chattering boys. One of them brushed against her, and I saw her move with the impact before he made his cheerful apology.

I was panting like a dog, breath coming in short sharp huffs of chilly air. Head pounding, I leaned against the rough trunk and tried to put my thoughts back in order.

She wasn't a ghost. Just someone with weird contact

lenses, a fetish for Victoriana, and bad manners. Any campus had its share of crazies who got their fun out of scaring the normal people.

"Hi, Ellie!" someone chirped behind me, and I screamed and whipped round, my hands ready to strike.

Iris Tsang stepped backward hastily, her sleek fall of black hair swinging back and forth across her shoulders. She looked alarmed, as well she might, with a giant girl screaming at her.

I leaned one hand against the tree and bent my head as the adrenaline subsided again, fighting the urge to pant some more. "Oh, my God! I'm sorry! Oh, God!" So much for polished and composed.

"It's okay. Are you all right? You're completely white!"

"I've always been white," I cracked feebly, and straightened to give her my usual envious once-over. I knew that "China doll" was racist, even just in my head, but I couldn't help thinking it. Iris had skin like fragile porcelain, dark eyes that tilted sweetly under a delicate fold of eyelid, and that gratuitously gorgeous hair. I was proud of my own hair, which was blond and straight, and the only thing that was vaguely pretty about me, but Iris had me beat without even trying. And *she* was wearing boots, knee-high black ones that looked great with her gray skirt and white sweater.

"What happened?"

I frowned. "Nothing. I was just...it's spooky, I guess. The fog."

She nodded sympathetically. "Well, come on in. We're in the lower common room tonight. Oh! Did you hear? We found a new Titania!"

I fell in beside her as we went down the hill and across the bridge over the creek. Passersby looked at us, and I bristled inwardly at the inevitable comparison, hunching down into my coat. "I didn't know you'd lost a Titania."

"Sarah pulled out *yesterday*, and with only three weeks to go, can you believe it? I thought we might have to promote one of the fairies. But Reka got a hold of me." She frowned a little. "She had some conditions...oh, well, I'll explain when I can talk to everyone. And thank *you* so much for helping! I just have no idea what to do with the fight scenes."

She really did look grateful. "No problem," I said, and resolved to be a nicer person, kind to animals and old people and irritatingly gorgeous nice girls who had never done me any harm.

The rehearsal room was filled with earnest, stretching people in white martial arts uniforms, which, unless Iris had vastly underestimated the fighting abilities of her cast, seemed out of the ordinary for a rehearsal. Kevin was just sticking a notice on the door when we arrived.

"We've been booted out by the karate club. We get the theater."

Iris sighed.

"Isn't that better?" I asked.

"It's freezing in the theater," Kevin explained. "Iris, why can't we do this outside? In summer?"

Iris smiled at him. "One, the only reason a mere first year is directing is because no one else wanted to take on a production this close to exams. Two, my directorial vision requires a decent set. And three, I want to do it now, and you're helping me out because you love me. Did I miss anything?"

Kevin's smile suddenly looked forced.

"Four, he's allergic to bees," I said quickly.

Iris turned to me, eyes shining brightly. "Oh, of course. Four, possible horrible death."

"Iris!" someone cried from behind us, and I twisted to see a pair of petite girls in the student uniform of sweatpants and pink polar fleece hoodies coming up the stairs. "Oh, how are we translated?" the smaller one asked, which made no sense to me at all.

"Transported, more like," Iris said, and pointed down the corridor. "To the theater."

We wandered through the smokers' lounge and past the photos of past student executives, beginning with the faded black and white photos of the early 1900s. Kevin tossed a mock salute at his missing Great-Uncle Bob when we passed his photo, and we had to stop so Kevin could explain the tragic story of his uncle's disappearance to the two girls. The photograph had been taken in 1939, a week before he'd gone missing. The boyish, handsome face was eerily similar to Kevin's—a bit darker, maybe—but some photographer's trick had given Robert Waldgrave's dark eyes an intense, suppressed excitement that Kevin had never demonstrated.

The girls made the expected sad noises at the story and then introduced themselves to me as Carrie and Carla. They were playing Helena and Hermia, and they were delighted that I was going to teach them how to catfight properly. I wondered if Iris had cast them for the alliteration, but she was staring pensively at Kevin, and I didn't ask. I began to edge forward, and the girls followed me, talking about the fight.

"I thought we could fall over things," blond Carrie said. "Like, maybe I break a walking stick on her, and then she tugs at my foot and we roll around. And then I kick her in the face!"

I pictured the impact of Carrie's flailing shoe against Carla's snub brown nose. "I'll work something out," I said diplomatically.

"Nothing that tears at clothes," Carla said. "We're renting all the Edwardian stuff."

"Carla's doing costumes," Kevin informed me. "Since the original costume designer quit."

"Do you want to be onstage too?" Iris said, perking up. "You could be a fairy, Ellie."

"What do fairies wear?"

"Bodysuits," Carla said promptly. "With *koru* designs drawn on them, and the girls get grass skirts."

I envisioned myself on stage, wearing spandex decorated in curling patterns and surrounded by tiny women like these. "Ah...no. Thanks."

"I'm glad I don't have to wear one," Carrie chirped, rubbing her flat stomach. "I've put on the first-year fifteen pounds since March!" I was probably imagining her sly look at my bulk, I told myself, uncomfortably aware that my "dinner" had comprised three chocolate chip cookies and four pieces of peanut butter toast. I *had* to get some exercise. My tae kwon do gear bag was in my wardrobe, untouched since I'd moved down in February. Maybe I could join the university karate club after the play. It might be interesting to see how they did it.

We had come to the end of the corridor, and entered the wide lobby. Kevin pushed on the wide, pale blue doors, emblazoned with "Ngaio Marsh Theatre" in flowing script, and ushered us in.

"Are any other—" I began, but I had spoken into one of those sudden silences that occasionally punctuate group conversations. All the strangers gathered on the stage looked up at us.

Empty, the theater was immense and intimidating. The black side curtains were tied up in enormous knots, and the undressed stage stretched all the way back to the brick wall. The group of shivering bodies clustered on the stage's scarred wooden floor barely covered a tenth of it.

I skirted the sunken orchestra pit and joined them, making abortive attempts to smooth down my hair.

Iris beamed at me. "Okay, guys, this is Ellie Spencer, from Mansfield, like Kevin! She's our fight choreographer!" She clapped. Everyone joined in.

"Hi," I said, through my teeth, hoping it looked like a smile. There *were* cute boys, but none of them looked enthused by my introduction as a mere high school kid. Probably not even my nice boots would have helped.

"It's good to see everyone here on time!" Iris said encouragingly.

"Sarah's not," Carrie pointed out.

"Sarah left," Iris told her, but before the groan from the other cast members could swell into real protest, she held out her hands. "It's okay! We have a new Titania lined up already. Reka Gordon."

"Why did Sarah quit?" one of the boys asked, looking disgruntled. I'd noticed him right away—he wasn't really tall enough for me, but I liked his brown curls and wide mouth.

Iris paused, a look of momentary confusion flickering over her face. "You'd have to ask her yourself," she said, then rallied. "But I'm sure it was a good reason."

"What's this Reka done?" he persisted.

Iris blinked again. "Oh, lots of things," she said. "She's just moved here, I think, so nothing recent...she *has* done *Dream* before, though, so that's a real bonus. Just one thing, though, before she joins us! She's allergic to the smell of cooked food. So we can't bring anything that smells to rehearsal." She picked up her notebook and smiled hopefully at the group.

Kevin raised his hand. "She's allergic to the *smell* of cooked food."

Iris nodded.

"That's—uh...I've never heard of that."

"Like, is she allergic to peanuts?" Carrie asked, pretty nose wrinkling. "Because that's airborne allergies. My cousin can't be around satay."

"Cooked food," Iris said swiftly. "All cooked food. Okay?" Her voice was composed, but I could see her hands tensing and relaxing in her lap. "She's joining us a little later. Let's get warmed up."

I squished myself into one of the seats in the row nearest the stage and watched as she marshaled everyone into a circle like a hyper-efficient sheepdog and took the cast through a series of increasingly bizarre physical, vocal, and mental warm-ups. I couldn't really see the point of making people howl, or asking them to visualize themselves dropping into a pool of black ink, or having them all clap in unison, but they did look more focused and intent when they were finished, so what did I know? And brown-curls boy looked even more interesting with his face screwed up in concentration.

"Okay, Ellie! How do you want to start?"

Panic swamped me. I'd been so intent on complaining about Kevin making me do this that I hadn't come up with any practicalities. "How about if I see the scenes like you've got them, and then come up with some ideas?"

Iris nodded as if that made perfect sense. "Okay! Act three, scene two. From Helena's entrance."

Carrie and Carla eagerly disappeared into the wings, and two boys whose names I had already forgotten began mock-punching each other, while another two sat at the back of the stage. Everyone else trooped into the auditorium, setting up camp in the front rows. Iris sat down beside me, so I took out a notebook and tried to look serious.

Carrie ran from the wings, pursued by one of the boys protesting his enchanted love for her. I'd studied *A Midsummer Night's Dream* in Year Eleven, but it was hard to follow Shakespeare's lines at speed. I thought that they were probably pretty good, though. Carrie's Helena was maybe a little too stagy, but Carla's Hermia was really distraught. Brown-curls boy was playing Puck, and he caught my eye more than once, smirking gnomishly to himself, or lifting his fingers in gestures that mocked the girls' earnest arguments.

Carla floated around in front of her Lysander in a pretty useless attempt to stop him dueling, then turned on Carrie, launching into the speech about their comparative heights. It came off oddly, since they were almost the same size, but I grimaced when she scorned Carrie's "tall personage."

"I am not yet so low but that my nails cannot reach unto

your eyes!" she declared in a rising shriek, and then stopped, looking expectantly at me. "And then we fight."

I nodded. "Just speak the lines you say during."

She looked disappointed, but they continued until the boys stormed off to duel and the girls followed in bemusement.

Iris twisted to smile at me. "Any ideas?"

To my surprise, I did have a few. It wouldn't be real training, but I could make them look a little less like actors and a little more like girls who genuinely wanted to hurt each other. "I think so. Is there someplace I can take them to try it?"

"The greenroom is back there," she said, pointing to the right wing.

Kevin tagged along, either to offer support or out of boredom. Backstage was dimly lit, and we walked cautiously around untidy piles of wood cut-offs and rolls of canvas. The chill air smelled of paint and sawdust, simultaneously sharp and musty. I shivered and tucked my numbing fingers into my coat pockets.

"How old are you, Ellie?" Carrie asked.

"Seventeen."

"Really? I thought you might be older. You're so tall."

"I noticed that myself," I said blandly, and watched her cover her fluster by reaching for the greenroom door.

The handle yanked out of her grip as the door swung abruptly back. Carrie stumbled forward, narrowly avoiding collision with the red-haired woman on the other side.

"Careful," she snapped, and strode through. She looked ready to move right through us, before she spotted Kevin and her whole demeanor changed. From the cool scorn of her lovely face she produced a beautiful smile, and aimed it directly at him.

Reflexively, Kevin smiled back.

The moment hung in the dusty air, and then the woman made a neat quarter-turn on the heel of her ankle boots and stepped surely onto the stage. The bare lighting edged her red hair with gold before she moved into the auditorium and out of sight.

Kevin stared after her.

"Is *that* Reka?" Carla wondered.

I was staring myself, but with the shock of recognition. In the fog she'd looked no age at all, and now she looked in her early twenties, just a few years older than me. But all the mystery of that odd encounter was explained—clearly an involvement in student theater was sufficient reason for strange clothes and weird contacts. Although she must have taken them out. The light from the green room had shown two perfectly normal pupils in her dark green eyes.

"She must be," I said. "Let's get started."

CHAPTER THREE
Sitting Inside My Head

The greenroom wasn't green. One of the sagging couches was, though, a sort of greenish-brown that I hoped was just faded upholstery, and not mold. The walls had once been off-white, now much more off than white, and the ragged curtains over the dressing room windows were black burlap, clearly there to ward off prying eyes during costume changes, and not as decoration. The three small dressing rooms didn't have doors, though, so apparently it was only outside eyes they were worried about. Or maybe shy people changed in the bathrooms.

It smelled comfortingly similar to the backstage of my Napier school hall-and-theater—closed air and old sweat, sweet baby powder and the sharp scent of cold cream. I took a deep whiff and tried to stop the irritation from showing on my face. We'd been practicing for half an hour, and they still wouldn't stop arguing with me.

"So I can't kick her in the face?" Carrie complained. I was beginning to think it was her default tone.

"It would be hard to look realistic without actually kicking her in the face. Especially since—you'll be wearing shoes, right?"

"Boots," Carla supplied, looking apprehensive. "Like those ones Reka was wearing."

I shook my head. "Bare feet can do more than enough damage."

"I'd be careful," Carrie insisted.

Muscles bunched in my jaw. "If you made contact, you could break her nose, cheekbones, teeth, jaw, or the orbit of her eye, give her a concussion or make her bite through her tongue. And if you missed very badly, you could crush her windpipe."

"And you probably wouldn't even see it from the fifth row back," Kevin added.

Carrie dropped her gaze. "I just want it to look good," she said, tugging her polar fleece hem with short, sharp motions.

"Let's practice the shoving again" Carla said quickly, going to stand between the boys. "Um, right. Lysander, whereto tends all this?"

"Away, you Ethiope!" Lysander scowled and gave her

a hearty shove that sent her stumbling halfway across the room.

"No!" I shouted. "Lysander—"

"Patrick."

"Right, Patrick—you can't just push her like that. The movement comes from her. You okay, Carla? Then let's try it again, *slowly*."

My brief temper tantrum had at least shut Carrie up for a while. We went through the rest of the scene until the bones of some decent work were there and I was sure they weren't going to hurt themselves or each other accidentally, then called a break.

On stage, Reka Gordon was cooing over the stocky dark boy who played Bottom. She was really, really good, and I didn't want her to be. I knew it wasn't fair to dislike her without giving her a chance, but my skin crawled unpleasantly when I thought of that meeting on the hill and her creepy eyes. We waited in the wings until she yawned delicately and curled gracefully into sleep around the boy. She raised her head and shot us an irritated glare when we came in anyway.

Iris was taking notes in her neat handwriting, but she immediately turned to me when I sat beside her.

"Did it go okay?" she whispered.

"It needs more practice," I whispered back. "It's pretty rough-looking up close."

Iris waved behind us at the vast expanse of the auditorium. "The forty-foot rule can take care of a lot of it," she said. "So, what do you think? Can you make it to the next three rehearsals?"

I nodded, and felt ashamed of myself for not liking her

more when she looked so grateful. "You're the best, Ellie!" She jumped to her feet. "Guys, it's costume fitting time! Come on back."

Everyone perked up and bounced toward the greenroom—except Reka, who apparently did not bounce; me, who was largely uninterested; and Kevin, who lagged behind to speak to me.

"Don't you want to play dress-up?" I asked.

"Oh, I do," he said, grinning. "I was holding out for Theseus in a feather cloak, but none of the local elders wanted to lend a *taonga* that precious to a bunch of ignorant students."

"Theseus is Māori?" I wondered.

Kevin pointed at his chest. "Duh. It's a reimagining of Shakespeare's classic comedy for extra extreme relevance to modern New Zealand audiences. Come on, I told you this. Last night."

"Oh, last night," I said pointedly. "I think I remember bits of it, before someone got me drunk and nearly expelled and dragged me into his play."

"Come on, don't lie. You love it."

I sighed and surrendered. "Okay. I like teaching."

"Say, 'Thank you, Kevin.'"

"Get stuffed, Kevin."

Throughout, I'd been conscious of Reka, waiting at my shoulder. She didn't fake patience very well, and the second the conversation lagged she stuck her hand out at Kevin. "Hello," she said, smiling. "I'm Reka Gordon." Her voice had an accent I couldn't place, part upper class English, part something that purred around the vowels. Her acting voice had been pure Royal Shakespeare Company.

Kevin's social training kicked in. He took her hand and gripped it firmly. "Kevin Waldgrave. And this is Ellie."

"We've met," I put in. "Briefly."

Reka's eyes flicked toward me, then back to Kevin's face. She was directing that beautiful smile at him again, and I wondered if I'd imagined that brief glimpse of surprise and malice in her glance at me. Kevin, unusually, hadn't let go of her hand as soon as was polite. He was smiling back, looking slightly dazed.

It wasn't fair. I was doomed to be surrounded by beautiful people being beautiful at each other.

"Come on," Iris called from the wings, and Kevin dropped Reka's hand. I thought Iris's mock frown wasn't entirely faked. "I want to see if Sarah's costume might fit you, Reka."

"Coming," Kevin said, and led the way to the greenroom.

The reason Iris had borrowed Kevin's car became apparent, as bags and boxes disgorged from Theodore's trunk and backseat. I did my bit, carrying in a long white cardboard box. It was light in my hands, and I thought it must contain something delicate, so I sat on the sagging couch with the box in my lap, balancing it over my knees. It was about the size of three of my Granny Spencer's old hatboxes stuck together, but much flatter.

The greenroom was crowded with activity. Some of the actors were already snatching up costumes, cooing over the lush fabrics and darting in and out of the dressing rooms in states of undress that might have made Samia blush. Well, definitely would have. She was very careful about being covered up in front of boys.

Iris was talking into her cell phone, looking increasingly

more strained, and I shamelessly eavesdropped. "Well, of course, your exams are important. Yes, yes, but you did say… all right, can you just give us everything you've already organized? … really. No, no, that's fine. I'm sure we'll find someone to take over. Thanks for letting me know." She snapped the phone closed and took a deep breath. "Well! Malika's quit." She shook her head and darted into one of the dressing rooms.

"Who's Malika?" I asked the room at large.

"The props mistress," sighed the guy who was playing Puck. He sat down beside me, wide mouth quirking. "This production is cursed. That's what we get for putting a first year in charge."

"If you didn't want a first year, why did you make Iris the director?" I asked tartly. "She looks like she's doing a good job to me. And how old are *you*?"

He grinned and waved spindly fingers. "Oh, I'm an ancient and world-wise twenty. Forgive the complaint; she's doing fine. She shouldn't even have to do all this, but the producer is useless. What's in the box?"

"All the evils sent to plague mankind."

"Hah! Someone's a classical scholar."

"I just like Greek myths," I said, absurdly pleased. It was ridiculous to be so thrilled just because a university student thought I'd said something clever. Too late, I remembered that Pandora had actually opened a jar, not a box, but he didn't seem to have noticed the slip.

Carrie waltzed over and sat in Puck's lap, wrapping one arm around his shoulders. I swallowed envy and tried not to let it show on my face. "This is a disaster," she moaned.

"Just a small one," he told her. "There's hope still." He winked at me, and I grinned back. Carrie, reacting to either the disagreement or the wink, glared at me.

"What's this?" she asked, and grabbed for the box on my lap. I let her take it and she ripped the lid off to reveal a pile of costume jewelry. I reached out curiously but she backed away. "Don't smudge them!"

"They're plastic, Carrie," Puck said, raising his thick eyebrows, and I decided to like him, girlfriend and all.

She hesitated, then inclined her head. "Sorry. I'm a bit stressed. This damn show." She handed the box to me and sat back in Puck's lap.

"Everything will be fine," Iris said, appearing out of nowhere like a perky jack-in-the-box. "Now, can anyone help me with props on Saturday afternoon?"

"I've got to study," Puck said.

"Me too," Carrie said, wriggling a little more into his lap.

Iris's shoulders bent infinitesimally. "Okay! I'm sure I can manage by myself."

"I can probably help," I blurted. "Where are we going?"

"Oh, *fantastic*. Just into Cathedral Square. Kevin said we can use Theodore, so it shouldn't take more than a couple of hours. Thank you so much!"

Oh, *God*. A city center full of people looking at Iris and me and making the inevitable comparison. "Sure," I said weakly. "No problem."

She whirled away again. Carrie shook her head and stalked off, bullying Lysander and Demetrius into helping her carry out bags.

Puck sighed happily and got up. "Show business," he said, and sauntered into the crowd.

Kevin came over to add my box of fake jewels to the pile in his arms. "I saw that. You'd better watch it; people might start to think you're nice."

I gestured at the chaos—Carla trying to duct tape a bodice onto busty Hippolyta, Demetrius and Lysander trying to whip each other with rolled-up scarves, Reka leaning against the wall and ignoring everything but Kevin—and screwed up my face. "Hardly. Kevin, I'm not sure if you've noticed this, but you and all of your friends are insane."

"Don't put yourself down, Ellie," he said, shaking his head wisely. "You need all the self-esteem you can get."

By nine-thirty the security guard had appeared to boot us all out and Puck had laughed at three more of my jokes.

Iris was the last to leave, locking the outside door of the greenroom with her own key, and stepping carefully down the narrow flight of stairs that slanted to the mist-dampened parking lot. I was huddled outside Theodore, waiting for Kevin to unlock the bloody doors. Reka was hanging around too, apparently trying to get Kevin to drop her home.

"Sure," he said easily. "You, then Iris, then Ellie and me. Where do you live?"

For the first time, that melting smile vanished while she

was looking at him. "Never mind," she said at last, putting her face back together. "It's not a bad night. I'll walk."

It was freezing, and wisps of fog still hung heavy in the air. Reka walked around the corner of the theater's foundations and disappeared. Kevin looked as if he might call her back, then shrugged and finally let us into the car. I hugged my cramped knees and shivered until the ancient heater warmed up.

Iris lived fairly close to the university and to Mansfield, along one of the roads that wound about the little rivers that cut through the city. On the way Kevin was less talkative than usual; Iris was much more so, chattering about blocking and budgets and set design. "Oh, look, Ellie," she interrupted herself, leaning over my shoulder and pointing. "That's Riccarton Bush. Have you ever been?"

I craned to make out the rounded heads of kahikatea trees rising over the dark houses. "No. That's the patch of original forest, right?"

"Yes. Right in the middle of Christchurch. They've stuck a big wire fence around it to keep bird predators out, so it's really left as it would have been before. The family of the first settlers left it to the city government on the condition that it never be cleared."

"The first *white* settlers," Kevin murmured, and took a right. The Bush dropped away behind us. "We should go in the summer, Ellie. There's a boardwalk, it's cool."

"We should definitely go," Iris agreed, and I fought the urge to say that *she* hadn't been invited. Kevin seemed to be working himself up to his promised confession, and being nasty to Iris right now would be even more than usually like kicking a cute but annoying puppy.

Sure enough, when we stopped outside Iris's neatly painted front door, Kevin offered to walk her to the door and in, shooting me a look that I had no trouble interpreting as an invitation to stay in the car with my book for company. At least he left me the keys, to drive the engine and keep the heat running.

I did more worrying than reading, biting at my already well gnawed nails. There were so many ways this could go wrong. Iris could react to Kevin's revelation like my parents had to Magda's. She could laugh at him, or insist he must be wrong, or tell him it was just a phase, or any number of other horrible, devastating things. Kevin was the second-bravest person I knew, I reflected. I wouldn't have had the guts to do it in a thousand years.

When he returned, Kevin's face was tight and closed in the car's internal light. I could see no trace of tears in the few seconds it took him to turn off the light and brace his arms against the wheel, bending his big head into the tense darkness there.

I was horribly curious, but it could definitely wait until tomorrow. "It's been a long day," I said.

Kevin sat up straight. I caught the white flash of teeth as he directed half a smile at me. "Yeah. Let's go home."

First period on Friday mornings was school assembly, where the principal made announcements and handed out awards to sporting, academic, and cultural high-achievers (not me).

Musically or dramatically talented students (definitely not me) were given an opportunity to perform for an audience of their bored and whispering peers. This week's performance was a skit by several fellow Year Thirteens, featuring students fearfully discussing which of the substitute teachers might be taking over their Geography class. It turned out it was only the Eyeslasher (Jeff Forbes, in a balaclava, with a knife I was betting he'd swiped from the kitchen) and they were all really relieved.

A lot of people thought this was hilarious, but I wasn't impressed. Real people with real families were dying, outside these walls. I leaned back into the uncomfortable wooden bench, trying not to crowd the people on either side of me, and wishing I hadn't eaten quite so many scrambled eggs that morning. I was relieved when we were finally allowed to stand and make our way through a limping rendition of the school song.

Second period on Friday mornings was Classics, which meant there were several good reasons to make it through assembly. I managed to snag one of the desks at the back, not too far from the best of those reasons, but my usual practice of picturing Mark Nolan with his shirt off was continually disrupted by a vague and traitorous memory. I couldn't actually remember what it was I wasn't remembering, but something about him was troubling, and it wasn't that he still hadn't washed his hair. My head started to ache again.

I forgot all about Mark when class started, and barely noticed my headache fading. Professor Gribaldi always demanded complete attention. Her braided hair was pinned into a black and silver crown that, in the harsh classroom lighting, assumed all the menace of a hoplite helmet. Her arms were bared to the shoulder and muscles bunched ominously under dark, smooth skin as she flung her hands about, all flowing yellow skirts and passion. I wondered, for a moment, what La Gribaldi might think of Demetrius's line about ugly Ethiopes. She was Eritrean by birth, not Ethiopian, but I thought the two countries were related somehow. I made a vague attempt at chasing the memory down, but it faded when she started reading from Homer's *Odyssey*.

The original text was well beyond us. Mansfield offered Latin as a language option (mostly for the prestige; hardly anyone actually took it), but not ancient Greek, an appalling oversight that clearly enraged La Gribaldi. But she'd won the battle to use Chapman's Homer instead of a more literal translation, informing us on the first day that, "Translation can never do more than approximate, so we shall, at least, be gloriously inaccurate." Today, her voice became Circe's voice, her American drawl transmuted into the witch's clever seduction. Not even daydreams about Mark Nolan's eyes could intrude very long into that.

Which was just as well. "Ms. Spencer," she snapped, flashing her rings at me. "What is the obvious thematic parallel in the presentation of Circe weaving?"

"With Penelope," I said, and waited to see if more was required. She folded her heavy arms over the bulk of her breasts and lifted an eyebrow, inviting expansion. "Well, Penelope's presented as the faithful wife, always with her loom," I said slowly, giving myself time to work it out as I went. "But Penelope's only weaving during the day and secretly undoing it at night so that she doesn't have to marry one of her suitors. So she's doing the work of a wife, but then she's destroying it, so no one will *make* her his wife. Oh, but she's just making ordinary cloth. Circe is weaving enchantments. And Circe's cooking is filled with herbs that transform men to beasts. She does complete the housework, but it's, uh, twisted." That sounded reasonably clever. Best to leave it there. "So, uh, yeah," I concluded masterfully.

"The sorcerous seductress as the perverted housewife," La Gribaldi said, slapping the book onto her desk. Her braided crown threatened to tumble down with the violence of the gesture. "Excellent, Ms. Spencer. Mr. Nolan, something to add?"

"Circe's pretty selfish," he offered, lowering his hand and glancing at me. "Penelope's selfless, but Circe just wants to control men. She gets what she wants from them, and then she doesn't care."

I wasn't going to let even a cute guy get away with that. "She wants to be safe," I argued. "You think the men would let her get away with being powerful? She has to protect herself. There're all those lines about her house being made of stone, and the wild animals under her command. Security precautions. Penelope wouldn't need to unpick her work every night if she had some other way to keep those guys off her back. But the Greeks didn't like women with magic — look at what happened to Medea and Ariadne."

Mark leaned forward. "They didn't really like anyone with magic."

"Orpheus is a magician as well as a musician," I pointed out. We were twisted in our seats, now, facing each other. The rest of the class was watching with interest. "But he's a good guy. When he goes into the underworld to rescue his dead wife, we're supposed to cheer for him, and sympathize when he turns to look at her before he's fully completed the walk back out. You're never supposed to cheer for women who use their magic to actually do anything. Naiads and dryads are allowed to be sympathetic, because they're pretty and passive, but we're never allowed to like enchantresses or witches."

Mark frowned and looked about to respond, but La Gribaldi cut him off with another wave. "Interesting points both, and I look forward to seeing them explored in your *Odyssey* assignments, due on Monday. No exceptions." She glanced at the clock. "For now, sadly, our time is up. Mr. Nolan, a brief word."

The rest of us escaped gratefully into the hall. Usually any mention of assignments came with one of La Gribaldi's famous spiels on how New Zealand students were lazy and underachieving compared to the competitive Advanced Placement students of her adopted country. I couldn't see the appeal of working yourself ragged and doing ten thousand extra-curriculars. So New Zealand only had seven universities, and most entrance courses required entrants to meet a bare minimum of standards. So what? How were you supposed to know what you were going to do for the rest of your life when you were only seventeen, anyway? Medicine and engineering were restricted-entry courses, and there were students at Mansfield killing themselves to make the grade. One student *had* killed herself a couple of years ago, a horrible event that was now a whispered cautionary tale. One of the science scholarships was named after her, which seemed a peculiar memorial to me.

With a start, I realized I was still hanging outside the class-room door, leaning against the cream-painted walls. Geography was in five minutes, and I hadn't done the homework. Why was I standing here noodling about poor suicidal Kathy someone? What was I—I'd wanted to talk to Mark. Or had he wanted to talk to me? I peered through the door's glass inset, rubbing at my aching temples. The wire mesh in the little rectangle made everything look fuzzy and undefined, but I could see La Gribaldi shaking her crowned head at Mark, big arms folded over her breasts again. Mark seemed to be pleading for something. An extension? La Gribaldi looked unconvinced. Abruptly, she moved toward the door, and I sprang back to lean against the corridor's far wall as she came out of the classroom, stiffening as she paused to stare at me. She surveyed me from toe to top, much as Reka had done in the mists, but her dark eyes met mine, a little puzzled, a little wary.

"Interesting," she murmured, and walked on.

Mark tried to scoot out after her, but I made my move, lurching to block his path like a transportable human wall. "Didn't you want to talk to me about something?" I asked. As conversational gambits go, it probably lacked a certain something.

He stopped, but didn't look at me. "No?"

"Oh," I said, confused all over again. Maybe I had wanted to talk to him? There had been *something*, damn it. I improvised: "Um, I was wondering. Do you want to study for the Classics midterm exam with me?"

Mark hesitated, pale face guarded. Something silver glinted at the wrist of his ragged sleeve. "When?"

"After school sometime? In the library?"

"I have a job after school. And on the weekends."

I didn't ask, *Then why do all your uniform pants have holes?* "Just an idea," I said, trying not to sound huffy about the rejection. What had I expected? That after crashing into him at the gates we were going to be best buds?

The headache eased and he nodded, smiling slightly. "It's not a bad idea. I'll think about it and let you know?"

I brightened. "Sure!"

"See you later."

I frowned after him. His final sentence was a perfectly normal farewell. Why did it sound so tantalizingly familiar?

Chapter Four

For What You Burn

Final period English was my only class with Kevin, science nerd that he was, and it was, to the joy of nearly everyone, a movie screening day. We'd had the option of *Heavenly Creatures*, *Once Were Warriors*, and *Rain* for the film section. Given the choice between teenage matricide, teenage suicide, and possible pedophilia, the class had voted overwhelmingly for matricide. I hadn't; I remembered the horrible months last year when my mother had struggled against the cancer and the chemo, and resented my classmates' enthusiasm for what was, after all, a true story about a nasty murder. When they caught the Eyeslasher, would Peter Jackson want the rights to that too?

Heavenly Creatures began with the patchy film of Christchurch in the 50s, looking even whiter and duller than now, and got progressively creepier. "There *are* New Zealand comedies," I whispered to Kevin, reasonably safe from Mr. Aaronsen in the dimmed light. Backseats by the radiators were even more in demand on film days, but Kevin had gotten there early, and saved one for me.

"Comedies aren't *art*, darling," he replied, in a fair posh English accent.

"I'd love to watch you tell that to Iris," I muttered, and was rewarded with a muffled laugh. "Everything okay?"

"Yeah." He thought about it. "We'll see."

"Well, she needs you for the play, so she can't get too pissy." I was trying to be reassuring, but I caught the flash of white as he rolled his eyes. "What?"

"She is actually my *friend*, Ellie. My friend who *likes* me, regardless of...stuff."

"Well, sure, I'm just saying—"

"If you lot are going to talk all through this—" Mr. Aaronson began, but the door opened before he could finish the threat. It was Mark Nolan, holding a strip of paper. I couldn't help straightening in my seat. Outlined in the light coming in the doorframe, he shone like a grubby angel, green eyes gleaming in his white face. He came in, and I began to breathe again. After a brief discussion with Mr. Aaronson, he folded his long legs under a desk at the front and stared impassively at the screen.

I was expecting Kevin to give me hell for the obviousness

of my crush, but he apparently had something else on his mind.

"Jesus," he muttered. "I swear he's stalking me."

"What?"

"Nolan's transferred into all my classes today—well, except Physics."

"*Seriously?*"

"God knows how he did it, but he did." He shrugged the mystery away and gave me his most irritating smirk. "This one worked out well for you, didn't it?"

I ignored him, leaned behind his wide shoulder and stole another look at Mark, who appeared totally oblivious to everything but the movie. In the white glare of the projector screen, his face was like a classical Greek sculpture, bleached of color after long years in the sun.

It didn't make any sense. Mark, I had pathetically worked out through careful deduction, took Classics, English, History, Latin, and Art History. How could he just transfer into Kevin's Chem and Calc classes, much less Māori? "You have Physics second period today, right? Fourth period Thursdays?"

"Yeah."

"That's when I have—"

Mr. Aaronson was rising in a clatter of remote controls. "Ms. Spencer! Are you the director of this film?"

I tried to shrink into my seat. "No, Mr. Aaronson."

"Then why do you insist on adding *commentary*?"

"Sorry, Mr. Aaronson," I said, staring at the floor so I wouldn't have to put faces to the people laughing at me.

Kevin gave me a comforting poke in the ribs when

everyone went back to the movie, but I was not in the mood to be consoled. I sulked in the warm darkness of the classroom until I went to sleep on my desk, and had to be hastily shaken awake before the lights went on. It wasn't an auspicious start to the weekend.

I was fully prepared to defend Kevin to Iris at rehearsal that night, but she foiled all my noble intentions by being typically warm and friendly to everyone, Kevin included. Reka was as warm and friendly as a glacier to everyone *but* Kevin, for whom she melted, chatting with him between their scenes as if he were an old friend. I didn't like the way she looked at him—sort of hungry and grasping—but it was hardly my business to protect Kevin's virtue, even if he had been inclined to give it away.

To make matters worse, Reka looked even more beautiful. She was wearing another anachronistic outfit, this one a crisp 40s-style dark gray skirt suit over a creamy, high-collared blouse. The fitted skirt cut off at the back of her knees, and she wore sheer black pantyhose underneath. In the crowds of students in jeans and layers of sweaters, she should have looked like an overdressed schoolmarm, but with her startling hair arranged in looped braids all over her skull, she resembled a barbarian princess in business drag. In that company, Iris's pristine gray wool dress and black stockings warranted barely a glance.

I ran the fights through for Iris's approval. The boys were

still too enthusiastic about their proposed punch-up, and I was worried they'd get hurt. The last thing this show needed was injured lovers. Maybe I could tell them some of my grislier training stories, like the one where I'd taken a sparring pad to the throat, and been unable to swallow solid food for a day. Or the one about the sidekick to the collarbone that had stopped me raising my right arm for weeks.

Iris called a break, and most of the cast scattered to get food somewhere where it wouldn't offend Reka's delicate constitution, sulking out loud about missing out on their Friday night. The vending machines downstairs were definitely calling to me—my dinner had been mashed potatoes and limp broccoli, and not much of either—but Kevin sat down beside me, and Reka with him. Iris slumped, then flicked open her newspaper to cover.

In the nearly empty theater, the silence was very obvious.

"So," I said, striving to make my tone light. "You're allergic to cooked food, is that right?"

Reka didn't bother to make eye contact with me, preferring to lean her arm on the armrest, beside Kevin's. "That's right."

"I guess that must make a social life pretty hard."

"Lay off, Ellie," Kevin ordered.

I blinked at him. "What do you—"

He put his hand over Reka's as if to comfort her. "Don't make fun of people's disabilities!"

"I wasn't—" I began, and then snapped my teeth together so hard they clicked. Kevin had never used that tone of voice, or looked at me like that. "Sorry."

"I accept your apology," Reka said, and squeezed Kevin's hand.

"What do you think about these Eyeslasher murders, Ellie?" Iris asked, tapping the newspaper's front page.

Even knowing she was trying to help couldn't stop my reply from being curt. "I think they're gross."

The headline read MĀORI ELDER MURDERED! and the story described the latest Eyeslasher victim as a pillar of the community; a general practitioner with a family practice, he had also been a respected *kaumātua*. There was a color photograph with the article, deliberately discordant against the description of the dead man's beaten and mutilated body. Looking steadily at the camera, a solid, grizzled man with a feathered cloak over his dark business suit stood in the middle of a crowd of kids in a *marae*, all of them with bare feet, dark eyes, and huge grins.

"He just went out to buy milk," Iris read. "That's so sad."

"It can't be that bad," I said sourly. "There's still room on the front page for the sheep that ran away and lived in a cave for six years." There was a picture of the sheep too. It was very woolly.

Reka leaned over and took the paper from Iris without asking, her looped braids nearly smacking me in the face. I caught a whiff of something that smelled like expensive fruit.

"Let's talk about something cheerful," Kevin suggested. "Such as exams."

I groaned.

"It's only two weeks until our midterms!" Iris said. "And they're right in the middle of the production run, which is why we keep losing everyone. Sometimes I think I'd like to just run away."

Kevin nodded. "Like Great-Uncle Robert."

"Oh, here we go," I said.

Reka went very still, and then, apparently realizing her cue, cocked her head at him. "Your great-uncle ran away from exams?"

"Nope. World War II, according to Grandad. Robert was a pacifist, and he vanished in his first year of university, a couple of days after war was declared on Germany. Grandad signed up, did manly, non-pacifist things in North Africa, and came back expecting his younger brother to turn up when the fighting was over."

"And he never did," Iris said, far too sad about something that wasn't *her* family tragedy.

"Nope. So Grandad named his son after his brother in case he wasn't a coward. Hedging his bets." He pointed at me. "But the *relevant* part is that Grandad blamed the drama club."

"Do tell," Reka said.

"It was only after Robert joined that he got all those weird ideas about how it might be nice not to shoot people."

"How enlightened," Reka said, nudging his hand with hers.

"A better life through theater," I said flippantly, and stood up, before things got any worse. "Well, there's a Snickers bar with my name on it."

"You need protein," Kevin said, but he didn't stand to join me.

"Snickers are packed with peanuts," I said, and loped up the stairs.

I ignored Iris's desperate look as Reka edged closer to Kevin. It was harder to ignore my own guilt. Iris and I weren't actually friends, I reminded myself. I wasn't obliged to deflect her imagined competition. And whether or not he came out to Reka was up to him, but if Kevin couldn't read the signals of interested persons and let them know he didn't reciprocate, it wasn't my job to fix the fallout.

Still, warned by some impulse, I turned to look at them just before I got to the exit. Reka was explaining something to Kevin, her hand on his arm, but she tilted her head to look me full in the face.

My skin prickled. It was probably a trick of the distance and the dim light, but for that brief moment, her eyes were dark from corner to corner, with no pupils or iris at all.

Even after a chocolate hit, I was in no mood to watch Reka be stunning and brilliant for the rest of the rehearsal, but it was full dark outside and I couldn't leave until Kevin did. Instead, I went to the greenroom and sulked in perfect privacy, picking holes in the collapsing couch instead of working on my *Odyssey* essay like a good Mansfield girl ought. This became less exciting after a while, especially when the tips of my fingers went numb with the cold. I shoved my hands into my jeans pockets and began poking around the little dressing rooms. The first two held Carla's sewing machine, the clothes they'd rented, and the costumes she'd been making herself, neatly hung on wheeled racks or folded onto rickety steel chairs.

In the last one, there was a bench built across two sides of the room. It was stained with makeup spills from the decades of actors who had sat in front of the four smeared mirrors to put on their faces. The box of costume jewelry was open there, beside a toolbox filled with half used makeup.

I sat down and pulled a strand of beads out of the box. It *was* only plastic, but the beads were a nice deep sapphire, and polished into irregular bobbles. I pulled the necklace over my head, pulled my hair out of its ponytail, and tossed it, smiling coquettishly into the mirror.

"Ellie?" someone said, and I jumped to my feet, turning guiltily toward the door.

It was Puck, whose real name I had still hadn't learned. He was staring, with an expression I didn't recognize at first, because it was so seldom directed at me. I was used to being invisible to guys. At best, I was a friend, a funny girl, a good laugh. But he was looking at me the way people sometimes looked at Kevin or Iris, the way I feared I looked at Mark.

"Sorry," I said, and put the necklace back. "I know I shouldn't mess with—"

He grinned and shook brown curls out of his eyes. "Don't pay any attention to Carrie," he said. "It'd set a terrible precedent." He stepped closer to me. My skin prickled. "I like your hair, Pandora."

"I washed it last night," I said, and then wanted to die.

He laughed. "Well, it looks good. Iris wants you there for notes."

"Thanks," I replied, and followed him back out to the stage, where everyone was pointedly waiting for us. Kevin raised an eyebrow at me, and I glared back. If Iris had notes for me, I didn't hear them, but I did catch Puck's name. It was Blake.

Carrie tried to catch my eye, but I decided staring at the floor was the better part of valor.

I didn't tie my hair back, though.

CHAPTER FIVE

Lament for the Numb

"Go do your essay," Kevin said on Saturday morning, trying to glare at me from his position in the Year Thirteen boarder lounge beanbag.

"I can't do my essay," I told him. "I'm doing my laundry."

"Not right at this moment."

"No, right at this moment I'm waiting for the midday news while the dryer does its thing." I eyed the beanbag enviously. The lounge was nearly full of students avoiding the dining hall's attempts at a hot lunch; Kevin must have been in here since the morning cartoons to have snagged it.

"You could do your essay while the dryer does its thing," he suggested.

"Kevin! It is vital that I keep myself up to date on current affairs."

"Is it vital that you watch *Ellen*?"

I scooped another forkful of two-minute noodles into my mouth and slurped defiantly. "Maybe. Besides, I've got all tomorrow to write it."

"We have rehearsal tomorrow night."

"About that. Does Iris really need me for—"

"Hang on, shut up," Kevin said, and turned up the TV. The lounge conversation died into silence as the solemn-voiced news reporter made her announcement.

Two more murders had been discovered. The victims had been a fifth-generation slaughterhouse worker from Lower Hutt and a Canadian journalist in Wellington, only recently emigrated. They'd both not come home last night, and were discovered dead this morning. And their eyes were gone.

The usual din of the lounge was subdued after the Eye-slasher story finished. I threw the rest of my noodles into the overflowing bin as the news ended with a final update on the very woolly sheep.

The laundry room was warm, if uncomfortably humid. I surrendered to the impulse to bury my face in the arm-ful of laundry, for the comfort of warm, clean fabric against my face. The sensation was only a little spoiled by the not-quite-lemon scent of the generic laundry powder Sheppard gave us.

When I straightened, there were wet spots on my white school blouses. There was no reason for me to cry; I hadn't known any of these people. Napier wasn't even on the list of places the Eyeslasher had struck. But looking at the fuzzy pictures of the man and woman on the crappy TV, I had felt an odd sense of connection; as if they were people whose names I had heard, once, and recognized.

I folded clothes into the basket, then hauled it back to my building. Samia and Gemma Chant were in the tiny living room, their accounting notes spread over the coffee table, and they didn't look up as I came in; I tiptoed past into my room and quietly shut the door.

It was my second load of laundry today, and the building designers had not been generous with storage space. I grabbed some of the folded jerseys and yanked open one of the drawers under the bed.

The contents clattered.

"Oh, crap," I breathed, staring at the empty beer cans. I'd completely forgotten about them. Three days later, even in my cold room, they were distinctly fragrant. I'd have to smuggle them out in my backpack, pretend I was going to the library, and dump them in a bin at school when no one was watching.

There was a sudden bustle in the living room, all the glad greetings and excitement that hadn't met my entrance.

"Ellie?" Gemma said. "She's in there."

I shoved the drawer closed, wincing at the sliding rattle, and dumped the jerseys on my bed.

"Ellie?" Iris called from outside my door.

I twisted on my knees. "Come in!"

She poked her head in. "Are you ready to go?"

"Go?" I wondered, then stood up, remembering. "Go! Oh, props shopping! Yes, just a minute."

"Am I interrupting? I can wait."

I emptied my backpack, shaking books onto the bed, and threw my wallet in. "No, not a problem." What the hell was wrong with my memory? I'd remembered Mark wanting to speak to me, only he hadn't; I didn't know the Eyeslasher victims, but it felt as if there was something in the way they'd died that I'd been warned about. But where the warning had come from, I couldn't remember. My head felt as if it were stuffed with used tissues.

Iris jingled the car keys while she waited, and I resisted the urge to snap at her. "Thanks so much for this," she said earnestly.

I tried a smile, aware that Samia and Gemma were watching and probably wondering why wonderful Iris Tsang was bothering with me. "No problem," I said, and hoped I wasn't lying.

The drive to town from Mansfield was a nice one. We coasted down Riccarton Road, the green mass of Riccarton Bush rising above the houses on our left, and then cut into the road that ran through Hagley Park. Iris parked outside the Arts Center, near the Botanic Gardens.

"Okay!" she said brightly. "I did some resourcing this morning, so we only need a few things from here. Some plastic tiki, and some kind of mask, for Pyramus. I thought the square market might be a good place to start."

We walked the few blocks up, and over the Avon Bridge. In spring and summer the punters took tourists up and down its sluggish waters, but their straw hats were nowhere in evidence today—only the green-brown of the water and a lot of desperate ducks. Iris described the set design ("A backdrop, you know, with the forest on it, but with indications of Edwardian influence") and didn't require my participation. I tried not to notice people noticing her, in her black pinstripe pants and careful makeup, and me, in my jeans and too-tight sweater.

On a Saturday afternoon, Cathedral Square was bustling, complete with people taking wedding pictures outside the cathedral, two young women playing with the giant chess set, and a crazy man preaching at passersby from the benches beside the cathedral. Stalls roofed in primary-colored tarpaulins displayed trinkets for tourists and for any locals looking for cheap gifts. I shot the souvlaki stand and its falafel a longing glance, but dutifully followed Iris to one of the stalls, where genuine greenstone pendants were carefully arrayed beside a box of green plastic tiki, red paint sloppily inscribed around the "carved" eyes.

"These are so fake," I said, running my fingers over the monstrous little faces.

"Forty-foot rule," Iris said. "And $2 each, which is good for the props budget." She handed over four gold coins and the stall owner tipped four of the tiki into a paper bag. "Can you see anything that might do for a mask? It doesn't need to be very good."

I nodded and wandered through the stalls, scanning them lazily. The wares were a mess of colors and items. Bone carvings, stuffed kiwi and tuatara dolls, handmade jewelry and mass-made sunglasses, colorful fire poi and painted ceramics. Masks.

I saw the right one immediately. Where the other masks were covered in feathers and lace and elaborate patterns of glittery paint, this one was a stark, bleached white with high, molded cheekbones and a small, pouty mouth. It stood out among the others on the stand, perfect in that simplicity. The empty eyes stared straight back into mine. Something jangled in my skull, a tingling shock that seemed somehow familiar. Without thinking, I reached out to touch the cool porcelain.

"Hey, no fingers," said the stall owner, pointing to a sign. "If you want to touch, that's a hundred and fifty dollars."

I couldn't afford it. Mum and Dad would kill me. But the idea of walking away without the mask was intolerable. I had to have it. I had to.

I pulled out my wallet.

After the exchange, I held the wrapped mask against my chest, half-dazed at my own craving. I walked toward the benches, where the crazy preacher was now delivering his sermon to a number of disinterested seagulls. He halted abruptly as he caught sight of me, but I avoided his eye and sat on the bench furthest from him.

I carefully eased the mask from its wrapping. There was a strange buzzing in my ears, like singing from someone else's headphones: something that had a coherent meaning, but only if you were close enough to hear it. When my fingers touched, just stroking around the edges of that beautiful face, it was like the completion of a circuit, or the moment before applause for a fine performance, or the hushed silence of Anzac Day dawn services, after the bugle sounded for the soliders who had never come home. The buzzing vanished, replaced by a sense of deep contentment. I turned it over, preparing to lift that perfect face onto my own.

"Excuse me," someone said, and I looked up. It was the crazy preacher. His skin was either naturally dark or deeply tanned, but either way it contrasted shockingly with the head of wispy white hair. The whites of his eyes were yellowy, and his breath smelled foul. But he was smooth-shaven and clean, and the crease of his dark blue pants was soldierly crisp. I wondered if he did the ironing himself, or if there was someone looking after him.

"I have a message for you," he said.

"Sorry," I said. "I have to get going."

His face tightened. "Are you lying? That's not godly." He leaned in close, and my repulsion was lost in a wave of sympathy. "People lie to me sometimes," he confided. "But they'll burn in hell. We're all sinners, you know." His lip trembled. "But now I'm redeemed. I escaped that woman's hell."

"Uh-huh," I said. The mask was calm and waiting in my hands. I reluctantly wrapped it and put it back in my bag, and then stood. "But I'm really going, see?" I tried to catch Iris's eye, but she was bent over her cell phone, frowning as she spoke.

The man's voice shook. "This is the message in the Bible," he said quietly. "'While I slept, my heart was awake.

I dreamed my lover knocked at the door. Let me come in, my darling, my sweetheart, my dove. My head is wet with dew and my hair is damp from the mist.'" He cocked his head at me. "Don't listen. She says it will be wonderful but she lies. She says you can go home but our lives will pass away like the traces of clouds and vanish like fog in the heat of the sun." He tapped his fingers on the briefcase, yellowing fingernails cracking against the worn black vinyl. "God warned me, but I didn't listen."

Iris had finished her conversation, I noted, relieved. She was heading toward me, frowning.

The man opened his briefcase and pulled out an equally decrepit book. "This is for you."

"No, thank you."

"You need it," he insisted, waving it at me. "It will save your soul."

"No," I said firmly, and began to turn away.

He grabbed me, chilblain-cracked fingers biting deep.

It was the first time I'd ever taken my training to the street, but I didn't have to think about it at all. I felt the pressure on my right wrist and twisted, my weight shifting automatically, my backpack swinging from my arm. Even before I fully understood what I was doing, I recognized the sure motion of my left hand as I raised it, knife-edged, and struck down my imprisoned arm to the fleshy spot between his thumb and fingers.

He let go, stumbling away. I held my weight on my back leg, fists raised.

"Let her go!" Iris shouted.

"Go away!" I said over her, staring into the man's eyes,

round with hurt surprise. He dropped the book and ran, unbuttoned jacket flapping around him like broken wings.

"Oh my God!" Iris yelped. She came up beside me; way too close for the adrenaline singing in my blood. "Are you okay?"

I stepped sideways. "I'm okay," I said, and covered for my shaking hands by picking up the book. "I'm fine." The man's dark eyes had been familiar, but I couldn't work out why.

"We can go to the police kiosk!"

"No!" I said. "He's just a crazy old guy. I don't think he was going to hurt me. He grabbed me, that's all. I can take care of myself."

She gave me a grin that lacked her usual polish. "I'll say. Could you teach them that for the play?"

I laughed. "Edwardian women who know how to break wrist grips? I don't think they taught them that in finishing schools."

She smiled, going pink. "It just looked really cool. Are you sure you're okay?"

I nodded and put the book in my bag. "Look! I got a mask."

I unwrapped it for her, and caught the tiny frown between her eyebrows. "That's really nice, but the props budget…"

"No," I said. "No, I bought it. It's mine. But I'll lend it to you for the play." The air buzzed and I frowned. I didn't really want to lend the mask to anyone. But that was why I'd bought it, right? I had that stuffed head feeling again.

"—you okay?" Iris was asking. "Do you need to sit down?"

"I think I'm catching something," I said slowly. "The last couple of days…"

She looked worried. "The marketing manager just called; I have to go pick up posters right now. Do you want me to drop you home afterward?"

"No, it's okay. Just give me a minute."

"You really don't look great. I can do the rest of the props myself."

"Okay. I'll catch the bus."

Her concern for me warred with concern for her play, and the former surrendered without much of a fight. "Okay," she said. "If you're sure."

I walked to the bus center, feeling better as the cold air helped clear my head and the last of the adrenaline rush eased. I was just in time to queue for the next bus leaving for the university end of the city, and rooted in my backpack for my wallet as the line decreased. The crazy man's book kept getting in my way, so I fished it out with one hand, dropped the coins into the driver's machine with the other, and sank into a seat near the back.

I glimpsed a flash of copper-red hair from the corner of my eye and looked up. Last in line, Mark Nolan was getting onto the bus.

He tilted his head at me as he made his way down the aisle. "Can I sit here?"

I grabbed the bag and book onto my lap, clearing the space beside me. "Sure. Were you in town?" Oh, God, *stupid*, of course, how else had he gotten on the bus in the first place?

"Yeah. So how's it going?" He was smiling at me, even white teeth gleaming behind his curved lips.

"Pretty good," I said, astounded. This was very nearly a conversation, like normal people had. He was sitting right beside me in the small seats, long thigh pressed against mine. I could feel it through my jeans, a line of heat that suffused my entire body.

His gaze had suddenly refocused to my lap, and he pointed. "What's that?"

I held up the book, realized too late that it was a Bible, and tried to indicate with a face that it wasn't mine. I didn't want Mark Nolan to think I was the sort of girl who read her Bible on the bus. Or the kind of girl who read a Bible at all. Gemma had that theory that he was a religious nut, which might mean that he liked girls with Bibles; but then I might not like him so much.

"Where did you get that?" He reached for the book too fast, and I tensed automatically, shifting back. His hand stopped, hovering over mine.

I cursed myself for being an overreactive idiot and pushed the book into his hand. "This crazy old guy in the square grabbed me. He wanted me to have it for some reason. You know, the one who stands on the cathedral steps preaching?"

Mark was turning the Bible over, apparently fascinated by it. "I know the one," he said. I peered at it, grubby and worn in his long, pale hands. The front cover was rubbing away to reveal the battered heavy cardboard underneath, but it was still possible to make out the illustration of well-scrubbed people of various ethnicities, all wearing bell-bottom jeans and huge smiles. The darker colors had flaked off, so that everyone with a skin tone darker than peach had skin of pale beige background with flecks of blacks and browns. Untouched by wear, wide white grins hung, Cheshire-like, on their faded faces.

"How's the *Odyssey* essay going?" he asked, dropping the book into his lap.

I wrinkled my nose. "I haven't started it. You?"

"Well, there are so many *Star Trek* reruns that require my attention."

I matched his poker face with my own deadpan expression. "Personally, I don't see how I could possibly concentrate on Homer's image clusters when my sock drawer is in such desperate need of reorganization."

He grinned—definitely a grin this time, not a smile. "Oh, you're a laundry procrastinator? I wouldn't have thought it."

"What would you think?"

"Oh, well, I figure being a Mansfield student's just a disguise. You're really undercover for an international spy ring. You only write essays in between running over rooftops and disarming bombs. Or maybe you're a member of the Justice League, or the Birds of Prey—"

"You read superhero comics?"

"Sometimes. Wait, you too?"

"I used to. I kind of got out of the habit last year." I sat back, shaking my head. "I can't believe you read comics!"

"Why not?"

"It seems so—" *normal*, I nearly said, and bit it back. "—not like you," I finished.

"Yeah? What do you know about me?" He was still smiling, but it suddenly looked a little forced.

"Oh, you're the original mystery man," I said flippantly, wanting the real smile back. "I know nothing."

"Maybe we could do something about that. I'd like to take you up on that study offer. If the offer's still open?" The look he slanted me was shy, but eager.

He was flirting. Mark Nolan was flirting with *me*.

"That would be great," I blurted, far too eagerly. I could feel a blush roaring up my throat and cast around for something to keep the conversation going before he noticed. Something to make me look cool and superhero-like. "I'm doing the fight choreography for a play at the university, so we'll have to work out a good time."

"Yeah? What's that like?"

"Oh, it's really—" I discarded *fun* and went for "—interesting."

"I bet there are some *interesting* people in theater." His head was bent and his hair was falling over his face. I wanted to brush it back to see his eyes again, but at least he wasn't staring at my red cheeks.

"Well, there's this one girl who's kind of off. She has these allergies, so I shouldn't be mean about her, but she's pretty much rude and nasty to everyone." Honesty made me add, "Well, except to Kevin."

His head came up sharply, but he still wasn't looking at me. "Kevin likes her?"

"Yeah, I think so," I admitted, and bit at my thumbnail. I should stop bitching about Reka before Mark decided I was an awful person. "And, hey, he has good taste in friends, so I should give her more of a chance. She's a really good actor." I looked out the window. "I hate this weather."

"Yeah, me too," he said absently.

I had totally turned him off. I kept prattling anyway. "Last night I dreamed that there was fog inside my room so thick I'd gone blind."

His half-hidden face went tight. "That sounds more like a nightmare. This is my stop." He lunged up and caught the red cord that dangled across the window, setting off the chime. "Can I get you to—"

I swung into the aisle to let him pass and caught a glimpse of something in his hand. "Oh. You've still got the Bible."

He turned his green-eyed stare on me, rubbing his wrist. "What Bible?"

The bus doors opened onto the foggy afternoon, and the smell of wet earth and rotting leaves rushed in. My head hurt. "You've got the...book," I said. "The...people, the faceless smiles."

"I'll catch you later, Spencer. We'll work out a time to study." He was hanging his coat over his arm. I caught a glimpse of something tucked against his side before it was shrouded.

"Sure," I said. "Weird weather."

Mark's eyes were strong with some unrecognizable emotion. "That it is. Gotta go."

He leapt down the steps and into the night. I slumped back into my seat, staring out the window. The view was totally obscured by fog droplets, and I smeared my coat sleeve across the glass, straightening as the cold shock of contact cleared my mind.

"The Bible!" I exclaimed, to the disapproving stare of the elderly woman in the seat opposite. I sank back, rubbing at my temples, and nearly missed my own stop. Getting off the bus, I paced down the damp street in time to the pounding in my skull. I couldn't work out why Mark had taken the book. Maybe he'd forgotten he had it. No, I'd reminded him. And he'd hidden it, under his coat.

Little sparks exploded, hanging in the air an inch before my eyes. I gasped and leaned against the stone sign at the entrance to Sheppard Hall. Even with my eyes closed, light flared in my skull.

"Hey," someone said sharply behind me. It was Kevin, full laundry basket on his hip. He must have been collecting clothes from the dryers. "Are you okay?"

"No," I said. "My head. Mark Nolan—" The wind shifted to bring the scent of the dining hall to my nose, the rich smell of grease cloying in my throat. I leaned over the sign and threw up into the flowerbed.

For some little time, all I could do was retch and cry and shake with the pain. I gradually became aware of Kevin's hands smoothing back my hair and his low, calm voice. "Did you eat something bad?" he was asking. "Is it the flu?"

"My head hurts," I said. My own voice sounded fuzzy in my ears. I spat, and spat again, and rubbed at my wet chin.

"Migraine?"

"Dunno. Never had one."

"Okay. Bed for you. And up we go."

I had never wanted so badly to be dainty and delicate. I could lean on Kevin, but I couldn't ask him to carry me, and each step through the Sheppard grounds reverberated, a jarring blow to the skull. When we finally made it, and he knocked on my building's door, I groaned at the noise. Samia opened the door, scarf wrapped hastily around her hair.

"What happened?" She peered at me. "Is she *drunk*?"

"Migraine," Kevin said. "Can I help her in?"

"Uh, sure," she said. "I've got some codeine if it's really bad."

I managed a half laugh at the conditional. If anything got worse than this, I didn't want to be alive while it happened.

I collapsed upon my bed amid the piles of folded laundry. Kevin and Samia held a low-voiced conversation outside the door and then he came back in to tug my shoes off and persuaded me to crawl under the covers.

Samia handed me a small white pill and water and hovered in the doorway. "Thank you," I managed.

Kevin tucked the covers up over me and drew the curtains, then turned out the light. "Go to sleep, you sad sack."

He closed the door softly behind him.

I gave it a slow ten count and stood up, staggering against the sharp white pain.

Mark had done something to me. He'd stolen the Bible, and made me forget, given me this agony as a deterrent against memory. And it wasn't the first time, I thought— there was something about standing by the bathrooms in the music center, trying to resist his quiet order...his order to... More pain, and I bit my lip against a scream.

Hypnotism or enchantment or drugs; I didn't know, and it didn't matter. This time I would not forget. I would not.

"Write it down," I muttered, and scrabbled on my desk. Kevin had thoughtfully piled my folded laundry onto the desk, on top of the scattered class notes and my battered laptop, a hand-me-down from Magda. The throbbing increased. I was going to vomit again. I was going to faint. My brains were going to explode and dribble out of my eyes.

I found a golf pencil I'd stolen from my mother and the back of a returned Geography assignment. There was an odd tension in the way the pencil left gray marks on the wrinkled paper, as if the paper itself was resisting.

MARK! I wrote. BIBLE! DON'T FORGET!

There.

I dropped the paper, not caring where it landed, and released the memory, stumbling back to bed.

The codeine lifted my head off my shoulders, and wrapped me in clouds of cotton wool. I curled around my pillow and let them carry me away.

Chapter Six

Love in the Air

I sat up and turned on my bedside lamp, alarmed awake by a half-familiar tune and wondering why I was so uncomfortable.

I switched on the bedside light and blinked. I was still in my sweater and jeans, and the irritating beeps were coming from my cell phone, muffled in the depths of my backpack. I stumbled to my feet and fished it out.

"Hello?"

"Hi!"

"Iris. Hi."

"Did you forget about the rehearsal this evening? Kevin said he thought you might come by later."

"No, I'll come." I jerked the curtain open one-handed and stared, appalled, into the black sky. "Wait, what time is it?"

"Five-thirty."

I'd slept almost twenty-four hours. "Oh, God! Iris, I'm so sorry. I had this massive migraine last night, and I've just woken up." My stomach chose that moment to rumble.

"If you're sick—"

"No, I'm fine now." Though there was something, trembling at the corner of my memories. My head hurt.

"Okay, then! We'll see you soon?"

I grimaced at the foggy night. The fifteen-minute walk alone seemed suddenly dangerous. I ignored the little voice that protested I'd crossed the fields at night at least a dozen times. "Could someone give me a ride?" My voice sounded weak, even to myself.

"Sure," Iris said, sounding surprised, and there was a muffled consultation before her voice returned. "We're taking a break. Kevin will be around in ten minutes or so. Okay?"

"Okay," I said, vastly relieved, and dropped the phone, sprinting for the bathroom. Wearing my jeans to bed had worn a red ridge into my belly that didn't fade in the hot water, and there was something pale and smelly encrusted in a strand of hair. Shuddering, I rubbed in shampoo until my scalp tingled. I was out of conditioner, but Gemma wasn't. I mentally promised to replace it.

Wrapped in a towel, my hair a wet mass down my back, I hurried back to my room. Clean clothes, fortunately, I had. I ducked under my desk to fetch my shoes.

My hand closed on a scrap of paper.

The tingle went up my arm like a spark of static electricity. The headache abruptly disappeared. I pulled the scrap free and stared at it.

In the untidy capitals of my own writing, pressed so deeply into the paper that it was torn in a couple of places, it read MARK! BIBLE! DON'T FORGET!

I closed my hand around the paper and stood, shaking with fury and fear, as my memories returned. Mark had asked me if I knew what I could be in the music center. He'd made me promise not to go out at night alone. And last night, somehow, he'd stolen the Bible, and the very thoughts out of my mind.

No wonder I'd had that head-stuffed feeling.

Someone knocked on my door.

"Just a second!" I yelled, and sought a good hiding place for my precious piece of paper. In the end I dropped the note on the keyboard of my battered laptop, and closed the screen onto it.

"I'm so sorry," I said, yanking the door open. "I can't believe I slept that long."

Kevin handed me a muesli bar. "How awesome am I?"

"You are God on Earth," I said, tearing the wrapper off and taking a huge bite.

He lowered his eyes modestly. "Maybe a lesser saint. Hey, you look a lot better. Now that you're not puking all over the flowers."

"Don't remind me." The words tugged at something I should be recalling, and I frowned.

"No worries; puke is probably good for flowers."

"You're so disgusting."

"Oh no, did I vomit into my hair?" he asked, eyes wide in pretended dismay, and dodged backward. "No punching! Are you really okay?"

I lowered my fist. "I feel fine." I didn't; I had that nagging suspicion I was forgetting something, and my head was beginning to ache. But both suspicion and headache cleared as we left Mansfield behind.

The cast was still on break when we got there, Iris holed up in the lighting booth with the technical producer. Greens and reds flickered over the stage while the fairies practiced their weird dance and Lysander and Demetrius scuffled good-naturedly in the wings. Iris had decreed it would add interest for them to fight hand to hand before they pulled out knives and Puck intervened to lead them astray, so I took them aside to practice the routine, with a few horror stories beforehand to stop them getting out of hand.

The stories made them cautious for a few minutes, but it didn't take long before they were careless and sloppy again. When long-limbed Demetrius clipped Lysander on the side of the head and sent him staggering, I'd had enough.

"Stop," I hissed, fits on hips. "Pay attention to what you're doing!"

Lysander, still rubbing his ear, looked inclined to take me seriously, but Demetrius shrugged. "Whatever, man. Sorry."

I clamped down hard on my temper. "No. Not whatever. I have an ethical responsibility to my art. Either you do it the way I showed you, with care, or I stop coaching you. Understand?"

Demetrius opened his mouth, caught my eye, and abandoned whatever he'd been about to say. His spine straightened and he nodded.

"Is there a problem?" Iris asked, popping up behind me.

"No problem," I said, wishing I'd had a mirror so I could reproduce whatever expression had made Demetrius shut it. It could come in handy in all sorts of situations. "We'll run this one more time and then I think it'll be good to go."

The boys behaved perfectly, and Iris assured me that I'd only have to come to the next rehearsal, when they were doing a full run with set and props. I was almost sorry. Annoying actors and rude prima donnas aside, working on the play had been fun. It felt good to *do* something.

"But of course you should come see it for free," she said. "Come on opening and closing nights and stick around! Those are the best parties."

"I haven't been to a party for a while," I said, trying to work out how long a while. Before the diagnosis? No, surely not, that was over eighteen months ago. "That'd be great."

Iris gave me the brightest of her many bright smiles, and turned back to the action on stage.

I had to wait for Kevin, so I wandered backstage again. I

explained to the short, sturdy stage manager that the chances of my climbing up rickety scaffolding to help her erect lights were exactly nil, evaded Carla's attempt to enlist me in the ranks of her sewing assistants, and escaped to sit on the stairs outside before anyone else could ask me to do anything.

I took a deep breath of frozen air, which burned all the way down, and huddled into my coat.

"Pandora! I've been looking for you!" curly-haired Blake said from the door. He descended to sit on the step behind me and I twisted to keep him in view, flattered at the spark in his eyes. "What do you think of the set?"

The backdrop had been painted with a wide frame that I guessed was meant to represent a doorway, pointed at the top. Half of it was in a style influenced by Māori art, curling koru and triangles and squat figures in red, white, and black. The other half resembled an old-fashioned European-style villa, with cream-colored wooden posts and some clumsy fretwork under the eaves. The space through the doorway was filled with a wild tangle of badly traced native forest. I wasn't really crazy about Iris's weird New Zealand-centered vision for the play, and I thought that even the forty-foot rule couldn't make the backdrop look anything more than amateur work.

But Blake had paint all over his hands. Clearly honesty wasn't called for.

"It's very symbolic," I said.

He laughed. "You think it's crap."

"No, no! It's just not exactly my style."

"We could discuss your style," he said. "After rehearsal. Over coffee."

I blinked at him. "Uh...would that be okay with Carrie?"

"Sure," he said easily. "I can make new friends, can't I?"

"Oh," I stammered. "I would love to. But I can't tonight."

He tilted his head at me, then nodded.

"I'm not brushing you off. I really can't; I have an essay due tomorrow and I haven't started it yet."

"Ah," he said. "Another time?"

"Yes, please," I said, like a polite kid to a friend's mother. New friends, of course, I told myself, even if Blake's interest didn't seem merely friendly. This was university—we could be adults.

"We're up, Blake," Carrie said loudly from the doorway, and I leaned back, feeling my cheeks heat. She wasn't glaring—her face was carefully blank—but I got the impression that she wasn't happy.

Blake looked mildly exasperated, then shrugged. "Tomorrow, then," he said and got up.

I concentrated on tying my hair back, taking much longer than necessary. The padded door swished shut.

I took a deep breath of frigid air and stood up, preparing to go back in, when a gangly, flame-haired figure appeared on the path from the bridge over the creek.

My skin tingled. I hesitated, wondering whether to play it cool and pretend I hadn't seen him, but by then Mark was at the foot of the steps, looking up at me.

"Hey, Spencer," he said. "What are you doing out here by yourself?" His voice was light and friendly, but he was not smiling.

I pointed at the noisy theater. "I'm not exactly alone."

"Still," he said.

"You're not one of those guys who thinks a girl needs an escort everywhere she goes, are you?" I asked. "Little bit sexist, Nolan."

His feathery eyebrows knit together and then smoothly relaxed. "Got me there," he said, and sat down, uninvited, at the bottom of the steps.

I was still standing, but there wasn't any question of going back inside now. I took a few steps down and sat behind him, politely tucking in my knees. "What about you? What are you doing here?"

He waved at the university buildings across the creek. "Oh... studying. For the *Odyssey* essay."

I made a face. "Yeah, I haven't started it yet. La Gribaldi's gonna kick my ass." Something was tugging at the corner of my mind, demanding attention, making me vaguely uneasy. This was how yesterday's conversation on the bus had started. But there was nothing about that conversation that could make me feel like this—we'd talked about procrastination and comics and it had gone really, *really* well.

"What?" I said, suddenly aware he'd asked me something.

Mark smiled and repeated: "So you're a theater girl?"

"Oh, no. No way. I'm a tae kwon do girl. They needed someone to choreograph the fights, and I guess I was the only sucker to say yes."

"Whoa, martial arts?"

"Yeah. I'm a black belt, first *dan*."

"I knew it," he said. "You really are a superhero."

I grinned. "It's not that impressive. But I like teaching. I used to assist Master Rosenberg-Katz at home."

He tucked his hair behind his ears. Something silver gleamed on his bony wrist, catching my eye, but he tugged the coat sleeve back down.

"Tae kwon do," I said, and stopped. Did I really want to start talking about this?

Mark's eyes opened wide, inviting.

"Well, the thing is," I said, hugging my knees, "my mum had cancer last year."

"Oh," he said, looking blank. "I'm so sorry."

"She's fine now," I said hastily. "Or, you know, she's in remission, you can never be *sure*, but for a while it looked as if she wasn't going to be fine at all. The mastectomy surgery was really painful and the chemo took a lot out of her and—anyway, it was all pretty bad. And I sort of stopped. I didn't—I had friends, and a guy who was sort of my boyfriend, but I didn't really go out much because Mum needed help and stuff had to get done and after a while I stopped going out at all. The only thing I really did—outside school—was tae kwon do. My dad started going back to church, and he wanted me to come with him, but I couldn't do that. I didn't have any faith in it. I didn't—" I stuttered to a halt, suddenly realizing that I was painting an entirely accurate picture of me as a pathetic no-mates who'd lost her boyfriend and her entire social life.

But Mark didn't seem to notice that I was confessing to being a loser. "So you're an atheist?"

This was a much better direction for the conversation. "I'm agnostic, I guess. I'd believe if I had proof."

"Some people find faith comforting," he said.

I resisted the urge to roll my eyes. "I know. It must be nice for them."

"You don't believe in anything out of the ordinary? Ghosts?"

I began to shake my head, then hesitated. "Well, I've never seen any. My grandmother said she saw ghosts all the time when she was a girl, but then she got married and had my dad, and they stopped showing themselves to her. But she believed in God too, so, I don't know."

"What would you do?" he asked. "If you found out the Greek gods or fauns or harpies or dryads were real?"

I laughed. "Stay the hell out of their way, jeez. You know the stories. Nothing good ever happens to humans who get mixed up in that stuff."

"That's sensible," he noted, the corner of his mouth twisting. "Anyway, sorry, go on. I didn't mean to start an interrogation."

I hesitated, but he nodded encouragingly. "Well, actually, it's kind of related. Master Rosenberg-Katz — she's amazing, she's a fourth *dan* — could see that I wasn't doing well, so she invited me to assist with teaching, and she'd talk to me after classes about *eum-yang*."

"Yin-yang?"

"That's the Chinese; this is Korean. Same concept. It's all about finding balance, physically and mentally. It really helped, last year." I shrugged, trying not to feel embarrassed at spilling my guts so very thoroughly. "So I guess I have faith in that; in trying to be balanced, even though I'm not very good at it. And trying to pass it on." I gestured at the theater. "Even through something like this."

Mark had twisted on his step so that his body was angled toward me, elegant shoulders leaning in. "That sounds really good," he said. It was an ordinary enough thing to say, but his voice was soft, and a little wistful, and sent a shiver through me that had nothing to do with the weather. "Listen, Spencer—"

The door banged open and I jumped, filled with instant hatred for whoever had interrupted this moment. So much for balance.

"Oops," Iris said, and grimaced apologetically. "So! We're closing up now."

"Right," I said, getting to my feet. Of course Kevin was right behind her, giving me incredibly subtle eyebrow-raising, twisty-mouthed, aha-I-see-you-there-with-your-eternal-crush faces. Of *course* he was.

And right behind him was Reka. She stopped, staring down at Mark, and though I took a step down, he refused to take the hint and move. We were all lined up on the steps, like that bit in *The Sound of Music* where the kids sing the goodnight song, except this was not cute and funny, but cold and weird. There was a prickly sensation in the air.

Reka's eyes went from Mark's face to mine and back again, absolutely blank. Then she smiled; not the beautiful one she reserved for Kevin, but something small and sharp and not very nice.

"How's it going, Nolan?" Kevin said.

"Hi," Mark said, eyes narrowing. He nodded slightly. "Okay. I'll see you later."

He didn't look at anyone in particular when he said it, but I decided that he was talking to me. I'd said things I'd said to no one but Kevin and my big sister, so he'd *better* have been talking to me.

"Good night," I said, and he got up and walked away.

In the parking lot, Reka cozied up to Kevin again as Iris locked the doors. She spoke quietly to him with her hand on his arm, the fog drifting around her stockinged legs like a caress. Didn't she have any pride? I leaned against Theodore's front passenger door, and sent Kevin glowering looks. Not that he noticed.

"Ellie," he said. "Reka needs a ride home."

I nodded.

"So you can walk," Reka said, without even looking at me.

My jaw dropped at her rudeness and then I straightened. "Actually, I can't."

Kevin was looking bemused, and Reka stepped closer to him. My skin prickled all the way down my spine. "You've walked home from the library by yourself plenty of times," he said slowly, as if he were talking out one of his trickier Calc problems.

"I promised Chappell," I said. "It's nearly time, come on."

"She can walk," Reka said, looking directly at him.

He blinked twice, and then pulled away from her. "What? No. I promised I'd drive her."

Reka's face was blank, but her fingers tightened in Kevin's

coat collar, twisting in the fabric. Then she let him go and stepped back. "Another time, then," she said, and smiled. "Sometime soon, I think."

The hairs rose on the back of my neck, but Kevin said goodnight as pleasantly as if she'd never said a thing out of place, and I couldn't exactly bitch about his new friend without being truthfully accused of envy and spite.

But though I replayed the highlights of the evening in my head, with first Blake and then Mark talking to me like someone they'd like to know better, I could not recover my previous good mood.

I managed to spend only half an hour reading in the living room before I resolved that I really would honestly and for true write the damn *Odyssey* essay now.

I went to my room, crammed my knees under the desk, and levered the laptop open.

There was a scrap of paper lying across the keyboard.

MARK! BIBLE! DON'T FORGET!

My head cleared as the memories jolted back into it.

"Shit," I whispered, and stared at the letters I'd inscribed, trying to think it through.

Mark had done something to me, and I couldn't come up with a logical explanation. So I went with the illogical one.

Magic.

Magic was *real*.

Humiliation smothered me. All this time Mark had been

talking to me like a normal person, like someone who *liked* me. But it had been an excuse, a way to make me stay in at night, or an opportunity to steal the Bible. Even tonight, at the theater, he must have been checking to see if his enchantment had held, while I babbled about tae kwon do and *eum-yang*. And I'd thought it was a happy coincidence that he'd been passing by. I'd thought I was *lucky*.

I'd told him about my mother.

The rage tasted hot and sour in my mouth. I got up to stalk around the room.

"Stupid," I hissed, clenching the note tight in one hand and pressing the cool palm of the other to my burning cheeks. "Ellie, you are so — *God*."

We had Classics the next day, which would provide ample opportunities for saying ludicrous things like, "So, are you a wizard, you *unbelievable dick*?" He'd bewitched me on a bus, which probably meant he wasn't worried about witnesses, but it would make *me* feel a lot better to be surrounded by curious students before I confronted him. And La Gribaldi would be there. She could probably stop a charging bull with a level look and a raised eyebrow, much less Mark — magic or no magic.

It seemed that if I was reading or touching the paper, I could remember what it said without Mark's damn headaches. I cautiously slipped the scrap into my back pocket and waited. The memories were still there.

It turned out that I *could* stop procrastinating on essay writing if I was using the essay to avoid thinking about something even more huge and intimidating. I worked steadily, touching the note in my pocket every now and then to make sure it was still there, like tonguing a sore tooth.

My usual sympathy for Circe's frustrating position in the *Odyssey* kept sliding into something more frightening as I wrote. A fear of a dangerous, beautiful woman controlling hapless men was so obviously ancient Greek paranoia. But my head was clear now, after days of fuzz and mixed-up memories. And if Mark could do magic—I touched the note again—why not Reka, with her sometimes-strange eyes? He'd asked me about her on the bus, I realized, without ever seeming to.

"Kevin likes her?" he'd asked.

And Mark had transferred into Kevin's classes, and come to the theater tonight, to participate in some weird standoff with Reka.

Too many questions, and far too many of them concerned my best friend. I pounded out a frankly shaky conclusion and emailed the completed essay to myself so that I could print it in the morning. My knees made horrible clicking noises when I got up, stiff from being crammed under the low desk for so long. The curtains were still open. No wonder my back was cold.

I went to close them and froze, staring out into the garden. It was dotted with wooden benches, and sitting on one was a tall figure, in a dark suit, white hair in wisps around his head like a dying dandelion, waving at me.

It was the crazy preacher from Cathedral Square. My fury returned, with an all-new target. He'd found out where I *lived*.

I hauled up the sash window and climbed out, not wasting time by putting on shoes or grabbing my coat. The wet grass soaked through my socks immediately, but I covered the ground in seconds. He stood as I approached and held out a *Good News Bible*, looking very serious.

"This is for you," he said. "To save your soul."

I stared at it. It was the same copy Mark had taken, I was sure, down to the blank faces and brilliant smiles.

"Where did you get that?" I demanded.

The man blinked at me. "It's mine. But you need it." He opened it to a passage underlined in red ink. "See? I marked it for you." He took a deep breath and began to read. "'While I slept, my heart was awake. I dreamed my lover knocked at the door.'"

"I don't want it!" I hissed, flicking a quick glance at the buildings behind us. As far as I could tell, mine was the only light on. "What do you know about Mark?"

"Mark?" he said vaguely. "Mark's a good boy."

I hesitated, then went for broke. "He's a magician, right?"

The man's eyelids shivered nervously. There were liver spots on his hands, dark against the brown skin. "Mark's a good boy," he repeated. "He can't help what he is. He tried. She's the demon."

I took a step toward him. I was on the brink of something important. "Who's the demon?"

"Back off, Spencer." Mark was suddenly moving toward us out of the shadowy trees, his hands thrust into the pockets of his long coat. He was glaring at me, as if I were the one in the wrong. I glared back, and had the satisfaction of seeing him flinch.

"You asshole! What did you do to me? What's going on with Kevin?"

Mark's expression went pleasantly blank, and he fumbled for the bracelet around his wrist. "I don't know what you're talking about. It's nothing, Spencer. Nothing."

I could feel a pressure at the back of my skull, but my memory stayed intact. I fished the note out and brandished it. "Mark! Bible! Don't forget!" I quoted savagely. "A *charm* bracelet! That's *hilarious*!"

Shock flashed in his eyes. "Shit," he said. "You made a memory aid." His hand made an abortive gesture that was nearly a grab; I stepped back, clearing kicking range.

"She needs guidance," the man persisted, turning to Mark as if to enlist his aid. "She nearly sees things."

"Through a glass darkly, and with extremely bad timing," Mark said, and sighed. "Spencer, this is my father. He is actually trying to help you. Dad, this is Ellie Spencer."

My mouth dropped open. I registered, again, the clean and ironed clothes.

Mark's father bent to grasp my free hand, and I was too shocked to resist. His palm was rough and dry. "What a charming young lady. I met a charming lady, once." He kissed my hand and straightened, giving me a smile of such sweetness I felt tears prickle at my eyes.

"So if you can stop harassing him…" Mark said, putting his arm around his father's shoulder.

"Why didn't you just say it was your dad's Bible? Why does he think I need help?" I tried to sharpen my voice, but the sunken sorrow of Mark's father blunted my most righteous efforts.

Mark ignored the second question and answered the first. "Because you said he grabbed you. And the last thing he needs is assault charges."

"I wouldn't do that," I muttered.

"Did I do something wrong?" Mark's father asked, hopeless and sad.

"No, Dad. I did." Mark lifted a shoulder, grimacing. "Sorry, Spencer. I should have just said."

It was ridiculous to feel mollified just because he'd baldly admitted to being in the wrong. And it wasn't the point anyway. I settled back onto my heels. "Why were you even talking to me? What did you do to me?"

He didn't bother to lie again. "I'm not going to tell you right now."

"Hypnotism?" I tested.

"Sure. If you like." He gestured at my note. "Can I have that?"

I smiled unpleasantly and tucked it back into my jeans. It seemed to vibrate faintly between my fingers. The soles of my feet were going numb, the toes tingling painfully in the chill, but I refused to dance from foot to foot with Mark bloody Nolan staring at me.

The old man held out the Bible again. "You need it," he said.

"You really don't." Mark sighed. "I don't think it can help you. Anyway, I'll take care of everything."

I started to ask him about "everything," but the old man began to cry. He wept like a child, noisy and unembarrassed, but with an agony that was entirely adult. I thought of my own father, so far from me, and flinched away.

"Oh, Dad," Mark said helplessly. "Please don't."

His father worked his hands together, dodging nervously away from Mark's embrace. Tears collected in his wrinkles, dropped onto the lapels of his jacket. "You see me now, but never again. If you look for me, I'll be gone. Don't let your people practice divination or look for omens or use spells or charms. You will know them by what they do! It's in the Bible!"

The whole situation, I decided, was well beyond awkward. When Mark's father tried to give me the Bible again, I took it from his calloused hands.

Mark didn't seem to care. He took off his scarf. "Here, put this on."

The old man let Mark wrap it around his neck and tuck the edges into his jacket. "Like a cloud that fades and is gone, we humans die and never return; we are forgotten by all who knew us."

"I know you, Dad. You did what you came to. You warned her. Let's go home."

"Home," the old man agreed, blinking at Mark. "You're a good boy. You can't help it."

Mark flinched. "Spencer," he said.

"Yes?"

"Just forget about it for now. I'll take care of it. Trust me."

"But I don't," I said, and saw him accept that with the same pained resignation he gave to his father's madness. He took his father's arm and they made their slow way out of that wavering circle of light.

I managed to climb back into my room without being enchanted or sick or falling off the windowsill, which felt like a minor miracle all on its own. The Bible went in my backpack, and two pairs of dry socks went on my feet. I tucked my memory aid into the socks, which was a bit tricky with shaking hands.

The mask went on the desk, the only beautiful thing in my cluttered, cramped room. So exhausted that I could barely think, I sat for a long time, staring blankly at that perfect face.

Eventually, I mustered the energy to get up, and closed the curtains, shutting out the cold, and the magic, and the blind, wet night.

CHAPTER SEVEN

Crazy? Yes! Dumb? No!

I woke before the alarm.

During the night, the note had had some lasting effect; I tested it by putting it on my pile of clothes when I undressed for the shower, but the memory of Mark's enchantment no longer dropped out of my mind or provoked those awful headaches when I let the paper go.

I traced my fingers over the letters, and thought about the way I'd written it, pressing the words into the paper, willing it to help me remember. And it had.

In the shower I let the warm water beat against my head

and back, formulating and rejecting questions for Mark as either too broad ("What can you tell me?"), too obvious ("So magic's for real?"), or too personal ("Is your crazy father magic too?"). Or too scary.

"Do you know what you are?" he'd asked me.

When I arrived at Classics for third period, having spent all twenty minutes of morning break struggling with the computer lab printers, a note taped to the door informed us that Professor Gribaldi was on leave; we were to have a study period instead.

I'd passed most of my classmates in the corridor but one of them—Hannah something—was scowling at the notice, her own essay crumpling slightly in her hand. "I was up until four on this," she said. It wasn't exactly to me, I thought, just a necessary burst of frustration. The skin under her eyes was dark and tight.

"I turned down coffee with a hot guy," I offered.

"Oh, that sucks! And after all her crap about dedication and sacrifice. I bet students in Virginia never take sick days."

"Are you kidding? Students in Virginia attend classes when they have the *plague.*"

She grinned. "I heard that one senior in Virginia died in the first term, and his decomposing corpse still attended all the classes."

"And got top grades," I said, nodding.

"And got into Yale, Harvard, and NYU."

"Unlike slack Mansfielders, who have no Advanced Placement and no Ivy Leagues to aim for and no work ethic whatsoever."

She laughed and shook her essay. "Four a.m.! I'm going to hand this in at the office. Want me to take yours?"

I handed it to her gratefully, and watched her leave with some surprise. Maybe I *could* make more friends.

A tall redheaded figure turned the corner, saw me, hesitated, and then spun on his heel. Too late. I could move when I wanted to.

I caught up with him just as he made it to the wide glass doors to the humanities building, closed against the winter chill. Outside, the skeletons of leaves danced over the bare concrete. There were no handy witnesses in case he tried anything. But I was not inclined to wait.

"So what am I?" I asked as he reached for the handle.

He stopped, hair falling into his face.

"It's a fair question," I insisted. I'd flicked through his father's Bible instead of going to breakfast; underlined with red were passages about witches, enchanters, and those who communed with the spirits of the dead. It had confirmed my general theories, but was frustratingly short on specifics.

He withdrew his hand slowly. "It is. You're Ellie Spencer."

I opened my mouth, just as he added, "And your eyes are opening."

"What does that mean?"

He ignored that, looking morose. "It's my fault. I didn't mean to. Be careful."

"Your fault?" I wondered, through the rising thrill of both excitement and terror, and he jingled his bracelet at me. I remembered falling against him, and the strange, electric tingle down my spine as my hair had caught in his charms. Yes, and only after that had he come to fog my head.

Only after that, in fact, had he noticed me at all.

"What are *you*? Do you know Reka?"

"I can't tell you," he said, and screwed up his nose. "Gribaldi's not sick," he offered.

"What? So?"

"One of her old students was killed by the Eyeslasher," he said. "She went to the funeral."

"What has that got to do with anything?"

"I mean—" he started, and then began to cough, great tearing bursts of sound that left him leaning on the wall and fighting for breath. He recovered and stood straight, reaching for the door again. "I've got to go. Don't go out at night. It's dangerous." He hesitated, shook his hair out of his eyes and looked straight at me. "Please?"

The effect of that level green gaze, both sincere and frightened for me, was enough that I abandoned my urge to kick him in the kneecap. But his secrecy was still *infuriating*. "You and I are going to have words," I promised.

He shrugged, and went out. The wind rushed in to tug at my skirt and hair, and then vanished, leaving only my shivers behind.

Rehearsal was a *nightmare*.

I had forgotten to bring the mask for the full props run, and Iris very nearly snapped at me before striding off to confiscate the short knives the fairies were poking at each other. Kevin and Reka spent all their time offstage together, whispering in the corners, and I spent most of mine spying on them and trying to pretend I wasn't. I didn't know if Reka was a witch, but I *did* know she was bad news. And whether by accident or by design, she kept me from taking Kevin away for a private conversation about Mark Nolan and hypnotism and possible witchery.

The first three acts were awful. The non-speaking fairies and Puck were supposed to do these intricate bits of physical theater representing magic in the world, but though Blake was perfect, the others fumbled and pushed and got out of time with the haunting flute music and, at one point, nearly dropped Bottom on his papier-mâché donkey head. The rude mechanicals still didn't know what they were saying, and didn't care. Iris was so tightly wound she was nearly vibrating, and her notes at the break went from encouraging statements to something that was pretty close to pleading.

But the fights went off okay, and Demetrius and Lysander were gratifyingly well behaved.

When the notes were over and everyone scattered to various tasks, Blake found me to remind me of our coffee date.

"Sure," I said absently, watching Reka stroke Kevin's arm, and then my brain caught up with my mouth. "I mean, I'm looking forward to it."

"I can guarantee she won't follow us there," he said, nodding at Reka.

I laughed. "To coffee? Definitely not."

Blake snorted. "Isn't that allergy stuff the most prima donna bullshit you ever heard?"

"It's not real?"

"Who ever heard of an allergy to hot food? To the *smell* of hot food? What does she do, eat raw fish and berries?"

"She's pretty strange," I ventured. "Has anything weird ever happened around her?"

"Weird? How do you mean?"

"Like...I don't know. Supernatural." I was beginning to blush.

He looked at me in alarm. "You don't believe in that stuff, do you? Vampires and unicorns and fairies at the bottom of the garden?"

"Of course not," I backtracked. "I was trying to set up a bad joke about her being such a witch."

Blake laughed. "Gotta say, if there was ever a candidate for getting a farmhouse dropped on her head—oh, here we go."

Carrie was walking onto the stage, a paper packet of hot fries in her arms. "I think I got enough for everyone," she announced, and began unfolding the layers of paper.

"Don't open it!" Reka's voice sliced through the appreciative hum like a scalpel. She was holding her hand over her nose, recoiling up the auditorium stairs. Her nails were long and unfashionably pointy, and I thought, unkindly, of claws. "Get that crap out of here," she ordered. "You *know* I'm allergic."

"I forgot," Carrie said apologetically, and pointed toward the wings. "How about if we eat in the greenroom?"

Reka's lip curled. "You leave, but the *stench* remains. Iris! I'm going home."

Iris leaned out of the lighting box. "We're going to run the second act," she said mildly.

"Not with me," she snapped. "I made it very clear what accommodations I required. *No cooked food.* If your cast can't respect that, I'm not certain I want to be a part of the production."

Opening night was less than two weeks away, and there were no understudies. Two pink spots appeared high on Iris's cheeks.

"That's not fair!" Carla said indignantly.

"*This* isn't fair," Kevin said, striding across the stage and snatching the greasy paper package from Carrie's unprotesting hands. She'd been shocked into stillness by Reka's fury, but she squeaked and jumped back as he took the food, eyes wide.

Kevin banged through the greenroom door. I was following him before I was entirely aware of it.

He was wrapping the fries in garbage bags, burying them in layer upon layer of bright blue plastic.

"What was that?" I demanded.

He tossed the package into the rubbish tin closest to the back door. "This crap makes Reka sick."

"Carrie said she was sorry. You scared the hell out of her!"

He wedged the back door open and started yanking the dressing room windows open. They shrieked in protest, rust showering the sills. The temperature dropped as the fog outside began seeping in.

"Kevin! It's freezing!"

"It makes Reka sick," he repeated. The expression he turned toward me wasn't entirely his own. His eyes glittered feverishly in the middle of a face usually so familiar that even his remarkable handsomeness was less noticeable. Now he looked beautiful and dangerous and nothing like the friend I knew.

The door swung open behind me and I jumped, half turning. I was keeping my feet hip-width apart, my arms up and braced over my rib cage. A defense stance. I hadn't known I was in it until I stepped smoothly to face what my body told me was a new threat.

Reka strode past me, her eyes trained on Kevin's face. Looking at her, he relaxed, that terrifying beauty transforming into slavish devotion. My stomach twisted.

Iris followed her, still protesting Reka's departure, but she lurched to a halt when she saw the two of them together. For a moment, I thought she was going to faint and stepped closer to offer support.

"Will you take me home?" Reka asked softly, laying long white fingers on the inside of Kevin's wrist.

He smiled down at her. "Of course."

They walked out together, both tall and beautiful, looking only at each other. Kevin didn't try to touch her, but he didn't shy away from her hands on him either.

The door swung shut behind them. Iris and I stared at each other.

"He said he was asexual," Iris whispered.

I swallowed hard at the anguish in her voice and looked away. "He is. I don't know what the hell he thinks he's doing."

She managed a mirthless little laugh. "This will sound bitter. But something strange is going on."

I thought about the way Reka had touched him, without any response in kind. "He's gone all protective. Knight-errant. Maybe it's some courtly love thing: no sex involved."

"But it's weird, right?" Iris said. Her face was tight and strained, as if some inner implosion was drawing her features together.

"It's weird," I admitted. "Hey, does Reka ever wear colored contact lenses?"

She pursed her lips. "I don't think so. Why?"

Blake poked his head through the door. "Is she gone, boss?"

"They both are," Iris said.

"Don't stress," he said. "Someone has a tantrum in every show. Usually it doesn't happen until dress rehearsal."

"Something to look forward to," Iris said, but she was smiling again.

"I guess we have the rest of the night off?" he asked, and winked at me.

Iris pursed her lips. "I suppose so," she said reluctantly, and went back to the stage.

"So," Blake said, leaning against the wall and grinning in a way that made my blood leap. "You need a ride home?"

I scowled at the door. "So it seems."

"My car and I are at your disposal. But before that: you, me, and the best coffee I can buy on a student loan?"

"It's a date," I said. "Well, not a *date*."

"A friendly date."

I smiled. "That."

We ended up in a small café in the central city. The place was decorated with hundreds of little kewpie dolls, all individually repainted. There was Pilot Kewpie and Pirate Kewpie and Prime Minister Kewpie, and a whole line of cancan-dancing kewpies, who watched us drink with cute and creepy smiles. Blake apologized for the coffee, but it tasted fine to me. When I said so, I got a ten-minute lecture on different beans and flavors, until he clapped his hands over his mouth and gave me an apologetic look.

"Sorry," he said, through his interlaced fingers. "Some things I'm passionate about, but there's no excuse for boring you. Tell me about yourself?"

I shrugged, feeling young and unworldly. "Not much to tell. I'm down here for a year while my parents are on holiday. Then it's back to Napier, and probably Waikato University." *Also, I'm apparently some kind of potential witch*, I thought, but I wasn't going to float that after he'd reacted with such disdain to the mere idea of the supernatural.

"Pity," Blake said, and it took a second for my brain to catch up. He meant me leaving after this year.

"But I might stay here and go to Canterbury University," I said recklessly. "If I can get used to the South Island winters."

"You North Islanders are all the same," he scoffed, taking a showy deep breath. "Taste that smoggy, muggy air! You can chew on it if you have to! It's invigorating." His brown eyes sparkled at me, challenging and inviting.

"Maybe if you're a South Island mutant," I parried. "Breathing smoke instead of oxygen."

He laughed. "Then you should definitely stay. Improve the stock."

I felt my cheeks heating, and looked away in an attempt to cover. My eye fell on the café's clock (installed in the stomach of a giant Kewpie) and I started. "I have to go."

"So soon?"

"Yeah, I have curfew." I was back to feeling like a kid again, but Blake merely nodded and stood, offering me his arm as we strolled to the cashier. I took it, tucking my fingers against his wiry forearm, and ignored the way I loomed over him.

"Together or separate?" asked the attendant.

"Separate," I said, and was pleased when Blake didn't demur. Making new friends suddenly didn't seem that hard.

We drove back toward Mansfield, but Blake asked to show me the scenic route, promising it wouldn't take that long.

"I love this city at night," he said. "Have you ever seen it from the Port Hills? The whole place spreads out like...a really pretty, shiny thing."

I laughed, and he shot me that wide smile before returning his attention to the route. "Hang on, I can do better than that. Okay, like a little galaxy, with every house light a personal guiding star."

"Oh, that was much better."

"I thought so," he said, and pulled over on a street I didn't recognize, released his seatbelt, and, hand on my cheek, guided me gently into a kiss.

His lips were chapped, but warm, and his hands were careful in my hair, fingers moving in feathery strokes down my neck and scalp. The last person to kiss me had been my sort-of ex-boyfriend, Eric Gould, over a year ago. I suspected that he'd partly asked me out because his two best friends had girlfriends, and he was sick of getting crap. He was a nice guy, but I'd drifted from him, like everyone else, when Mum got sick.

Blake was a much, much better kisser. I sank into the sensation, my eyelids fluttering closed. It took some effort to put my hands on his shoulders and move back.

"Wait a minute," I said, half laughing. "What about Carrie?"

Blake blinked at me, still well over toward my side of the car. "What about her?"

I blinked, suddenly unsure. "Isn't she your girlfriend?"

He grimaced. "She thinks so."

"Is she right?" I was really, really hoping for a denial, but his heavy sigh was a bad sign.

"Well, sort of. I can't break up with her right now, you know? She's having a tough time with her classes. And it'd really mess up the play."

"So what are you doing with *me*?" I asked, feeling my temper start to burn.

He leaned in, breath warm on my face. "I like you. You're sexy."

For a moment I hesitated, remembering the trembling

heat of my lips meeting his. What did I owe Carrie? I didn't even *like* her.

But I didn't want to kiss someone capable of doing this to her. "No."

"Come on," he wheedled, and brushed my cheek with one hand, the other landing on my knee.

I moved closer to the door, and his hands fell away. "Really, no. But we can stay friends, right?"

He was still smiling. "No one would ever have to know," he said, and trailed his fingers up my thigh. Then he squeezed, hard.

All of my alarms went off at once.

Adrenaline coursed through me as I reared back, scrambling for the seatbelt release. My bag was at my feet. While he half-fell across my lap, unbalanced by my sudden retreat, I scooped it up and opened the door, yanking myself out into damp and chilly air. "I said *no*!"

"Oh, for God's sake, Ellie. Jesus! Get back in the car."

"Not a chance!"

Blake lunged across the seat as I tried to slam the door, holding it open. "What are you going to do, walk home? The Eyeslasher's moving south, you know."

Fear quivered for a moment, but it was drowning in my increasing anger, at him and at myself. Mark had told me to not to go into the dark alone; but even if I could trust him, and I wasn't sure I could, I *was* capable of taking care of myself. And being in a car with someone who'd already ignored a no was the more immediate danger.

"I'll drive you home. I won't touch you; I won't even speak. You can't just walk around this late!"

I started walking, my sneakers smacking into the pavement with the force of my steps. I was glad, for the first time in a long time, that I was so big. If Blake got out to press the situation, I knew I could deal with him.

He didn't. "Fine!" he yelled. "You crazy bitch, you can just *be* a drama queen! Don't come crying to me if you get yourself raped!"

I sucked in a breath of pure rage, and whirled, ready to spit out something poisonous, but he yanked the passenger door closed and started the ignition. I turned on my heel again and, stiff-backed, ignored his roaring retreat.

"*Kia ora!* This is Kevin's toaster. Kevin's phone is busy right now. You could leave a message with me, but don't blame Kevin if he doesn't get it. I'm really much better at toast."

"Call me as soon as you get this," I said, striding down the road. "I'm angry at you, you asshole, but I won't yell. I promise. Call me! Please! I'm stranded!"

I cycled through the other numbers on my contacts list, all of them useless to me. Mum and Dad. Friends in Napier. I hesitated at Iris's number, but she didn't have a car. Even if I could swallow my pride enough to call her, she couldn't help me. I hit the end of the list and threw my phone back into my bag.

It was a horrible confirmation of just how alone and friendless I was in Christchurch. If I'd made even a little effort, I could have had Mansfielder friends, ready to help me get home, ready to sympathize with my situation, ready to share my anger with Blake.

But there was no one but Kevin.

And that meant that, right now, there was no one but me.

Out of the twisty little streets at last, I found one of the main roads and the right direction, and set off grimly. It would be a long time until I got home, and Chappell was going to hang me out to dry when she checked the sign-in log in the morning. I huddled into my coat as I walked against the cold wind and worried about Kevin, out in the dark with someone I was convinced meant him harm.

I paid the car no attention until it pulled alongside, engine revving as the driver let it crawl along at my pace. His passenger leaned out the open window, and I summed him up in one glance. Mid-twenties, rugby jersey, cropped hair above a face that might have been handsome if it hadn't been leering.

"Hey! Need a ride?"

Oh, for fuck's sake. "No."

He held up his hands, mock hurt. "Hey, hey! Just being friendly. You should be careful. The Eyeslasher guy killed a girl in Kaikoura. They say he's moving south."

I gritted my teeth at this reminder of Blake and lengthened my stride. "I live just down here." The street branched. I turned the next corner to give support to my lie, resolutely not looking over my shoulder, and trying to walk as if I owned the area.

The car followed. "I'm Liam. What's your name?" The driver laughed and muttered something I couldn't hear, and the passenger whispered back.

Two of them, and big guys. If they both got out, I was in trouble.

I glanced ahead, my heart jerking unpleasantly. The road was a cul-de-sac, blank-windowed houses curling around the blunted road. But it wasn't quite a dead-end. At the highest point of the road's curve, the opening to a narrow asphalt path opened in a chain-link fence, leading into what looked like a park. A car couldn't fit down there.

"Hey! Be polite! What's your name?"

"Iris."

"That's a pretty name. We'll give you a ride home, Iris."

I didn't respond and sped up again, trying to look casual as I gauged the distance to the gap in the fence.

"Come on. We'll look after you. Get you home safe."

I stopped, and the car stopped too. It wasn't fair. Being huge and unfeminine was popularly supposed to prevent this sort of situation, but instead the perpetrators inevitably expected me to be *grateful*. I remembered the malice in Blake's parting shot. I was *not* going to give him the satisfaction.

"Just keep driving," I said, gauging the give in my jeans, and trying not to flinch at the nasty promise in their laughter.

"Come on," Liam said. "We'll all have some fun." His door swung open.

"Go fuck yourself," I suggested, in lieu of a battle cry and stepped clear. I'd always been good at side kicks.

The impact jarred up my foot as the door slammed back on his leg with a wet, satisfying thud. I had time to see the shock and pain blur his features.

Then I ran.

There were shouts and curses behind me, but I didn't look back as I pounded down the road and turned onto the narrow path. It was slick with wet leaves and I skidded in my worn sneakers, recovering my balance with a jolt that strained my knees. I could hear the rush of their chase, but no shouting; they were hunting now. I left the lit path and headed for the shadows, running between copses of trees as silently as I could. When I couldn't hear anything more and cramps stabbed at my side, I scrambled under a tree and waited, listening through the thrumming of my blood in my ears.

I stayed there for a long time, counting the seconds in my head, and crouching against the reassuring solidity of the trunk until even a slow pursuer would have appeared. I let the terror go through me then, in a spate of quiet, vicious curses, most of them directed at Liam, with a few left over for Blake. They got repetitive very fast, but it made me feel better. If I'd taken Latin I would have more variety, I thought, and had to fight back inappropriate giggles. Maybe I could take it at university next year. If I *did* stay in Christchurch.

I slid from my hiding place to work out exactly how lost I was.

Three steps away stood a high wire fence, dimly lit at intervals. The trees towering over the top of the fence weren't the spreading bare limbs of European imports, but the damp green tangles of native foliage, crowned by the kahikatea trees thrusting bare trunks far into the sky before the rounded leafy heads appeared. They were so tall that the security lamps illuminated almost nothing; I could only make out the tree outlines as dark shapes against the fog.

I was outside the Riccarton Bush, where Kevin had

suggested we go in the summer. My stomach hurt, and it wasn't just the running.

But the wet smell of the bush was reassuring. Heedless of the mud squelching under my boots, I trudged to the edge of the fence and leaned in, brushing the tips of my fingers along a leaf.

Only a body's length to my left, wearing nothing but her skin, Reka Gordon walked out of the mists.

I didn't waste time trying to deny my instincts or the evidence of my eyes. She hadn't been there a moment ago; and now she was, naked and perfect and terrifying. She looked me over, up and down, green eyes gleaming in her fine-boned face. Her pupils were missing.

"Ellie," she said. "So *you're* the one skulking at my borders. Have you been reading fairy tales?"

Fear fluttered in my throat, but my voice came out strongly. "What are you doing here?"

Her laugh was a pealing cascade, cold as a waterfall over dark stone. "This is my home. And I don't like intruders. Spying was very stupid of you."

Unbound, her hair was longer than I'd have thought possible, hanging straight and shining to the backs of her knees. Her face was as ageless as I'd seen it first, before I'd talked myself into believing she was an ordinary woman. Now I only wondered that I'd ever thought her even remotely human.

"I wasn't spying," I said, through a mouth dry with terror.

"As you say," she said, in mocking disbelief. "Why else would you come here?"

Since she obviously wasn't going to believe me, I went to the most urgent question. "Where's Kevin?"

She sniffed. "I'm sure I don't know."

"Leave him alone!"

"I need him," she said, implacable. "His protections fade. I *will* have him." She shrugged, in dismissal of me and my protests, and began humming a tune all in minors.

I was sweating, even in the cold. That song wasn't natural. "What protections? What do you need him *for*? Sex? Trust me, he's not interested!"

She looked thoughtful at that, and I had the terrible notion that I'd just handed her a vital piece of information. But she didn't stop humming, and the mist drifted around our legs in thickening strands of white. When something ran over my foot, I squeaked, and kicked. A tiny green lizard leaped away, landing neatly on Reka's bare shoulder and climbing down to sit in her outstretched hand.

Her humming intensified. The gecko sat in her palm, swaying slightly, tongue testing the air as it stared unblinking at me. I felt another weight on my shoe and then, to my disgust, another gecko ran up my leg. I hit at it, and it leapt onto my arm, more tiny feet on my other leg.

The mist thickened until I could see nothing, and Reka vanished into that blank whiteness. But I could hear her, chanting something that might have been Māori. I wasn't really listening. More geckos were climbing onto me, faster than I could shake them off. I tried to scream for help, and a gecko thrust its head into my open mouth. I felt the tiny bones crunch as I bit down, and gagged on the bitter, spurting fluids. I clamped my teeth together as other geckos crawled wet-footed over my face and nudged at my mouth. They were clinging to my hair, settling on my eyelids, crawling over me until I couldn't breathe for the terror of their tiny limbs.

I wasn't *moving*. My feet were rooted as Reka's song rose. Numbed, I heard my fate in her voice—not death, but the long, wooden life of tree and bush, sleeping away winters and rising in the spring to thrust mindless to the sun. I might live a century or more until the rot claimed me, and never remember that I had once been a girl, with limbs instead of branches, who had fought, and run, and kissed.

Anger faded into placid acceptance as her voice sang out the final phrase and hung, questioning, on the last word.

I began to sigh my consent.

She wants Kevin.

No!

Fury brought me back to myself, body motionless and covered in small, sticky feet, but mind unfogged. I didn't know how long I'd been standing there, but now there were two voices chanting in the mists—Reka's, and a male voice, speaking another language I didn't recognize at all.

The geckos were still. Some pressure on me eased as the voice that wasn't Reka's got louder.

The speakers paused, their chants fading.

I strained. My fingers jerked.

There was a quieter conversation, in the rhythms of English, and then silence. Small bodies streamed down mine and ran into the mists.

The owner of the other voice came out of the fog, lanky

body careful and slow. He splayed the long fingers of his pale hand across my cheek and muttered something, and the last of the enchantment holding me motionless wavered and broke.

His eyes were cautious. "Spencer. You okay?"

"Fuck you, Nolan," I said, and fell.

CHAPTER EIGHT

Violent

I'd been really looking forward to passing out, but the shock of landing in cold mud turned out to be a wonderful remedy for a fuzzy head.

Mark bent and offered me his hand. A little closer to my face, and I'd have been able to bite it. Instead, I pushed myself back to my feet, wiping grime off my hands. My jeans were sodden. I'd have to dry-clean the coat.

"That was exciting," I said. The remnants of gecko were still sour in my mouth. I spat into the mud. "What was it?"

"Hypnotism?" he offered, smiling slightly.

My brittle composure snapped.

"Stop lying to me! What is going *on*?" I drove both hands into his shoulders and pushed, hard.

He staggered back. "Oh, you're welcome," he said bitterly, spreading his hands. "I did everything I could to keep you out of it."

"You gave me a migraine!"

He grimaced and held up his hand flat. "I know. I'm sorry. I thought you'd stop trying to remember before it got that bad."

I wanted to stamp my foot like a three-year-old. "What the hell is she?"

Mark looked more tired than anything else. "I can't tell you."

I shoved him again, bouncing him off the fence. "Then I'll tell you what *I* know." There were tears welling out of my eyes. I ignored them.

"I know she tried to *kill* me, and that she's after my best friend, and that this is nearly the worst night of my life. And I know that I don't owe you any favors. If you don't tell me something right now, I'm going to *make* you." Pain flickered across his face when I shoved him again. I smelled smoke and the wet scent of growing things, and under it, the acrid tang of my own sweat. "So!"

He closed his eyes. "So what?"

Fury roared through my head, drowning out the small, inner voice that protested. I pulled my fingers back and drove the heel of my palm under his chin.

The strike snapped his head back and he sagged against the fence, wrapping his fingers against the wire.

"Tell me," I said.

His pale eyelashes fluttered like nervous moths. "I can't."

I threw a two-knuckle punch across his face. His lip split under the blow, dribbling blood down his chin. "Tell me!"

"I can't!"

That inner voice was screaming, and I tried to ignore it. I couldn't kick for the jaw; if I broke it he wouldn't talk well and if I missed, I might kill him. But I could hit the shins or gut, and after he regained his breath, he'd talk to stop it happening again. "Tell me," I said again, and prepared the kick.

His eyelids snapped open, and the look in his eyes drove me back a step. "I. Can't."

Can't, the inner voice howled. *He's saying he* can't*!* I lowered my hands in sudden understanding. "Wait. Not that you won't."

He closed his eyes wearily. "Right." He dabbed at his bleeding lip. "You can't help like this. If you knew a little more—" He broke into a hacking cough, his eyes streaming as he gagged on the words.

I waited a minute, but it was clear he wasn't faking either his attempt to speak or whatever was preventing him from doing so. "It's okay," I said.

He shot me a grateful look, then stared at the blood on his fingertips as if it were an interesting puzzle.

I looked away. "Why didn't you fight back?"

"I don't know how."

"Not even with magic?"

I'd scored a hit; he ducked his head and sighed. "Maybe

I hoped you could beat it out of me. But it seems you can't. So. We're done here?" He glanced over his shoulder, and I pictured Reka lurking unseen in the Bush, and nodded.

We walked silently back toward the sanity of the city night. The richly appointed houses made geometric shapes against the cloudy sky. Until tonight, I'd thought I preferred the softer shadows of trees.

Mark had a car, which pretty much guaranteed that he had in fact followed me onto the bus that day. It was an old Toyota with mud on the wheels and bugs on the windshield. He unlocked the passenger side door first, but I hesitated.

He didn't seem offended. "Your choice."

I shrugged. "It's been a rough night."

He gazed uneasily at me. "It's up to you. But you might—" He started to say something else, then sputtered again, shrugging helplessly as the cough rolled through him.

Well, I already knew I could handle him physically. I swung the stiff door open, reassured by its resistance to my hand. "What about Kevin?"

"Nothing should change until tomorrow night," he said. The words were strained. "If you want to know more, why don't you—" he coughed, clutching at the steering wheel. "Tomorrow morning—the university library," he got out, and then convulsed, fighting for air. I caught his shoulder and squeezed it, helpless to do anything else. The chain bracelet jangled as he jerked, odd charms dancing.

My hair was still knotted around the silver links.

I yanked his hand up, glaring at him. "What's *this*? Is this how you followed me? Did you get this from me on purpose?"

"No! I mean yes, I used it to find you, but I told you, waking you up was an accident. I didn't even know you had latent talent until then."

"Talent," I said flatly. "*Magical* talent." I started picking the blond strand free from the bracelet.

He half smiled. "Don't get too excited. You're not all the way there yet, and even then, you can only work by instinct until you train it."

"Yeah? Will you do that?"

He hesitated. "Maybe. If I can." He took back his hand and inspected the chain. "You got it all."

"You can't follow me?"

"No."

"Good," I said, ignoring the part of me very excited about training in magic. Training with *Mark*. "Because that's really creepy." I stuffed the torn hair in my coat pocket and pulled the seatbelt across my chest. "Take me back to Mansfield. I want to see Kevin."

I made Mark park outside the fence by the Sheppard garden, rather than risk walking past Chappell's residential flat late and covered in mud. Mark didn't look much better than I felt; bruises were already beginning to appear around his perfect mouth.

I touched my own jaw in sympathy. "I'm sorry about that."

"Forget it. I mean…don't worry about it." He hesitated. "I'm sorry about Reka."

I closed my eyes for a long moment, tired of mysteries. "But you can't tell me about that either. Not yet."

He shook his head, and we waited each for the other to fill the silence. Carefully, checking my expression for protest, he leaned forward and touched my face again, the same cool spread of fingertips against my cheekbone that had dispelled Reka's enchantment. My breath stuttered.

"Tomorrow," he said, half question, half promise.

I nodded and swung out of the car without speaking. I didn't trust myself not to say anything stupid.

There were still lights on in my building, and I decided that it would be best to avoid awkward questions about late reappearances and being covered in mud. The best plan would be to climb into my bedroom window, then sneak to the bathroom when the coast was clear to get the worst of the mud off. Then I could take the long way back through the garden and down the road to get to Kevin's building in Pomare.

Under the circumstances, I was pretty proud of myself for coming up with such a good plan, but it all fell apart when I climbed in and found Kevin asleep on my bed.

"Ellie?" he mumbled, sitting up.

"Oh, thank God," I said, and dropped onto the foot of the bed.

He switched on the bedside light and stared at me. "Hell! What happened to you?"

I managed a laugh. "So it turns out Blake's kind of a dick," I began, and explained everything up until Reka walking out of the night. In this version of my evening, I had hidden until the men went away, and then walked home.

Kevin was silent as I went along, but his face gradually went dark red with anger. "I'll kill him," he said when I finished.

I snorted. "Yeah, big man, you're a hero. *I'll* kill him."

"Why all the mud?"

His fists were clenching and unclenching, and I was reminded of the rage he'd unleashed on Carrie over the packet of chips. The memory was uncomfortable, but it was sort of reassuring to have that fury on my side.

"I fell over when I ran." A weird sense of guilt made me add: "He did say he'd drive me safely home. It was me who stayed out of the car."

"You did exactly right," he said indignantly. "He made a move, you said no, he tried again. You didn't know those other two were going to turn up. You *did* know he'd already pushed it once."

I tried to take a breath, but my chest heaved and it came out in hiccups. "I flirted with him," I said, my voice stuttering. "Even though I knew he had a girlfriend. I feel like I asked for it—"

"No!"

"I feel so *stupid*."

Kevin made a distressed noise and hugged me hard, heedless of the mud that got all over his shirt. "You said no," he repeated. "That is the absolute opposite of asking for it, Ellie."

I leaned on him until I could breathe properly again, and wiped tears away when I pulled back. Then I punched his shoulder. "Why are you here? Where the hell did you go with Reka? Didn't you get my message?"

"Phone out of money," he said vaguely, and grimaced. "I was kind of a dick to you tonight. I thought I should apologize."

I sniffed. "Yeah?"

"Yeah." He gestured at his backpack. "So I went to the supermarket and got you some dick-apology wine. But I'm broke right now, so it's *urine d'chat*. Normally I'd recommend getting drunk before you open it."

I tried to smile. "Oh, well, if there's wine I forgive you. What happened with Reka?" My voice sounded false in my ears, just a little too casual.

He long nose wrinkled with distaste. "She tried to kiss me. We were getting on great until then." He paused. "Actually, I don't think she wanted to take no for an answer either. But she did."

"I bet she's not used to hearing it." I must have sounded too sharp.

He gave me a hard look. "She doesn't know many people here. And it's difficult for her, with her allergies. She's a great person, really." His voice rang with conviction; so much so that I winced at his volume and made exaggerated keep-it-down gestures.

"I know, I know. I was only..." *Terrified for you.* "...wondering where you were."

He relaxed, losing some of his evangelical air, and pointed at my desk, and the white mask propped on a pile of notes. "Is that the mask for *Dream*?"

"That's it," I said absently, and then blinked. The mask seemed different, somehow. That buzzing in my ears was back, but it was more like the purr of a contented cat, pleased to have me home. A chill went through me.

"I can take it on Wednesday."

"No!" I said. "I mean...I can take it."

"I thought you didn't have to come to any more rehearsals?"

"The girls still haven't quite got it," I lied.

He shrugged and waved the wine bottle at me. "So. Are we going to drink this?"

I dragged my eyes toward his, and then away. "It's been a long night. School tomorrow."

He handed me the bottle. "In your own time, then. Sorry I was a dick."

"Shut up," I said. "I'm going to hug you again."

"Okay," he said agreeably, and let me lean into his warm solidity, my arms moving in and out with the steady rhythm of his breath. "You sure you're all right? I can stay."

I discovered that I was trembling. "It's—" I began, then sighed, suddenly aware of how tired I was. "It's been a weird week."

"When aren't they?" he said. "It's a Mansfield tradition." He squeezed me and stepped back to pull up the window. "Good night, Ellie."

I watched to make sure he was gone, and then went straight to the mask. It warmed in my hands, and the humming purr traveled up my fingers, akin to but not exactly like the shock I'd got from Mark's bracelet. For God's sake, were these magical things lying about everywhere? Frustrated as I was, I put it down carefully, in what was nearly a caress. My dirty fingers should certainly have left marks, but the mask's face was as smooth and clean as ever. I ignored the urge to put it on and see what happened—I'd walked into enough dangerous situations by following my impulses for one night—and resolved to ask Mark about it tomorrow.

But the mask didn't *feel* dangerous. Not to me.

I chewed on my thumbnail, gagged on the mud, put the bottle of wine into the drawer that held the empty beer cans, and went to the bathroom.

A shower was so normal a thing. There was nothing fanciful about the grumbling pipes or the strange pink stain up the tiled wall. I used the final squeezings of my toothpaste and scrubbed until my tongue was numb.

Dropping off to sleep at last, I could still taste the memory of gecko in my mouth.

Mark's assurances aside, I had no intention of just letting Kevin wander around unsupervised while I researched in the university library. He was probably okay during school, but what about afterward? Who knew what he could get up to without someone to keep an eye on him? Unfortunately, the only solution I could come up with was personally humiliating.

"Hi, Iris? It's Ellie."

"Hi!" Iris sounded startled. "How are you?"

I'm awful, I thought. *Last night I got sexually harassed—twice!—and then I was nearly turned into a tree, and now I've got to skip school and go to the university library in my uniform, where everyone will stare at me, and try to research something I can't even name.* I took a deep breath. "This is a bit weird. But can you do me a big favor I can't tell you anything about?"

Iris hesitated, which was a perfectly sensible reaction to being asked for a favor by a not-exactly-friend at seven in the morning.

"It's about Kevin and Reka," I added. "I'm sorry to bother you, but there's just no one else."

"I'll help," she said instantly. "What do you need?"

I sagged. "Okay. After school, can you take him to your place to hang out? As if it's your idea? Try and keep him there, and if Reka shows up call me right away. And if she tries to get him to go anywhere, don't let her."

"Why?"

"Uh—"

"I have a paper on Māori Urban Migration due on Monday. And exams in two weeks and a show that keeps hemorrhaging cast and crew. I'd like to help, Ellie, but I'd also like an explanation."

"It's really important," I begged. "You know that something's up. You said so yourself."

Iris was too polite to sigh wearily, but I could almost hear her struggling not to. "But you say you can't tell me anything," she said.

"Not now. I don't know enough." I cracked a bitter smile

at Mark's words in my mouth. "I'm trying to find out now." I ran my fingers through my hair, getting caught in tangles before I'd gone three inches. Brushing promised to be painful. "Uh. And can you give me your university system username and password?"

The pause was much longer this time, and I tore another fingernail down to the quick with my teeth, afraid to speak again in case I tipped her the wrong way. "Will you tell me when you *do* know?" she asked.

Really, what were my options? And it wasn't like Mark's love affair with secrecy had helped me any. "Yes," I said. "I'll tell you."

When she let out her breath, it wasn't quite a sigh. "Okay. I'll do it. After school?"

"After school. *Thank* you."

For once, I made it to the dining hall in plenty of time for breakfast, and ate with Samia and Gemma. Samia, who had to get up for dawn prayer, had thoroughly woken up by then and was far bubblier than anyone should have been at 7:30.

"Ellie, did you finish the Geo assignment?" she asked, biting into her toast.

There hadn't seemed much point, since I was going to skip anyway. "Sort of," I hedged. "You?"

"Yes," she said. "But it's awful. I have no idea why I even did Geo this year."

Gemma rolled her eyes. "Because it's handy for a journalist

to know which country is where?" she suggested. Obviously not a morning person.

Samia rolled her eyes back. "Maybe I'll do law instead. What do you want to do, Ellie?"

"Teaching," I said automatically, and then, "or maybe Classics at Canterbury."

Samia nodded. "I heard you were good at Classics. Maybe you can take out the cup this year, instead of Nolan." She filched Gemma's last piece of toast as Gemma turned to wave at her boyfriend across the hall. "At least you'll be there to pick it up."

Gemma turned back and made a strangled cry, grabbing at the crust in Samia's hand. "Thieving bitch! Which *reminds* me, did you use my conditioner?"

"Ugh, no! Why would I want to smell of fake flowers all day?"

I smiled weakly and filled my mouth with scrambled eggs, hoping that Gemma wasn't close enough to me to catch the scent of her hair products.

After breakfast I checked my mailbox, and was unsurprised to find a note requesting that I meet with Mrs. Chappell after school. I pocketed it, and went across the road with the girls, pretending that I wanted to do some homework in the library.

As the corridors filled, I hid in a sciences building bathroom, and escaped out one of the back gates when everyone else was attending morning group, feeling a little smug. There was no way to avoid being marked absent, but I had successfully evaded premature capture.

It was one of Christchurch's clear winter days, with not

a wisp of fog. Given the circumstances, that was more than usually comforting. But the Antarctic wind numbed my nose and fingers in minutes. I joggled in place on the icy stone steps of the library, cursing everyone who'd invented mornings.

The gangly boy who unlocked the doors did a double take at my uniform and then smiled at me. "Bunking off school?"

"At the *library*? No. Special study."

"Jeez, you're eager," he said, but pulled the door open.

I'd meant to wait for Mark outside, but it wasn't worth the frostbite, nor the time wasted. I took the lift up to the fifth-floor computer lab and began.

The search engines were not helpful.

I hadn't really expected a webpage or citation for the Legend of the Vampire Witch Ghost That Haunts The Riccarton Bush. Anything like that would have passed through Mansfield's impressive gossip system, increasing in horror with each retelling. But I had hoped for some evidence of Reka's existence, some idea of what she was, the scope of her abilities, and, most importantly, what I could do to stop her.

There were plenty of stories about the history of the Riccarton Bush, but none of them talked about a mysterious woman living there. There were listings for Reka Gordons, but none of them referred to the woman I was seeking. It didn't surprise me that she wasn't in the White Pages, but she also wasn't mentioned on the drama club's threadbare website, nor in the university listing of enrolled students. When I thought about it, I realized I wasn't even sure if she *was* a student, or what she did if she wasn't. Iris had said that she'd just moved to Christchurch, but it was as if she'd come from nowhere, unnoticed.

Maybe she had.

She'd mocked me for reading fairy tales, which might mean there was something more useful in the stacks, but I was horribly aware I didn't have time to prowl aimlessly through the shelves on the fourth floor devoted to mythology and folklore. Mark had promised me Kevin's safety until tonight, and sunset would come, the newspaper website assured me, at 5:04 p.m.

The lab began to fill up as I browsed through tabs, and every time the door opened I craned to see. But it was never Mark. Doubt wormed at me. Maybe this "research" was just another ploy to get me out of the way. Maybe he'd lied to me about everything, and was even now plotting with Reka.

I clamped down hard on the rising paranoia and went on.

Sometime after noon, I pushed back from the screen and pressed the heels of my hands to my eyes, my stomach gurgling. It had been a long time since breakfast, and I was beginning to have wistful visions of the vending machines in the basement.

Desperate and bored, I tried naming dictionaries. Gordon was a traditional and very common Scottish clan name, not at all special unless you were the type of person who liked to go around claiming your ancestors were once Highland kings. Reka was listed as a few things, including the Māori word for "sweet."

I sat up so fast my wheeled chair skidded backward, making me clutch at the heavy desk for balance.

"I'm an idiot," I said out loud, and ignored the vicious glare from the engineering student on my left. Reka was paler than I was, and I'd assumed she was Pākehā too. But her song had been Māori, or something very like it.

Māori Vampire, I typed. Nothing. Well, that was stupid anyway. I'd seen her in daylight. Māori witch sent me off on a survey of *tohunga*, the religious guardians and special craftsmen, whose knowledge had been handed down verbally for hundreds of years. It would have been fascinating if I hadn't been in such a hurry, and I wondered if some of the stories about curses and transformations could possibly be true. Until this last week, reading *The Lord of the Rings* six times in one school holiday when I was fourteen had been the closest I'd come to dealings with the supernatural.

But if women could walk out of the night and try to turn me into a tree, why couldn't all the rest of it be real? Including my father's lapsed faith?

This was no time for a religious crisis. I tried Māori Immortal, and got a bewildering number of pages dealing with cosmology and the intricate, contradicting myth cycles. I scanned through a few of them anyway. There was a little bit on Tāne-mahuta, God of Forest and Man, journeying to the uppermost of the twelve heavens and bringing back the three baskets of great knowledge from the God of all creation, but it didn't seem applicable. Anyway, if Reka was a big-G God, I was sunk. There were more pages concerning the trickster hero Māui trying to permanently secure immortality from the Goddess of Night and failing badly, but that didn't seem right either.

My heart thudded.

Hidden in an asterisked hyperlink on one of the Māui stories, there was a brief note referring to the long-lived, fair-skinned, bright-haired fairy people who lived in the mists, and created great magic with their songs.

"Yes!" I crowed, and stabbed my finger at the screen.

"Do you *mind*?" the woman next to me snapped, the beads in her dark braids clicking against each other as she whipped her head around.

"Sorry," I whispered, and tried to keep further yelps of triumph internal.

Chapter Nine

All Ready Now

I printed out a list of texts that looked promising and took the stairs down to the fourth floor two at a time. I was terrified and excited, and incapable of waiting for anything, much less the slow library elevators.

I slowed my mad dash to a fast walk when I pushed open the heavy fire door. The desks lining the walls and clustered in the open spaces between rows of shelves were packed with harried people finishing assignments and staring blankly at heavy books, and, at one desk, huddled up and crying quietly over her Japanese text. This would be me, in a year.

Well, hopefully not the crying.

Hunching with my arms at my sides, in a vain attempt to be less intrusive, I made my way between desks and bags and legs tangled uncomfortably around chairs to the right section.

The bright red hair shone in the florescent lights, looking even more halo-like than usual. Mark was sitting slumped at a desk overlooking a window at the very end of the Folklore row, past the shelves on Māori and Polynesian Mythology. Something flared hot and glad in my stomach, even above my resentment that *he* wasn't in uniform. He hadn't lied to me this time. *And* he'd washed his hair.

I tiptoed up and tapped him on the shoulder. "Hi," I whispered.

He twisted, and the anger in his face drove me back a step. His bruises had developed nicely overnight, decorating his lips and chin in shades of blue and purple, edging toward black in the middle.

"Where the hell have you been?" he demanded tightly. "You said you—" He waved at the stacks. "This isn't a game!"

"I've been researching," I said, confused.

"No, you haven't! I've been here since it opened!"

I snapped my jaw shut and thrust the sheaf of papers in my hand into his chest, a little harder than I'd meant to. He rocked in his chair, automatically clutching at them. "What's this?"

"I was *researching*," I snapped. "With databases and search engines. It's the twenty-first century, Mark! And you haven't been at the library since it opened, because I was waiting outside when they opened the bloody door!"

"Shut UP!" an anguished male voice howled from the stacks.

Mark ignored him. "So what did you find?" His tone was still terse, but there was a pink stain spreading across his high cheek-bones, and the paper in his hands shook like leaves in a breeze.

This was more important than my temper. I swallowed my anger, and carefully sounded out the syllables. "She's... pa-tu-pa-i-a-re-he."

Mark took a deep breath. "Yes!" he said. "*Patupaiarehe.* Yes."

Satisfaction stretched my face into a grin.

Mark touched his parted lips with two fingers, eyes blank and unbelieving. "I can say it," he said, and burst into tears.

Girls crying quietly in the library before exams mightn't be so unusual; a boy sobbing noisily was attracting a lot of attention. Mark gasped and shook, and didn't seem to be able to stop. Worried about librarian interference, I hustled him into the elevator and headed for the eleventh floor, under the hope it would be less crowded.

Fortunately, a clump of girls in headscarves cleared out of one of the group study rooms just as we arrived. I shoved him in before the next group could arrive. When they did, I didn't even have to come up with an excuse—the three boys took one look at the tears streaming down Mark's face and backed away, looking more appalled than annoyed.

I sat at the wide table in the middle of the tiny room. From this vantage point, I could see most of the city's west side, and the farmland beyond, out to the hazy outline of the Southern Alps.

Behind me, Mark hiccupped a few times and drew in some long breaths. I gave him another minute, staring at the misted mountains, before I turned to face him.

"Okay?" I asked.

He blew his nose. "Yeah. Sorry." He didn't look sorry. He clutched the printouts and smiled as if I were some sort of dazzling divinity—Athena bringing Perseus his Gorgon-slaying sword, maybe. Or Māui beating the sun into submission so that his family could have enough light.

"She really is?" I said. "A Māori *fairy*?"

He shook his head. "Fairy's an English word. She's patupaiarehe. Or you could say *tūrehu* or *tiramāka*, or one of the other names. There are different stories. And they're not Māori. They're not human at all."

"What does she want from Kevin?"

"The same thing she wanted from his great-uncle. The one who vanished."

"Robert Waldgrave?" I gasped, feeling my way toward the answers. "Well, what was that?"

"She had his child," he said, and touched his breastbone.

I stared at him—the pale skin, the thick red hair, so like his mother's—and was unable to form a single coherent question from the dozens crowding my head.

I could feel my own face going peculiar, and very red. I tried a few responses out in my head, but settled for, "She wants another child."

"At least one."

"Ambitious. And what happens to Kevin?"

He grimaced and held my eyes.

I thought of Mark's father — Kevin's great-uncle — ranting on the steps of the cathedral; weeping and mad outside my dorm. My fists clenched. "No."

"We're going to stop her," Mark said. His voice was grim, but so earnest he sounded oddly young. I suddenly realized I had no guarantee he *was* young. Reka looked only a few years older than me, but if she'd been around since Robert Waldgrave had disappeared...that was just before the Second World War.

And Mark was her son.

The wariness must have showed on my face, because he stiffened, then sighed. "Believe me, I'm not on her side."

"I don't have much choice but to trust you," I said, which was entirely true, but probably not very comforting.

Mark stared at the ceiling for a moment, then drummed his fingers against the table. "Okay. Some history, then. She's of a species that made New Zealand their home centuries before humans settled here. When humans started migrating, her people withdrew almost entirely to the mists."

"First question," I said, raising my hand, and he nodded.

"The mists are...sort of a real place and sort of not," he said. "They're connected to real places, in the bush and mountains and by the sea. Patupaiarehe can go deep into the mists and move through them, but others can't unless they're very powerful, or have something very powerful. And..." he hesitated. "They're real places to patupaiarehe. They make them real out of their belief. But if you go in and you don't *know* what you'll find, you could find yourself in any kind of place. You bring your own history, your own mythology with you."

I resolved to think this over later and tried to look as if I understood.

"Time works differently there, but they still get old, eventually, and die. Her father was human, but he married a patupaiarehe woman, and Reka was raised patupaiarehe. She's nearly the last patupaiarehe in the South Island. The last of her family."

"Well, not quite," I pointed out.

He waved that off and went on. "In 1939, she joined the drama club to get closer to my father. From what I've worked out from Dad, she didn't have to make him love her. He really fell hard." He rubbed at his eyes. "And then she took him away into the mists.

"They weren't a good place for a Pākehā-raised Christian boy who didn't believe in magic. He was more than half-mad by the time she was pregnant. Then she brought him back, and finding out how much time had passed did the rest. It was the mid-sixties, and he still looked nineteen. His parents were dead. His brother was in his fifties. I think Dad thought he'd been in hell. Trapped by a demon."

"He tried to warn me," I said slowly.

"Yeah. He has…potential. Latent power. That's why she took him; to wake him to his power, and make sure that her children had it. But she never really taught him how to do anything, and now he's too mixed up to learn. He can only see magic, and after I woke you, he saw you had it. He thought your soul was in danger."

I shivered, suddenly understanding the underlined passages in the Bible. "Is it?"

He gave me a small smile. "I wouldn't know."

I thought of Reka's fingers on Kevin's wrist, the bright smile that she gave only to him. "Did she love him?"

Mark scowled. "Love is a human thing. She says she did, because that's the word humans use for things they think are beautiful."

I shuddered.

"I was born in the mists. I was seven or so before I saw anyone except Reka. When I asked, she took me to visit Dad." He laughed bitterly. "If she wasn't what she was, we'd never have found him. When he wasn't in an institution, the Salvation Army took care of him, and no one anywhere knew his real name.

"She taught me patupaiarehe knowledge. I guess *spells* or *prayers* is the closest English. Chants, blessings, curses. But she's half-human by blood, and I'm three-quarters. We're in-between. Time in both worlds helped our power." He paused. "I don't use that power now."

I remembered his voice in the fog, chanting in a language I didn't recognize, not Reka's Māori. "But you do magic."

He nodded and twisted his bracelet around his wrist. "A different kind of magic. Anyway, when I was a kid, we lived here for a while, like a normal mother and son. Playing human is sort of a hobby for her. She stole everything we needed, and more: clothes, jewelry. I had a lot of toys. She likes human things." He shook his head. "We went back to the mists, but I asked to come and visit Dad more often. And after our last visit, five years ago, I just stayed. I got Dad into a house and I stayed with him."

"She couldn't make you go back?"

"Oh, she could have. Probably. She didn't try."

"Why?"

His face closed again. "She said it was because she loved me."

There didn't seem to be an answer to that.

"So she made sure I wouldn't tell anyone what I was or what she was—" he touched his throat. "And mostly left me alone. She thought I'd come back to her in my own time. Once I got tired of looking after Dad, and looking after myself. But I didn't. I saw normal families, human families, and I knew she wasn't right."

He took a deep breath. "And then I saw Kevin. He'd just come to Mansfield. And she saw him too. Even then, he looked like Dad used to. He has the same latent power. And she wanted him the same way."

My stomach tightened. "She—*God*."

"He's my *family*. I knew I had to protect him, and it wouldn't have happened if I hadn't left her. I'm the disappointment, you see. I'm not loyal, and I don't even use patupaiarehe power any more. She wants another child of power, to carry on her birthright."

"That's disgusting," I said.

He went on, relentless. "I knew I had a couple of years; she doesn't like children that way, so she'd wait for him to get older. And I knew she couldn't take him from his home; that's *his* place. But Mansfield isn't a home. So I enrolled there, and I put protections around him, as much as I could without looking obvious, and I did a lot of studying, trying to find a permanent solution."

He pounded his fist into his palm. "He's *safe* there. But

he had to do that bloody play. She just keeps wearing all his defenses down!"

"That's why you switched into all his classes?" I asked. "So you could prop them up again?"

He nodded, looking exhausted.

I sat there for a moment, trying to fathom the immensity of Mark's lonely watch. He'd started school the same time as Kevin—nearly five years of guarding his cousin from his mother. However time passed in the mists, he must have looked like a thirteen-year-old kid when his work began; a scrawny, beautiful kid who never made friends, or took part in school events, or even collected the awards he'd won. A kid looking after his father, who never came to Parents' Days.

"I think that's the bravest thing I've ever heard," I said.

He looked wary, as if he thought that I might have been making fun of him.

"I mean it," I insisted, and then abruptly remembered something important. "Kevin's not going to be at Mansfield after school today!" I said, feeling panic rise. "I made a friend of his take him. But she's going to call me if Reka turns up."

Mark frowned out the window, at the sun. "It should be okay, so long as he's back before dark. Reka will need to take him into the mists and it's much easier to do at night. Everything's easier for them at night."

"So. What's the plan? Did you find your permanent solution?"

He nodded. "I think I've found something that'll work,

but it's risky. When she tries to take him I cast a spell that will force her to give up her claim. Then he'll be safe always."

"But she has to try first," I said.

"Yeah."

"Then what do you need me for?" I asked, as lightly as I could.

"You're the distraction," he said. "I might not be able to take her by surprise, but she should have a harder time with both of us there. You're untrained, but you can see her. You'll puzzle her; enough that she'll be wary of you." His eyes flickered in some internal calculation.

I tried to hide my disappointment. Just the distraction. Right. "It sounds so crazy. What do we tell Kevin, afterward?"

He rattled his bracelet again, tapping the little paperclip man. "Afterward, he won't remember it ever happened."

"Hey! No!"

"Yes," he said inexorably. "I can't explain it to him without choking on the truth—not until he's already worked it out. Maybe you could; I wouldn't bet on it. But even if you can, do you think you'll get anywhere? They wouldn't stick you in an institution for believing things that aren't real; not these days, not if you're harmless. They'd just give you some antipsychotics and a session a week with a concerned and overworked psychiatrist." He spread his hands. "You'll soon find out that it's easier this way."

I thought about him enrolling in one of the snootiest high schools in the country, with no birth certificate or sane legal guardian. Magic must have made life a lot easier for Mark. What could it do for me?

Or for Kevin?

"You could wake him up," I said. "Like you did to me. He'd have to believe me then."

He looked impatient. "I did it to you by *accident*. I'm not going to try and wake his power unless I have to. Now, this friend you mentioned. What does he know?"

"She," I said, trying not to be resentful about the way he pushed my suggestions aside. "Just that Reka's bad news."

"Can she fight?"

I tried to imagine Iris flinging her handbag away and set- tling into a stance, which rapidly became an image of Iris fall- ing out of her shiny three-inch heels. "I really doubt it. And she's—" *a China doll* "—little. Iris Tsang, you know? She was at Mansfield until this year. At the theater last night?"

"Oh, the short girl. Well, I have to finish preparing." He stood, and I stood with him. "Reka'll probably try for him tonight. Let's meet at your friend's house at four-thirty. Here's my phone number."

I nodded and wrote down Iris's address for him. "I guess I'll read up on this stuff."

He took the scrap of paper, his fingers brushing against mine. He hesitated at the contact, and then stepped toward me, spreading his arms.

I moved sideways, raising my arms for a block.

We both froze. Mark's hands drifted slowly to his sides. I unclenched my fists.

"I was going to hug you," he said carefully.

I flushed. "Oh."

"Sorry. It was stupid. You just found out I'm a freak."

"You're not a freak."

"What would you call it? I'm all in-between. Not human. Not patupaiarehe." His lip curled. "I'm a chimera."

I squinted at him. "Maybe you should see the school nurse about that."

He let out a shocked laugh. "Ellie. Look at me."

The air in the small room was suddenly cold and clammy. I looked up into his strong-boned face and watched as his pupils were swallowed in glossy green.

I let it scare me for a dreary moment, while my skin prickled in the sudden chill. Then something quivered and untwisted in my head, and I saw that Mark's face wasn't actually expressionless. It was still and hard, and the blank eyes made it more difficult to read his emotions, but they were there, just under the skin, pulling his temples tight with pain and hope, tensing around the corners of his lips in defiant vulnerability.

"I'm looking," I said. "I can see you." I fumbled for the words to bridge the gap between us.

Words weren't going to do it.

I wrapped my arms around him, and felt the shudder that ran down his bones. "I can see you," I repeated, and this time he breathed out a shaky laugh against my shoulder, and when I dared to look again, the solid mass of his eyes was not blind to me.

We stayed like that for only a moment, and then I drew back, suddenly shy of his blinding smile. My chest was squeezing in a way that I tried very hard to ignore.

"Four-thirty, then," I said, and cleared his path to the door.

"It's good that you know," he said shyly. "You asked what I needed you for? I think what I most needed was for someone else to know. I'm lucky that it's you."

He left. I slumped over the table, and thought hazy, confused things about the way his head had felt heavy and hard against my shoulder, about how he twisted his fingers while he talked and retreated behind his hair when he didn't want to answer questions. The thoughts got mixed up with thoughts of Blake kissing me in the car, and how I had wanted him at first, tainted memories that made me feel grubby and ashamed.

In any case, I couldn't fall for Mark now. I had to concentrate on my research.

Most of the books on my printed list were still on the dull metal shelves of the Folklore section. I took them all down, settled myself at a spare desk nearby, and tried to concentrate over the thrumming in my veins.

The results weren't reassuring. Not every book mentioned the fairy people, but those that did all mentioned their immense magical power and incredible sacredness. Cooked food or its smell were non-sacred, and could drive them off or keep them away, which explained Reka's "allergy." The books were vague about their appearance. Sometimes they were supposed to have reddish skin and blue or black eyes. Sometimes they were pale skinned and light haired. Mostly, the books agreed that they were beautiful, but there were plenty of more monstrous figures too, like men with huge claws for fingers and a taste for human flesh. There was a story about a giant patupaiarehe woman who had a beak for a mouth and speared birds upon it, and one about a man who took the form of a giant lizard, although another book with the same story classed that one as a *taniwha*, one of the huge, man-eating water monster–guardians.

The patupaiarehe were reputed to sometimes steal human wives or husbands, to live in the thick fogs of the forests and coasts, and to be visible only at dusk and dawn. They were musicians and singers, and their music was magic, capable of curse or transformation. Clearly, though, it was possible to beat Reka. In most of the stories, the humans encountering patupaiarehe avoided potential disaster.

Even as I finished that thought, I saw the problem with my smugness. Of course, I could only read the stories based on the tales of survivors. How many people had simply vanished, their stories never told? I flipped through the titles. And how come so many Māori stories were written down by people with Pākehā names? How much of this was worth believing?

It took longer than I'd thought, even skimming through repeated material, and it all began to blur in my head. I drifted off into unpleasant visions of Reka turning me into something horrible and yanking Kevin into the mists, and I came back to myself with a jerk. I was ostensibly reading one of the stories of Māui and his brothers. The trickster-hero had been human, sort of, but he'd known many spells, and used various magical items that he'd stolen or been given by his ancestors. That wasn't very useful for my purposes, unless I could find someone willing and able to cram years of lore into my head in an afternoon, and then produce my grandmother's sacred jawbone. I imagined Nanny Spencer pulling herself out of her ransacked grave to shamble after me, scolding with her unhinged skull. *Eleanor, you thieving magpie! I should have known you'd come to a bad end! Your sister would never disrespect me so!*

I was trying to stifle my half-hysterical giggles when my cell phone rang.

Everyone in close proximity twisted in their seat and glared as I fumbled for it.

I glanced at the caller ID and hunched over it. "Iris?" I whispered.

Her voice was sharp with alarm. "She's *here*. She got here just after we did, and Kevin's acting really *weird*. Ellie, what the hell is—"

"I'm on my way," I said. "If Mark Nolan turns up, he's there to help. Let him in. Okay?"

"Mark *Nolan*? Ellie!"

I clicked the phone shut on her panic and punched in Mark's number.

"She's at Iris's," I snarled. "With Kevin, *now!*"

"Coming," he snapped. "Go!"

I abandoned my books, grabbed my bag, and ran like hell, ignoring the death glares from the library's patrons.

I jumped down the bus steps before the door had even finished opening, and raced around the corner to Iris's place. The faded green door was locked. I pounded on it with both fists, and nearly overbalanced when Iris pulled it open.

She was still small and delicate, still neatly dressed in a black skirt and white cashmere cardigan, but she looked undone in a way that was foreign to her. There were two red spots in her cheeks, and her eyes were wild, her mouth tight with fear.

"Is he okay?" I demanded.

She nodded and grabbed for my hand. I let her do it, drawing me over the threshold. The air inside felt different, charged with something that prickled down my spine. I shut the door behind me, leaving the lock open for a fast getaway.

"What *is* she?" she whispered.

"Bad news," I said, and remembered that one of Iris's majors was Māori. Maybe she'd worked it out.

But no epiphany showed on her frightened face: "We're going over lines."

"No. We're leaving." I strode down the hall to the living room.

Iris had an allowance from her parents and lived by herself in the tiny house. I usually considered that yet another reason to be envious and hateful, but today I was just grateful she didn't have nosy roommates to get in the way.

The two of them were sitting around the glass-topped coffee table, Kevin in his favorite chair, Reka on the couch, in the space closest to him. Her head snapped round when I entered. She was wearing brown today: a burnished copper dress that pooled around her feet, and a darker half cloak that swung over one shoulder. She glanced up sharply as I came in, and despite all my rage, I nearly stepped back.

Menace drifted from her like smoke on a still day.

Kevin finished a speech and cocked his head at Reka like a puppy awaiting a treat.

"Kevin, I need you," I said. "Please, come home with me."

He looked vaguely troubled. Reka put her hand on his knee and his face settled into pleased contentment. My jaw clenched.

"We're rehearsing," Reka said.

"We're rehearsing," he agreed.

"Kevin, *please*." My voice cracked with the force of the plea. Reka snatched her hand back as if it stung. I deliberately stepped into the gap between her chair and Kevin's. I heard her breath hiss between her teeth, but didn't dare turn to meet her eyes, focusing all my attention on Kevin. My body felt like such a fragile barrier.

Kevin frowned. "What's wrong?" he asked, sounding more like himself.

I paused, caught.

"Could you get me a glass of water?" Reka asked sweetly.

Kevin leapt to his feet and hurried into the kitchen before I could grab his arm. I spun, staggered backward into his chair, and kicked it away. It crashed into the wall, but Kevin didn't charge back in. I heard the pipes complain, and then the gurgle of running water.

Reka leaned back on the gilded throne and regarded me with mild interest. "Goodness, Ellie, are you stupid or just mad?"

"Apparently insanity is your specialty."

Her face went glassy smooth. "Mark's father is no business of yours." She spread her hands in what could have been regret. "Kevin is stronger. He believes in many of the old ways. He won't suffer so much."

Iris was edging behind her, in the doorway to the hall. Three-inch heels or not, she looked ready to leap across the gap and wrap her manicured hands around Reka's elegant neck.

Reka must have felt the hatred aimed at the back of her skull. She shifted to keep us both in view. "Did Mark bother to tell you why I need Kevin?"

"You want kids. You incredible bitch." The faucet was still gushing. Was he trying to find an appropriate glass for his lady love, or was he getting his head clear? I edged closer to the kitchen door.

Reka sniffed and uncrossed her legs. "I could be doing a great deal more than taking one man for a short time. Really, you girls have no idea how much I love your grubby little species."

My lip curled. "We're a *hobby*."

"Don't trust Mark too much, Eleanor. He's got his own goals." Abruptly, her eyes blanked out to that solid green. "Oh, I'm tired of both of you. Eleanor Spencer, you are a lumbering waste of half a talent, and as for you, Iris Tsang, you simpering, *useless*—"

Her words brought pain, a stinging impact that scalded my skin. I saw Iris pale and stagger against the doorframe, but Reka's eyes were trained on me, and her sheer presence pinned me against the wall. My skin felt as if it were being peeled away to expose the quivering flesh beneath.

The doorbell rang.

"Speaking of useless," she said lightly and rose in a rustle of skirts. "'Twere good he were spoken with; for he may strew dangerous conjectures in ill-breeding minds. Let him come in."

Mark didn't wait for anyone to answer the bell. He came down the hall at a dead run and caught Iris under the elbow before she toppled. Her face was drawn tight with pain, but she steadied herself against the doorframe.

He yelled something in the heavy syllables of ancient Rome, and the scalding sensation vanished. I sagged against the wall.

"I really should have taken Latin," I said, and was surprised to hear my voice come out so evenly. Mark released Iris's arm and stepped slightly in front of her to stare at his mother. I didn't need to ask to see that something had gone wrong; his earlier confidence had vanished into a look of tight strain.

Iris slipped off her shoes and planted her tiny hose-clad feet on the floor with all the deliberation of a Sumo wrestler.

"Kevin," Reka said. "Come here."

The faucet shut off. The air was suddenly dead with the absence of rushing water.

Kevin walked through the kitchen door like a toy soldier. I planted myself in front of him. "Stop," I said firmly, and braced.

He tried to walk through me, but I strained my full weight against him, my hands solid at his hips, and he didn't have the momentum to push through. Behind me Iris squeaked with outrage, and something went flying past my ear, accompanied by Reka's surprised exclamation.

It was a shoe. Not a bad weapon, really; the chunky heel might have done some serious damage if it had actually hit her. Instead it scattered cards as it skidded across the coffee table and came to rest against the bowl of peanuts in the center.

"Kevin!" Iris cried with real anguish.

Kevin stopped straining against me, and his face flashed with lucidity. I put my hand up to his eyes. "Stop," I said again.

"Oh, sit down then," Reka said as if it was a minor irritant, but I caught the strain wavering under her voice. It cheered me, even as Kevin blanked out again and walked mechanically to the couch. This much opposition wasn't in her battle plan.

Over Kevin's shoulder, the kowhai tree in the backyard was an inky outline scrawled against the dimming sky. I stared uncertainly. Was that water condensing outside, or just an illusion of the dirty glass?

Whether she was also aware of the coming night or not, Reka showed no qualms when I turned around. Iris was holding her other shoe and squinting speculatively.

"Let him go," Mark suggested. "Give up your claim. Before I make you."

Reka sat down and crossed her ankles, still managing to

suggest she was the tallest person in the room. "That would be very stupid. And even more stupid for you to make me. Don't you care for your people?"

He flinched. "Which people? You made sure I wasn't either."

Reka slammed her hands against the coffee table and we all jumped at the sound. "You foolish child! You did *that* yourself! And now they will come for you!" Her voice came a little undone on the last words, and I realized that she was genuinely scared for him. But of what?

The question must have shown on my face, because Mark glanced at me and said something in fast Māori.

Iris coughed. "It isn't the right place to speak about this," she translated. I gave Mark a hard stare.

Reka smirked at her son. "Yours to explain to your accomplices," she said. "Since you will not accept *my* help."

"Your help comes at a price."

"So does everything, Mark." She thrust her hand out at Kevin, voice softening. "Look at him. He could be so strong."

Mark didn't take his eyes off Reka's face, but as soon as she said it, I saw that she was right. Kevin's face was still eerily pleasant and blank, but the potential for power hummed in his bones like a giant cat purring in sleep. The right stimulus might wake him.

Tendrils of mist brushed against the window.

Reka's voice went on, smooth and calm. "I wouldn't harm him. And you could have brothers and sisters. A family."

"Shut up!" he shouted.

Her mouth hardened. "I must have him, Mark."

His face settled into that stark, potent stillness and he began a low chant in another language. It wasn't Latin; that was about all I could tell. Iris tensed beside him. I half-stepped back, clearing room for an axe kick. If I hit with enough force, I'd break her neck. The thought clenched in my belly like a fist, but my balance was steady.

Reka flicked a glance over my shoulder at the gathering mists, then gasped as Mark's chant increased in volume.

"Your foreign power won't save you," she said, placing a hand on the coffee table for support. Her pale fingers gleamed against the glass. "They'll come for you. You lost what you were born with. You don't count to them. So they'll take your foreign power and your eyes and your life. If you don't want to die, you'll need my help then."

"No," he said brutally. "I don't want anything you have to offer."

Her eyes glinted with something that might have been grief, and then she moved, dolphin quick. Snatching up Iris's shoe, she hurled it with a breathy command—Iris squeaked—Mark shouted—and the living room window exploded outward into splinters of glass.

The mist rolled in. Long-nailed hands lengthening into the claws of legend, stone-hard eyes gleaming in her beautiful face, Reka came for Kevin.

But I was ready, turning to drop over him even as my vision blanked in the thick white air. I landed hard, with his knee slamming into my thigh and my chest awkward against his shoulder, but I landed in time. A clawed hand brushed my back, groping for a hold. I grabbed it and twisted as hard as I could. No finesse, no technique; but something broke with a wet-sounding crunch.

She snarled and tugged free, landing her slippered foot in my back. It knocked the breath out of me and hurt like hell, but I craned my chin over the top of Kevin's unmoving head and held on.

Mark was shouting again, more syllables I couldn't make into words. The smell of something burning, thick and sweet, hung in the air.

Reka screamed like a hawk and raked the nails of her good hand down my back. I kicked back, and her shriek cut off with a gasp as I hit something soft. I felt the wet flow of blood over my skin before I felt the pain, and then it was worse than almost anything; worse than breaking three toes with a bad front kick; worse than dislocating my shoulder in a tournament; worse than blistering sunburn after a ski trip. Only the migraine Mark had inflicted had hurt more. I hissed, because I didn't have the air to scream, and huddled tighter around Kevin.

Mark shouted the same phrase three times, his voice increasing in volume.

"Have him, then!" Reka cried, as if the words had been torn out of her, and vanished, and the mist with her.

My eyes stung in the sudden light as I straightened and turned. Mark was sagging against the doorframe, looking like he'd run a marathon and lost. Iris was standing beside him, staring at me in horror.

"Oh, God," she whispered. "Ellie, your *back*."

I twisted to see over my shoulder, the pain of the move-ment forcing air out through gritted teeth. The back of my blazer was shredded, stuck to my back with my own blood. I couldn't see the extent of the damage, but I was sure I didn't want to.

"Who—" Kevin said, and we turned to stare at him in his chair. "Ellie! What's happened to the window?"

Chapter Ten

Together Alone

Iris crouched by Kevin. "Are you okay?" she asked urgently. "How many fingers am I holding up? What day is it?"

I left her to it and stepped toward Mark. "Reka was scared for you."

He pulled back, hair falling over his face. "That's not my problem."

"What 'they' was she talking about?" I persisted. "They'll take your *eyes*?" A nasty suspicion was forming. "Mark! Does this have something to do with the Eyeslasher?"

"What the hell is going on?" Kevin roared, attempting to get up. Iris sprawled half into his lap and made a small pained sound. Kevin patted her arm absently and jerked his chin at Mark. "What are you doing here?"

"I think Reka drugged you!" Iris said, and peered into his face. "Your pupils are dilated!"

They weren't, but Kevin was diverted from rage into bewilderment.

"I feel weird," he admitted, and rubbed at his forehead. Mark was staring intently at him, fingers moving over the key charm on his bracelet.

"Maybe you should rest?" I suggested. The pain in my back flared into agony as Kevin slung one arm around my waist, but he noticed neither my flinch nor the blood staining his green sleeve as I helped him into the bedroom and onto Iris's bed. Unlike the rumpled sheets of a normal person, it was neatly made, with crisp white linens and a pretty flowered throw.

"Did something happen?" Kevin asked muzzily. "Something happened."

I knelt to tug off his shoes and settled the throw over him. "You should sleep. You'll feel better if you don't try to think about it."

He struggled onto one elbow. "Ellie? Tell me."

I hesitated in the doorway, no longer able to avoid his eyes. They were full of confusion, and pain, and trust that I wouldn't leave him in the dark.

"Sleep well," I said, and switched off the light.

Iris was all spiky angles when I came back, thin elbows thrusting aggressively out from the fists on her tilted hips. She was still holding her other shoe. Mark was slumped against the back of the couch, pinching the bridge of his nose.

"We should get going," he said. "I'll give you a ride."

"Is it safe to leave him?" I asked.

"It's fine," Mark said. "I made Reka give him up. Once done, it's done. She can't claim him again."

I frowned. "Iris, you're staying, right?"

"No," she said. "I want to know about the patupaiarehe."

I deflected Mark's sharp look with an outstretched palm; directed him back to her.

"Oh, come on," she said irritably. "I'm a Drama and Māori major. I read books."

"Books," Mark said, raising an eyebrow at me.

I gave him the finger. He ignored me and stared out of the broken window.

"Mark," I said, softer. "I need to know. I'm stumbling around blind."

"And she promised she'd tell me everything," Iris put in.

Green eyes bored into mine. "You said that if you found out this stuff was real, you'd try to stay the hell out of it."

"That was before I knew I was already in it," I said. Whatever was going on, even knowing that Reka's irritating hints were designed to make me drag it out of him couldn't stop me. This *did* have something to do with the Eyeslasher. "It's too late. You can't stop now." I'd meant it for me, but Iris nodded, folding her arms again.

Under our twin stares, Mark sagged against the doorframe and tilted his bruised face to me. "Just out of interest, Spencer, if I don't tell you everything you want to know, will you beat it out of me?"

I jerked back. "No."

"But I might," Iris said thoughtfully. "I've still got another shoe."

Mark raked his hair out of his face, and looked into the middle distance. "Okay. Come with me."

Before we left, I inspected my back in the bathroom. Reka's claws had cut right through my blazer and blouse so that they hung awkwardly off my shoulders. Iris gave me a big T-shirt that she probably slept in, and I grabbed Kevin's jacket. My bra was also ruined, only hanging on by a few threads, and I took it off, glad for the first time that my breasts hadn't increased much with the rest of me. The cuts were shallow, but long, and naturally, they hurt more the moment I saw them: five angry streaks, curving from under my right shoulder blade to above my left hip. I awkwardly squeezed antibacterial lotion into the wounds and hissed, bracing over the sink with locked arms, trembling until the burning stopped.

It would have been easier with help. But I didn't trust Mark at my back right then, and I didn't want either him or Iris to see me half-naked.

Kevin was hidden in Iris's bed, a small, snoring mountain. I tiptoed in and dropped a kiss on his forehead. It hurt to close the door on him, and even more to hear the front door lock snap as I tugged it shut behind me and went to join the others in the car.

Iris had left me the front passenger seat of Mark's shabby Toyota, and spent most of the ride staring out the back window, lips shaping silent arguments. I sat forward so my back didn't rest against the seat, and tried to stop flicking glances at Mark. He drove pretty well for someone I was almost certain didn't have a real license, staring at the road with a furrowed intensity.

"Where are we going?" I asked.

"The Gardens," he said tersely.

"Why?"

"You'll find out when we get there." He relaxed a little, and noticed me noticing. "I was checking on Dad." He lifted his left hand from the wheel and held it out for me. The furry white tuft was hair, not wool. "He's preaching."

"Neat trick," I said, instead of *Should you be doing that while you drive?*

"What else can you do?" Iris asked. "Since you can't do what Reka does."

Mark must have filled her in on some of his history while I was doctoring my back. That made sense. It was stupid to feel jealous about it.

He pulled into the parking lot before he answered, and sat there for a minute with the engine running, his fingers turning over his charms. "I can do lots of things. Suppress memories. Tangle your feet into falling. Make lightning in my hands and send it to kill you."

Iris made a noise that wasn't quite a gasp. I didn't say anything, but I must have looked as shocked as I felt, because he twisted in his seat and gave me the full impact of his green stare. "I've never killed anyone," he said quietly. "But I could. Ellie, after this, you won't be able to go back. You'll never be normal again. Are you *sure?*"

He meant it. I stared into the misty parking lot and thought about the electric thrill that had gone down me the moment I made contact with his charm bracelet, the determination with which I'd clung to the memory of his bewitching me, fighting to make my pathetic scrap of paper a talisman for my memory. I thought about Reka's song in the night, and the pain burning down my back, and the risk Kevin had run, all-unknowing. I thought about Mark, strong enough to make a life for himself and keep Reka away. And I thought about the mask on my desk, warm and welcoming and perfect.

"Yes," I said.

"Yes," said Iris.

Mark sighed and pushed his door open. "Your choice," he said, and I couldn't tell whether he thought it was the wrong one.

The Botanic Gardens closed at sunset every night. We walked up to the gates just as a security guard was rattling the locked gate. Mark turned smoothly to pace beside the fence, and we walked on in silence until the blue-striped Armorguard car purred past us.

Climbing over the gates wasn't fun. My school skirt was wide enough to not restrict my movement, but my back screamed as I lifted my arms, and howled as I automatically bent to take the landing with my knees. Iris climbed surprisingly well, though she insisted I check for people watching before she hiked her pencil skirt up to her hips. She'd changed to silky black ballet-style slippers, which were only slightly more practical than her heels, but matched her skirt and little handbag perfectly. She didn't need to instruct Mark to keep his eyes closed—he had hoisted his lanky body over with ease and was leaning against the fence of the Peacock Fountain, staring into the water. The fountain was a Victorian ironwork monstrosity with hideous wrought-iron animals gape-mouthed all over it, and it was much improved by the mist's partial concealment.

"They rebuilt this," he said when we joined him. "It was on a little island in the river, but the island sank under the weight, and it rusted."

I wondered if the designers had wanted the horrible thing to crumble quickly. Otherwise, putting cast iron in a river that flooded regularly seemed to lack a certain amount of foresight.

Mark led us further into the park, toward the river. The trees lining the pale gravel path were mostly non-natives, oak and pine thrusting massively out of the earth. I shuddered, remembering Reka's sung invitation to vegetable life.

Mark reached out without looking at me and caught my uninjured shoulder. I couldn't decide on a reaction before he squeezed gently and withdrew. After a few minutes we came to the grassy riverbank and squelched our way down.

Mark was staring at the river, twisting his charm bracelet over his wrist link by link. "Sit down."

I gave up my school skirt for dead and sank onto the bank beside him. Iris eyed the muddy grass for a moment longer, then sat, crossing her ankles. We looked expectantly at Mark at the same time, and I felt a reluctant liking for her. Really, she was being much better about this than anyone had a right to expect.

"The full story," I said. "And explain why Reka said they would take your *eyes*."

The corner of his mouth crinkled. "Actually...the full story wouldn't be a bad place to start. Okay. In the beginning..." He hesitated, then shook his head. "Look. This is a dubious version of the myth. It isn't the whole story, or an entirely true one, and there's no way to get around it. I can't even tell it to you in the right language, because you don't speak it."

"Chapman's Homer?" I suggested.

He slanted a tight smile at me. "Heh. Close enough."

"So," I said, and half bowed, trying to mimic Professor Gribaldi's drawl. "At least be *gloriously* inaccurate."

He returned the bow with an arm flourish that set his charms jingling, and tried again.

"Okay," he said. "This is a story of how mankind was made, and how death entered the world. A long time *after* the beginning, there are Papa-tuanuku, who is the Earth-Mother, and Rangi-nui, who is the Sky-Father. So strong is their affection that they cannot bear to be apart, and remain always in loving embrace. They bring forth many children, but will not relinquish their grip on each other. Those brought forth from Earth's womb are forced to crawl upon her surface, while their father presses against her. There is only close, moist darkness and suffocating warmth. Like everyone, these children want to stretch and grow without the constraints laid upon them by their parents."

I gaped at him. The words had rolled out in a low, passionate flow, his usually ordinary voice becoming something rich and compelling, lightly accented. In that voice, the familiar story was transformed into a living epic of intense fascination. Iris's eyes had acquired a familiar glint. If Mark wasn't careful, he was going to end up with a starring role in her next production.

"Some of their sons gather to decide what should be done. One of the brothers says that they should kill their parents, but he is shouted down. Another proposes they do nothing at all and be content in their closeness, but no one listens to him. As always happens in such meetings, the most charismatic speaker wins the argument. One by one, five of the brothers, crawling in their claustrophobic prison-home, set their shoulders against their father and push. And finally, the last of the brothers, the tallest and strongest, lies on his back and pushes with his mighty legs, and measure by tiny measure, their father's body moves.

"Rangi-nui calls to Papa-tuanuku, and they cleave ever tighter to each other. But they have seeded their own destruction, and the six brothers fight for every finger of space until their father is a torso's length from their mother. Then a body's length. Then as far as they can reach with their arms outstretched. And then, with one final heave, they hurl their father high above the loving reach of their mother's embrace.

169

"And Sky-Father weeps in his grief and Earth-Mother tosses and rumbles in her anger, but it is done, and nothing they can do can ever reverse it.

"The brothers look around and shake out their long hair, stretching freely for the first time in their long lives. The tallest, strongest brother, Tāne-te-toko-o-te-rangi, Tāne the prop of the sky, is disconcerted by his father's nakedness, hanging above them. He gathers lights in a basket, and sets them in his father's cloak, to shine down at night. But the brother who protested this violation is angry with his siblings. He joins his father in the sky, to be the God of Wind and Storm, and he is an enemy to the descendants of his brothers still today."

He rotated his shoulders, and I startled. The vivid images his voice had conjured faded. "With me so far?" he asked.

Iris nodded, her lips parted in admiration.

"But I know this," I said, resenting him and his beautiful voice and his beautiful face and body. They kept tricking me into thinking I could trust him, when most of the evidence suggested the opposite. "It's the Māori origin myth; everyone knows this."

"You've got to know the very basics. Or nothing will make any sense. Ready?"

I tried to ignore the dank sensation of muddy grass against my butt, and nodded.

"Right, then," he said. "After a long time, Tāne makes a woman out of earth, and brings her to life. She is beautiful, and he takes her to wife. Their daughter is the first woman born, Hine-titama, the girl who brings the dawn. Innocent, she does not know her father is her father. He takes her to wife also, and they have many children. Tāne is the God of birds, of forests, and now the creator of man, and this is the beginning of humankind.

"But this incest is wrong, and one day Hine-titama discovers she is daughter-wife to her husband-father. She flees from him, to live in the underworld, and when he tries to fetch her home, he cannot. She has grown strong and fierce in the darkness. She is no longer the dawn maiden, but Hine-nui-te-pō, the woman of the night. She tells her father-husband that he must care for their children in life. She, in turn, will wait to receive them when death enters the world, and protect them, in death, from all evil.

"Tāne grieves, but he must accept her words."

"This story is so sexist," Iris said abruptly. She was working her thumbs into her palms in slow circles, no longer so enthralled by Mark's voice.

I nodded at her. "You get that in a lot of origin myths. The Greeks go crazy for it."

Mark blinked. "You think it's sexist? I always thought the bit where she told him to go away was empowering."

I snorted. "Sure. After the incest he initiated and lied about, she gets to hide underground and be the goddess of dead people, and he gets to be the god of the living."

His eyebrows drew down. "Well, regardless of modern readings of ancient mores" — Iris sniffed — "that's our story: the origin of humankind. The children of Tāne and Hine-titama have children of their own, and those children spread and have children of their own. They are human, but immortal; they do not know death from age. And from their descendents, many years later, Māui is born.

"He is the youngest son, born premature, and, wrapped in his mother's hair, he is tossed into the sea. But he lives. Protected by the ocean guardians and befriended by birds, he finds his way home. He makes his mother acknowledge him and finds his father by following his mother on her nightly visits. When people complain that the days go too quickly, he makes his brothers catch the sun in a net, and he beats it so that it goes slower across the sky. He takes the flaming fingernails of his ancestress, which ends by bringing the secret of fire back to the world. He goes fishing with the sacred jawbone of his grandmother and hauls up a giant fish. His brothers, who are envious of his strength and power, disregard his warnings and beat the fish in his absence, making hills and valleys of flesh. It becomes Te Ika a Māui, the North Island of New Zealand. Māui's boat, Te Waka a Māui, becomes the South Island. He is a trickster and a hero, feared and loved, almost a god himself. He's unbeatable."

He fell silent for a moment, then returned to storyteller mode. "But finally, Māui hears that the immortality enjoyed by the descendents of Tāne and Hine-titama will one day end, unless one brave man can prevent it. And surely, that man is he, who tamed the sun, and dragged land from the sea.

"Accompanied by the small birds, who are always his friends and allies, he goes into the underworld, to the cave of Hine-nui-te-pō, who was once in ages past the maiden of the dawn, and who now guards the dead while she sleeps. She is enormous in her slumber, sitting against the wall with her giant legs splayed. Māui can see sharp teeth of greenstone and obsidian at the junction of her thighs. He knows that to conquer death for all time, he must make a reversal of birth.

"Before he makes this attempt, he swears his bird companions to absolute silence. One breath of sound might wake the goddess. They all promise to keep quiet. And then, while she snores, he crawls into the cave between her legs.

"But he looks so ridiculous, wriggling his way into her, with his legs sticking out and his feet squirming in the air. The birds take deep breath after deep breath, until all their cheeks puff up and they are dying with the need to laugh.

"And then the fantail surrenders to this need, and lets out a trilling burst of mocking song."

Mark brought his hands sharply together. "At once Hine-nui-te-pō wakes, and crushes the impudent man between her thighs. He dies in shame. Worse, in trying to prevent death, he invites it. And ever since, all living things are mortal and must die, to be received and protected by the guardian of the dead, who was once the dawn maiden, in accordance with the agreement she made with her father-husband. And that is the end of the story." His voice fell on the last words, winding away into a tenuous finality.

We waited for a moment, but he said nothing else.

"Are you saying this actually *happened*?" Iris demanded.

Mark hesitated. "Not... a lot of people know the story, do you get it? It's the shape of the story that matters, the way belief forms around it. The story has real weight." He pointed at himself. "Patupaiarehe look like monsters in some stories, but they're beautiful in a lot. I guess people believed more in the beautiful version. And the ideal of beauty changes. If I'd been born two hundred years ago, I bet I wouldn't look like this. The stories shaped me. They shape everyone, inside and out, but me more than most, because I'm magic."

Iris looked mildly perplexed.

He was tugging at his bracelet again. I put my hand over his to still the movement. There was a sense of motion in my head, of important things sliding into new places, forming new structures. "You said 'all living things must die,'" I repeated. "Including the patupaiarehe?"

"Yes. They live a long time, especially if they stay in the mists. But they age, and eventually, they die. They used to be immortal. They don't see why they should pay for a man's arrogant mistake."

"Are you saying they think there's a way to get immortality again?" I couldn't see what this had to do with anything. Good luck to them.

Mark's face was weary. "There might be. This is *living* legend. Hine-nui-te-pō is always there, guarding the dead in her sleep, but maybe she could be, uh... mystically overworked? If the patupaiarehe can burden her with enough work to make her sleep very soundly, they might be able to do what Māui tried to, and regain their immortality."

I suddenly grasped the implications of what he was saying, and gaped at him.

Iris had apparently been a step ahead. "You're saying Reka wants to kill a lot of people?" she said flatly.

Mark smiled bitterly. "That's... not her style. It's other patupaiarehe, in the North Island."

I felt empty. "Can't they just sit and wait for a really bad flu season?"

He shook his head. "They don't have the time. There's maybe three dozen left. They're a dying race."

"What will they do?" Iris asked. She sounded practical

and calm, but her fingers were combing frantically through the ends of her hair.

"I've been trying to work that out for five years. Reka didn't know specifics, so I started researching, making some contacts. Nukes are probably out. But it could be an epidemic—like flu. Or maybe SARS." He took a deep breath. "Whatever they've planned, I think they've already started preparing for it."

I stared at him, that same sliding feeling in my head outlining the shape of some enormous revelation. I almost knew what he would say before he pointed at me.

"You were right, Ellie. But the Eyeslasher isn't just one person. It's a dying species, cannibalizing the power to commit mass murder."

"Oh my God," I said, as the outline became clear. "When they take the eyes, they're taking power, aren't they? That's why you tried to keep me from going out at night. They've been killing magicians for days."

Mark winced, as if in pain, and then, slowly, inclined his head.

In the silence, ducks made their way up the river, small wakes spreading in the dirty water behind their churning feet.

"Magicians like . . . us?" I asked at last.

He nodded, looking slightly sick. "Like both of us. To them, I don't count as patupaiarehe any more."

"But not Kevin?" I pressed.

"No. He's still latent. Not even half-woken, like you."

"Is this why Reka tried to get him now? Before they did whatever they're trying to do?"

Mark's mouth hung open slightly. "Huh. Maybe. I never thought of that."

"This is insane," Iris said. "This is not happening."

My own head was spinning. The stories were true on some level, okay. There really were patupaiarehe; I had seen that for myself. That they were killing real people, in the real world, and stealing their power I could definitely believe. Those dead people on the news had been very real. But that the patupaiarehe were planning to use that stolen power to precipitate a disaster so catastrophic that the guardian of the dead wouldn't notice one of them crawling between her thighs to reclaim immortality for their species—*that* was a bit much.

Still, I forced myself to believe.

"You wanted your eyes opened," Mark said, and rose to his feet. "This should complete that process."

"What are you doing?"

"There's someone I want you to meet." He held out his hand to the river and cried out something long and ceremonial-sounding in Māori.

I raised an eyebrow at Iris.

"I don't understand it all," she said quietly. "I caught greetings. And an apology for the disturbance."

Mark's voice died away. The dark water churned, white froth washing violently against the banks. Gleaming darkly, water cascading from its stately flanks, something rose slowly from the river.

The *something* was immense, and so alien that I could barely comprehend its dimensions. On the long, twisting body, I saw scales grown over with furry algae and jagged spikes like greenstone spear-heads thrusting up from the spine. But it was the face that held most of my attention—a knotted, twisted thing with a nose that was merely two nostril slits and, most arresting, the pupil-less eyes. They weren't patupaiarehe green, but iridescent and as many-colored as opal or the inner shell of an abalone.

"This is my grandfather," Mark said. "Be careful. Show him respect."

Something crumbled in my head; some final remaining barrier between the ordinary person I had been, and my access to the secret potential I carried within me. I barely noticed its disintegration. Instead, I stared up at the taniwha, and wondered if vomiting in terror might be considered rude.

"Wow," Iris breathed, edging closer to me. Her small hand was colder even than mine, but I didn't pull away when she wrapped it around my fingers.

"Did you feel it, Ellie?" Mark asked.

"In my head, like walls crumbling? Yes."

He smiled, and I understood that I had passed a test. It did little to alleviate my terror when the taniwha opened its mouth.

In shape and sequence, the black teeth were those of sharks, marching back in rows, but the smallest was as large as my hand, and they gleamed like obsidian mirrors. The pink tongue was pointed and rough, like a cat's. I waited for some menacing roar or reptilian hiss, but it spoke to Mark in Māori. That jagged mouth apparently had no difficulty forming the sonorous syllables, and the rolling voice was beautiful and low, rippling like water. It sounded real. It sounded human.

In less than a day, I had been harassed, enchanted, shouted at, cried on, and clawed. I'd been cold, scared, dirty, exhausted, hungry, and miserable. And up until now, I'd been mildly impressed with my ability to cope.

But the taniwha's voice finally broke me. It was not the monstrosity, but that which was not monstrous, coming out of that awful mouth. Alive with animal panic that rose directly from my darkest instincts, I turned and pelted up the bank in my heavy shoes, Iris's hand still tight in mine.

"Ellie," Mark shouted. "Don't!"

My shoulder jerked hard as Iris skidded in the mud and my back was aflame, but the fear left no space for anything else, and the pain was like an uninteresting conversation in another room. My shoulder eased as Iris found her feet. She was missing one of her shoes, but I did not relinquish my grip, yanking her over the gravel path and into the misty concealment of the huge, old trees.

One conifer was right before us, its down-spreading branches promising the illusion of safety. I ran us both under it. Iris was gasping for air, her breath coming in noisy pants.

I tugged her into a crouch and clamped my hand over her mouth. "Breathe through your nose," I hissed, and waited until she gave me a wide-eyed nod before I released her to follow my own advice.

I wrapped my arms around my shoulders and shook. Reka had been frightening and evil, but close enough to human, with desires and motivations that shadowed those of humanity. The thing in the water had abruptly convinced me I wanted nothing to do with Mark's secret war.

Except the patupaiarehe needed human lives.

But what could I do to stop them? I couldn't wrap myself around every threatened life and hold on.

"Wasn't it beautiful?" Iris whispered, slipping off her other shoe.

I shivered, trying to fit that description to the monster as big as a house, and the beautiful baritone voice coming from between those teeth. "It's just... when it *spoke*."

Her face went completely blank.

"Iris?" I said quietly.

"Mark's calling me," she explained easily. I grabbed at her wrist as she ducked under the branches. She didn't struggle, but when I made contact my hand stung as if I'd grasped a nettle. I snatched it back, and she scrambled forward, moving carefully but steadily over the uneven ground in her bare feet, ridiculous handbag swinging from her shoulder.

"Oh no," I whispered, and followed her, sticking close to the trees in a probably vain hope of watching without being noticed. A ninja I was not.

Mark was leaning against the Fountain fence again, fiddling with his bracelet and only partially concealed from the view of anyone who happened to peer through the gates. I spared an irritated thought for this impracticality before I remembered I was furious with him.

Iris walked straight up to Mark until she was close enough to touch him, her head reaching neatly to just under his collarbone. They looked like something out of a fairy tale; his flaming hair set against her glossy lengths of black. He put his hand on her shoulder and she shook her head hard, then gasped up at him.

"How—"

"Shhh." His eyes searched the mists. I clung to my tree trunk. "Ellie?"

"What did you *do?*" Iris demanded, and kicked him in the shin.

Mark jumped back, yelping out a curse, and Iris yelped too, grabbing at her stockinged foot. She overbalanced hard into the rim of the fountain with a thump that echoed dully and then lurched upright again, landing a wild punch on his shoulder. He evaded the next one, but he was no longer looking for me.

"I'm trying to help you! Ellie, please come out!"

"What are you going to do?" Iris demanded, limping toward him again. She swung her handbag at him and he danced out of her clumsy, if enthusiastic, reach. "Are you going to bewitch her?"

"I can't! I just want to explain. Ellie, please! It's safe, I promise!"

"I'm right here," I called, and waded through the fog.

He favored me with a tight smile. "Good. We were just about to start pulling hair."

I folded my arms and didn't smile back. Iris was still bristling, but she'd stopped trying to smack him as soon as I appeared. "You enchanted my friend," I snapped.

"You insulted my grandfather," Mark said.

"Some warning might have been nice!" I paused. "Grandfather? Seriously?"

"Reka's father. His wife was patupaiarehe but he was

human before he died. Sometimes, if the land needs you, you can come back as something else."

"Something like *that*?"

Mark's pale cheeks flushed. "He can take human shape if he wants to."

"Then why does he look like a taniwha?"

"Because that's what he is!" he shouted. "You wanted answers! Did you think they would be *nice*? You ran away!"

"Yeah? Well, now I'm walking away," I said, and forced down the voice which said I wasn't being fair. "The buses are still running, Iris."

Iris finished pulling off her muddy pantyhose. "I want to know more, still."

I shuddered. "But it's so —"

"*He*," Mark insisted. "He's the guardian of this place." He kicked the fountain fence. "This poisoned him. But he's strong. He rusted it." His voice was defensive.

Iris nodded as if that made perfect sense. "Cast iron in the water. Like chemical warfare."

Mark nodded, in a stiff imitation of his usual blankness. But I could read his face now, read the genuine hurt that tugged at the corners of his mouth.

I couldn't shake the feeling that I was responsible.

But still. "Taniwha *eat people*, and it's not the sort of thing you can spring on me unprepared," I said, and marched up to the gates. The gravel crunched under my shoes. Iris came after me, skirting the path on the grass. "We'll call you tomorrow, Nolan," I added. "Or you'll call me. Or stalk me. I'll give you more hair if you need it."

"It's not safe," he said quietly. "You'll show up on their radar now."

He was standing by the fountain with his hands thrust into his pockets. Weird mist slow-time aside, he was probably twice my age, I reminded myself. He wasn't some lost kid in need of a home.

His eyes narrowed over my shoulder. Wet air prickled along my skin like a spider walking down my spine.

"Get back!" he shouted, but I was already moving, wrenching at Iris's wrist to tug her away from the entrance.

I thrust her stumbling toward Mark, and spun to face the threat on the other side of the black cast-iron gates.

I'd known danger was there, but not what form it would take. Yet that sense of something otherworldly and strange resonated like a struck bell in my head, and I was not surprised when I saw the five strange patupaiarehe, armed and unsmiling, step silently out of the mists.

Part Two

CHAPTER ELEVEN
Pink Frost

There were four males and one female and they were all naked and pale and inexpressibly gorgeous. If Mark, with his human ancestry, was just incredibly good-looking, and Reka, with hers, edged into the territory usually occupied by supermodels and movie stars, then no human blood had dimmed the radiant, painful presence of these five. The red and yellow hair of the males was tied up in fat knots. The female's hair fell in shining platinum waves across her breasts and back, and reached down to her waist. She might have looked grandmotherly, if any wrinkles had appeared on that ageless face.

I was momentarily so stunned by their beauty that I didn't notice the weapons until they lifted them. Each of the men carried a *taiaha*, the long wooden staffs with their flat-bladed ends and sharp thrusting points fitting easily to their hands. The woman had a bone *mere* dangling from her wrist, the polished surface of the curved club marred with ugly brown stains.

I took it in, the beauty and the terror, as they turned their pupil-less eyes on me. There was a humming thrill in the air, and I thought that perhaps I could speak with these beautiful people and be loved by them.

Then I broke free of the impulse that told me to stay, as stupid as any bird in a trap, and pelted back toward the others.

Iris was running beside the gravel, flying ahead toward the river, but Mark was waiting for me.

His outstretched hand circled my wrist. "Run!" he shouted. Answering shouts rose behind us, and were abruptly replaced by unnerving silence.

I wasn't slow, even in my stiff black school shoes, but Mark was ahead, and yanking me off-balance. I twisted my wrist free through the gap in his fingers, and sped up to run beside him. We caught up with Iris in the half a minute it took to cover the distance, and skidded down the bank together, ungainly and undignified on the wet grass. I hadn't forgotten what was in the river, but at least we'd been introduced.

Mark caught my hand again and tucked his arm securely

about Iris, propelling us into the icy-cold water. My skirt floated up, twisting in the strong current; I spared one hand to shove it back down again and felt an algae-covered rock turn slickly under my shoe. After that, I abandoned the skirt and used my free arm for balance. Iris was swearing like a sailor as we waded forward, almost absentmindedly. English curses apparently exhausted, she switched to Chinese.

I was chest-deep in the center of the river, Iris clinging to Mark to keep her head above the water, when the patupaiarehe appeared and ran smoothly down the bank.

"Mark," I said, hating the way it came out in a squeak.

"Don't let go," he said, something humming through his voice. I stopped twisting the hand he held, and tried to think as the patupaiarehe stepped into the water.

I could slow them down while he and Iris escaped. The women's hospital was just a short run from the other bank, and if they could get through the fence they might be safe in there. Of course, I wouldn't be. One out-of-practice tae kwon do first *dan* black belt trying to take five armed warriors was an extremely stupid idea, but if Mark didn't come up with a better plan very soon, I was going to put it into action anyway.

All five of them were in the water, wading carefully toward us, well balanced, with their weapons ready. We craned over our shoulders, unable to turn without releasing our grip on each other. Iris let out a high noise, splashed, and went silent again.

Something long and dark flowed between us and the advance.

Mark's grandfather reared, water cascading from his flanks as his massive jaws closed halfway down the torso of the blond male leading our attackers. The patupaiarehe shrieked once, and then the taniwha shook his head, like a dog worrying a rat. Gore sprayed across the water as the legs collapsed and tumbled down the slope and the air was suddenly saturated with the sweet scent of blood overlaying a richer, more stomach-turning stench. Something warm and wet spattered against my cheek. I touched it with my free hand. It was too thick to be blood.

My held breath puffed out in a low sigh, but I was screaming internally. On Mark's other side, Iris began swearing again, in a voice on the ragged edge of full-blown hysteria.

Mark was silent.

The remaining patupaiarehe were, briefly, as shocked as we were. Then they howled in ragged chorus and flung themselves at the taniwha's sinuous body, thrusting their taiaha at its throat and darting away. The woman floundered back to shore, letting her shorter weapon swing from her wrist by its cord. The taniwha roared and twisted, flinging the full weight of its spiked mass at them. In the faint, wet light of the fog, I could see two taiaha broken off in its body. Another patupaiarehe shrieked as he was smashed into the water by the monster's bulk. He floated there, broken, and didn't rise again.

The woman on the shore pointed her mere at us, voice rising in eerie song. The air crackled.

"Don't let go!" Mark said.

The taniwha whirled, faster than anything so huge should, and cocked his head at Mark.

"Yes," he whispered to it, and yanked us into the river.

I closed my mouth and eyes before the freezing water closed over my head, schooled by childhood beach summers of being dunked by my sister and her friends. But they'd never thrown me in during the winter. I kicked down, and felt no rocks beneath us.

I opened my eyes.

I could see nothing at all; not even light and shapes blurred by water; not even myself. There was the sensation of motion, a fast rushing through solidity as if I was insubstantial, but I felt no pressure or pain, even from my wounded back. I was anchored only by Mark's hand, the one real thing in this blind flight.

I tried to scream and made no noise. I wasn't breathing. I wasn't sure I had lungs to draw breath with, or a mouth to shape my terror.

Mark tugged me up. Rising, I saw, before I clenched my eyes shut again, the reddish-brown of clay and soft gray silt.

Then we were standing in the middle of a creek that came up to my knees, long river grasses winding about my calves. Iris moaned, a low, wavering noise that cut off into abrupt sobs. Bare-limbed European trees stood on the banks, with the odd patch of green indicating a cabbage tree or pine. I peered through them and made out a familiar squat, large structure, lit up by harsh white lights—the student association building. We were in the part of the creek that the pub overlooked, but it seemed that no one had been out on the cold terrace at the time we appeared. At any rate, there weren't any cries of alarm.

Mark staggered and fell against me, dragging Iris with him.

I stood, somehow, against their double weight, and shoved back until we were all righted again, and splashing toward the bank. We collapsed in a tangle of cold wet limbs and bruises.

"Shelter," Mark gasped.

"We went under the earth," I said.

"My grandfather's work," Mark said. "I couldn't do it." His face was next to mine, his lips twisting bleakly. "We need to find somewhere to shelter. They can't easily come into a building ungreeted. It breaks protocol, saps their power."

Shelter was a good idea for more than one reason. I was shivering so hard I had to clench my teeth against their chattering.

Iris hiccupped, and abruptly drew herself up. "I've still got my keys," she said. "We'll go to the theater."

The student union side of the riverbank was right by the pub, and in order to make it harder for drunk students to drown themselves, it was fenced off. We had to climb out on the university side and go the long way around, heading for the bridge. Iris had scraped her foot on something running barefoot, and couldn't walk properly. Over her weak protests, I got her to jump onto Mark's back.

I took her handbag, feeling a bizarre affection for the absurd scrap of black satin. It was soaked and stained, but it had, unlike my abandoned backpack, survived the evening.

The moon was nearly full and reassuringly clear in the sky, unclouded by tendrils of fog. I stared up at it as we began to trudge along, clutching the bag in numb fingers, humming along to the music the pub was pumping into the still air. Then I jolted to a halt.

"Mark."

"Yes?"

"There's a woman in the moon."

I could see her. She was clutching a scrubby tree, the roots dangling from her desperate grip. Enormous dark eyes seemed to meet mine, filled with an immense despair.

"Yep," Mark said. "There is."

"But that's—" I shied away from *impossible*. "She'd be too big!"

Iris looked. "I don't see anything, Ellie," she said apologetically.

I walked forward, still staring. When I blinked the woman was gone, replaced by the familiar near-circle of the waxing moon. I blinked again and she reappeared, dark hair falling around her face. "She's so sad."

"She can't get back down," Mark said. "She cursed the moon on a cloudy night, and so the offended moon took her away."

"I know the story," I said absently. "She stubbed her toe."

"I know how she felt," Iris said.

"Look at the stars," Mark suggested.

I did. They were only stars, at first, a misty swirl across the dark sky. It took a moment to make out the shapes between them, the curves suggested by their shadows, but when I saw the true picture I stopped walking altogether.

The sky was the body of a man, so large he defied comprehension, massive arms stretching yearningly toward the earth. He was clothed in a cloak woven of light. The stars were a gift, created by a son for his sorrowing father. Tears welled in my eyes and I had to look away. Mark's eyes met mine with ironic understanding.

"Are all the stories true?" I asked. "Am I going to see this everywhere, all the time?"

"You'll see the big stories, the ones that have formed the shape of the world around you. And you carry your own mythologies with you, so you can see the stories that are important to you, the ones that parts of you believe."

I thought of the tall shelf of Māori and Pacific Folklore, the Greek and Roman myths and legends that I'd devoured since I was seven, the Christian iconography I'd absorbed through my father's faith and from living in the West. Maybe even my old Superman comics. "*Only* those ones?"

His face was wistful. "It can be controlled."

I shivered and turned to gaze again at Rangi the Sky-Father, poised above his unreachable wife in eternal solitude, and was not reassured.

It was impossible to look away from the radiance of the sky for long. Iris kept twisting to watch me anxiously, while Mark scanned the trees on either side of the road, fingers tugging at his charms.

"Will they come after us again?" Iris asked, as we started over the footbridge.

"Probably not you, if you stay away from us. They only want people with magic. People like Ellie." He grimaced. "And me. Damn. She was right."

"At least your grandfather killed two." She looked even paler. "When he bit them."

"Deep breaths," Mark said quickly.

"Oh, God, the *smell*." She scrambled off Mark's back and hung over the railing, retching in convulsive shudders. Mark pulled her wet hair out of the way. Stirred by some vague impulse toward comforting her, I patted her back.

After a moment she wiped at her mouth. "I'm sorry."

"Don't be," I said. "It was the grossest thing I've ever seen." Clouds were blotting out the beautiful sky, and I found it easier to tear myself back to earth. Something twinged at the edge of my awareness. "Mark?"

Fog drifted up from the damp road, turning into a thick bank behind us. I could see two dark outlines coalescing in it. "Mark! They're here!"

He pushed past me and ran back to the road to guard the entrance to the bridge, braceleted arm up like a shield.

The taniwha had evidently taken out one more of the male patupaiarehe. The last of them came out of the mist limping on a torn calf, the blood almost as bright as his hair against his pale skin. His taiaha had been snapped to half its length; dark, viscous liquid gleamed on the broken end. But the silver-haired woman was whole and unharmed. She held her mere and watched Mark with calm certainty. The man stepped in front of her, brandished his spear-shaft, and issued a low cry of challenge.

Iris had made it to the end of the bridge by hauling herself along the railing, but she fell trying to make her wounded feet take her weight. I reached for her.

"I can't," she panted. "I can't, I can't, please, just run!"

I shoved the handbag into her hands and hauled her to her feet, thrusting my arm around her waist, my shoulder screaming at the strain. The scratches on my back were aflame, new agony with a harder edge, and I unceremoniously dropped her on the wet asphalt. I was suddenly terrified that I would faint and certain that if I lifted her again, we'd both go down.

"Mark!" I shrieked.

He whirled, his braceleted wrist flung out toward us, and shouted a word. It gave Iris strength; she tore from my grip and sped straight for the theater's back door, pale feet flashing in the murky air like fish glimpsed darting through a silted creek. I spared no further thought on the miracle.

Belly clenching in fear, I ran back over the bridge to stand with Mark as the red-haired man attacked.

I'd never been in a real fight before, not with weapons and people who wanted me dead, and my first panicked impulse was to throw myself forward and batter at them blindly. But years of training held firm, and I slid into place, perfectly balanced.

The patupaiarehe's taiaha spun and struck and thrust, and I managed not to die. It helped that he was already hurt, and that he wasn't used to the shorter length of his weapon, but he was still insanely quick and unhesitatingly fierce. I blocked three blows to my head that smacked my right arm numb from elbow to wrist, and deflected a stab to my gut with my left hand. Brain whirring automatically through the forms, I tried to follow with a strike, but he stepped back to the limit of his weapon range, far beyond where my feet and fists could reach him. Even with the broken taiaha, he could bring me down long before I could land a blow on him.

I screamed a war cry, desperately denying that I was about to die.

"Down," Mark said behind me, magic burring through the eerie calm of his voice and I dropped awkwardly to the gravel. White light crackled over my head and tore the taiaha from my enemy's hand.

He was shocked for one second too long, and fear gave me speed.

With screaming muscles and throbbing back I rose, big hips twisting, and sank my left foot into his gut. He folded over as sweetly as any opponent in the ring, and I flowed smoothly into the axe-kick I would never use in a proper match—one with pads and headgear and no one trying to kill me or my friends. Remorseless, my heel in its heavy black shoe crashed down on his bare skull.

He flopped facedown onto the asphalt path, blood from his wounded leg spreading watery pink over the frost.

I twisted to face my next opponent, sobbing, but the silver-haired woman was gone, vanished back into the mists.

"Run," Mark said calmly, and together we pelted up over the bridge and up the theater steps, where Iris was watching, and holding the door open for us.

Mark dragged the couch in front of the glass door and then slumped onto it with Iris. We were dripping everywhere, and our breath hung white in the frigid air of the green room.

"Showers," I said. "Showers and fresh clothes."

"What clothes?" Iris said vaguely, and then sat up, indignation cutting through the fatigue. "Ellie! Not the costumes!"

"It's that or hypothermia," I said ruthlessly, and went hunting through the dressing rooms. Mark was easy—Demetrius was stouter and shorter, but a close enough fit, and his Edwardian layers would be warm enough. Iris could wear one of the fairy bodysuits, and Carrie's skirts and blouses. Kevin's Theseus costume wasn't finished; I had to settle for the trousers and rough shirts and jackets of the rude mechanicals. Typical.

I gave them their clothes and sent them into the two shower stalls. Mark went in willingly enough, but Iris hopped out again in a moment, looking at the floor. "I can't quite manage the buttons," she said, trying to laugh. "My fingers are too shivery. Sorry, but could you lend me a hand? Or some fingers?"

I could. Her skin was clammy and cold against my hands, like meat from a refrigerator, a sensation that had always made me nauseated. Underneath the stark black and white of her outerwear, she wore a scarlet camisole and panties set, small yellow flowers embroidered around the neckline and waist. I didn't feel up to peeling them off her, and her fingers were too numb to manage it, so I turned the shower on and helped her in, underwear and all, to sit on its floor.

"You're still wet too," she called through the curtain, over the creaking in the pipes.

I was. My hair was drying at the edges, wisps escaping to fly witchily about my head. "I'm next," I said, false cheery.

"What happened after I ran?"

I grimaced, and told her how Mark and I had escaped that final assault.

"Did you kill him?" she asked, her voice matter-of-fact.

I'd been wondering that myself, with a distant queasiness. "Probably not. It's pretty hard to kill with one blow." I swallowed, remembering the litany of possible injuries I'd so blithely recited to Carrie, when she'd wanted to fake kicking Carla in the face. "But it happens. I don't know."

She shut the water off with another clanking, and thrust the curtain aside, her pinkening face appearing around the edge. "I shouldn't have made Mark take me along."

I blinked. "Where did that come from?"

"I slowed you down. I don't even have magic."

"Stop that. You were great."

Still looking gloomy, she wrung the water out of her hair and took the threadbare theater towel I handed her.

"I haven't been very fair to you," I said, as I unzipped Kevin's jacket. I moved carefully; the cold had numbed the wounds in my back, but movement made everything throb and sting again. "I'm sorry."

Inky strands of wet hair clung to Iris's cheeks. She pulled them back impatiently and wouldn't meet my eyes. "Ditto."

I had the horrible impulse to ask what she had thought of me, or said about me, and what she thought about me now. Instead, I sealed the apology with a smile, and waited until she smiled back and politely turned away, letting me peel off my clothes like a sodden second skin.

By the time I came out, Mark had found the theater's first aid kit and presented me with more salve for my scratches, bandages for Iris's torn foot, and a bottle of painkillers. There wasn't any food or heat, but we had light, and places to sit, and a complete lack of frightening murderers, and that turned out to be enough for now.

Mark stood in the corner while Iris sorted old curtains and cloaks from her perch on the couch. He was running his fingers over the white tuft of hair on his charm bracelet and frowning.

"Everything okay?" I asked, feeling the painkillers take hold with a great rush of relief.

"I guess so. I can't get a fix on him." He half smiled. "I'm running on fumes, really. The bracelet's good, but I've been using it hard. It needs to fill up again."

I nodded seriously. "Like Green Lantern's ring."

He shot me a startled glance, and then his whole face relaxed. "Well, I don't need to recharge it with a magic lantern. It only needs time; it should be fine by noon tomorrow. Plus, I can use it on things that are made out of wood."

"Hey, that's only Golden Age Lantern," I said. "Modern Lanterns can use it on anything."

"Geeks," Iris said amiably, and curled herself into a pile of material ends like a sleek cat.

"Here," Mark said, and offered his wrist to me. "See what I mean?"

I could feel myself flushing again, but I reached for the bracelet, trying not to brush against his skin. As soon as I touched the metal I could feel it; the sense of power exhausted, like a laptop switching to power save mode. But there was no sense of personality, just the thrumming power of a useful tool. The bracelet had been made for Mark, but not by him, and it would work for anyone. It would work for me.

My fingers traced around the curve of his wrist, and I discovered that my fingers could divine what each charm was for. This plastic lightning bolt had called the crackling magelight that had torn the patupaiarehe's taiaha from his grasp. The rusty steel key could muddy the memory and encourage forgetfulness. The pebble would turn flesh to stone.

Mark was watching me. "You can tell which is which?"

"I think so," I said, suddenly aware that I was, more or less, holding his hand. But he didn't try to take it back. I kept talking, in the hope that he wasn't fully aware of how I reacted to touching him. "And the whole thing's like a power source, right? You can use it to power other spells that don't already have charms."

He nodded. "I think you have a knack for objects of power. Like this, or that paper you made. That's why contact with the bracelet woke you. It's a valuable talent."

"There's this mask," I began, reminded, but there was a sharp rapping at the greenroom door, and I jolted at the sound, dropping Mark's wrist. The figure of the woman on the other side of the glass was indistinct through the grimy glass, but still recognizable.

"Mark," Reka demanded through the glass. "Mark, let me in."

Iris slid out of her nest to stand on one foot, looking grim.

"Go away!" Mark shouted.

"It's about your father," she insisted, and Mark jerked, and looked at me.

I picked up a piece of wood left over from building the backdrop frame. "Go on."

He dragged the couch out of the way and stood ready as the door swung open. My hands clenched on the wood as she stepped across the threshold.

I felt her power blow across my skin like the hot breath of some massive beast, half saw it shimmer around her like steam rising from baked asphalt after summer rain. There was blood on Reka's right hand, oozing from the split skin on her knuckles, and her left arm was in a makeshift sling. Two of her long claws were broken off jagged.

I stilled as Reka's eyes met mine. Her face was drawn tight with pain. I had seen her angry, afraid, and surprised, but never unbalanced. Now, she wavered.

"You," she said, and for a moment I thought my presence was the cause of her unnerving lack of cohesion.

Mark moved to stand at my left shoulder. I could feel his exhaustion like a damp wind, as tangible as the scratches down my spine, now flaring at the sight of Reka's broken nails. If she attacked now, we would die.

Her blank green eyes swept over my shoulder and settled

firmly on Mark's face. The wet gleam in her eyes was not supernatural.

With real horror, I realized Reka was crying.

"Oh, my son," she said, voice suffused with pain. "Your father is dead."

CHAPTER TWELVE

Body-Shaped Box

"You—" Mark said, and knocked agony into my back when he pushed me aside to get at her.

His first blow was a tight-fisted punch to the ribs, and it took her by surprise. Badly aimed and careless, it must have hurt, but not so badly that she couldn't sidestep the second, nor block the third. She moved around his clumsy strikes as if it were all some complex dance she was leading. When he tried to kick, awkward and low, she caught his foot in her slim hand and flipped him easily onto his back.

He landed hard, breath breaking out of him.

"I did not kill Robert!" she snapped.

I tried to help Mark up, but he staggered away to stand alone. "When we came here," he said, his mouth twisting. "While I *showered*—"

Reka jerked her chin at his bracelet. "I told you not to put so much trust in your toys," she said brutally, and I wanted to hit her myself. "Your grandfather told me you had run from them, and I came to help you. You were not at your home." She rubbed the back of her hand across her forehead. There was a dark stain on her wide copper sleeve. "But Robert lay outside." Her voice lifted fiercely. "They should not have touched him. He was mine!"

She spoke as of a prized possession that had been despoiled by vandals. But Mark had loved his father, and not just as a beautiful means to an end. He stumbled, clutching blindly for the wall to keep steady.

I braced him under the elbow, ludicrously reminded of bumping into him only a few days ago, when the worst I'd had to worry about was helping out with Kevin's play. Now it was all murder and monsters. It wasn't the sort of thing they advertised in the Mansfield prospectus.

"Mark," Reka said, insistently.

"Can't you leave him alone for a minute?" I snapped.

She shook her head, ignoring her own tears, and darted back out onto the steps. She reentered the greenroom backward, dragging something with both arms.

It was the male patupaiarehe I'd knocked down, dead-weight in Reka's grip. His throat was a torn crimson mess, and the side of his head was crushed, bloody pieces of scalp and worse jiggling obscenely as his head bounced along the worn floorboards.

Well, I thought, cold all over, *that answers Iris's question.* I hadn't killed him. I hadn't gone for the throat, nor broken the skull. But I'd left him there, unconscious, for Reka to find, and turn a breathing body into this atrocity.

"Now I will know what he knows," Reka said, self-satisfied. I had just time to wonder how she intended to get information from a corpse before she dipped her hand into the hole in his skull and raised the befouled fingers to her mouth.

Iris yipped, high and breathy. My head spun and I staggered backward. Mark made some inarticulate sound of protest, cut off by Reka's surprised look.

"I need to *know*," she said.

Mark grabbed my shoulder, and it was all I could do not to scream at the contact. He shuffled me back through the stage door, collecting Iris on the way.

We shut the soundproofed door on Reka's grisly feast and huddled in the darkness of backstage.

"That was—" Iris whispered, and then went fumbling for the lights at the stage manager's desk. When they came on, I could see the tears tracking down Mark's face.

"Oh, Mark. I'm so sorry about your dad," Iris said.

I wrapped both arms around him, ignoring the twinges in my back, and held on.

"Hello?" someone called from the theater entrance. It was the elderly security guard.

Iris took a deep breath and smoothed back her damp hair.

It was eerie, watching her face reposition itself into a bright and smiling mask. "Stay here," she whispered, motioning to a pile of rolled up canvas in the wing, and went out into the theater. After a second her voice came back, all sweet apologies; they were just doing some costume work in the greenroom, of course she'd lock up when they left, sorry for the bother.

I hadn't eaten in hours. My head hurt and my back throbbed. I didn't want to be this vulnerable anywhere near Reka, but I was too tired to be sensible. I lay beside Mark as he sobbed into the dusty material, tucking my feet around his, looping my arm over his waist. My thoughts were fuzzing around the edges, as if my body had given in and said *No, enough, no more, be still.*

I fell, sore and sad, into deep and silent sleep.

I woke up when Mark tried to slide out from under my arm.

Reka was standing over us. In the daze of my awakening, I thought I could see the cannibalized power around her like smudges on a charcoal drawing.

I sat up slowly, muscles creaking, and was grateful that Mark didn't stand or move away from me. Instead, he took my hand in his own and squeezed.

Iris appeared from the stage. She must have slept in the theater seats. Her hair had left red marks on her cheek, like the delicate threads of a leaf skeleton. From her approving smile, I was pretty sure she noticed our linked hands.

Reka ignored her, staring directly at Mark, and at me next to him. She looked smug, so I was gratified to see that she'd taken the sling off, revealing that two of the fingers on her left hand were bruised and swollen, probably broken. I'd done that.

"Did you find out what they're planning?" I asked.

"Yes," she said, and tapped her right hand against her thigh. "They meant to kill you for your foreign power, Mark." She frowned at me. "Her too."

"I guessed that," he said, watching her steadily. "What's going on? Do I need to carry the fight to them? Go up north?"

She snorted. "Hardly. They plan to wake Te Ika a Māui from his slow decline. They mean to tug at Māui's hook and bring his fish into the fast fury of the final death throes. The North Island is no place for you."

Mark went very still. Iris gasped.

"Te Ika a Māui *is* the North Island," I said stupidly.

"Yes," Reka said impatiently.

It hit me like a blow. "Oh, God. An earthquake."

Every child knew the score, from school projects and news reports and countless alarm drills: New Zealand balanced precariously over a fault line, and the next killer quake was only a matter of time. The Wairarapa earthquake had lifted acres of land straight out of the sea. The 1931 Hawke's Bay quake had killed hundreds in my hometown and destroyed most of the city. In my mind's eye I saw Napier's graceful Art Deco buildings collapsing as the earth roared and danced. I saw my friends' bodies, sprawled under the rubble of the high school.

Mark was shaking his head slowly. "No," he said. "Worse than that."

"What could be *worse*?" I demanded.

"Māui's fish is old," Reka said. "He will not survive such violence, to float in this present stupor. The earth will not merely quake, Eleanor Spencer. The land will crumble and sink, back to the depths from which it was drawn out. You see, Mark, you cannot carry your foolish *fight* north. You must stay here, and be safe." She folded her arms across her chest, as in the gesture of a successful closing argument.

I sat there, in the dusty grime of the theater, holding the hand of a myth, and wondered if three million human deaths would so occupy the guardian of the dead that the patupaiarehe could reclaim the immortality they had lost.

And if even one of them had ever balked at the cost.

We were still with the shock for a little time.

"I have friends in the North Island," Iris said eventually.

"Me too," I forced out, through numb lips. "My cousins, my hometown—"

"I wasn't trying to one-up you—"

"I know. It's just too big."

"Yes," Reka said. "Too big to fight." Some of the smugness was vanishing from her voice as she watched Mark's motionless face. "Mark?"

His hand was sweaty in mine. "I've been learning," he said hoarsely. "As much as I could. I could—"

Reka's remaining poise shattered. "You could do *what*? They'll kill you! Eleanor knows nothing, and you're half-crippled. You can't even enter the mists, and you plan to face them alone?"

Mark got up. "Not alone," he said.

She sneered at him. "Will you go to the one you asked to *cure* you? You seemed unsatisfied with that bargain!"

"There are plenty beside him," he said patiently. "You just never bothered to learn about them."

"Men of every creed and race," Iris sang weakly. She giggled nervously when we all looked at her. "From the national anthem. One of the later verses. I always thought it was weird that it's such a peaceful song. 'Guard Pacific's triple star from the shafts of strife and war.'"

"'God defend New Zealand,'" I said. "But since he's not around right now, it'll have to be us." It sounded good, but my voice felt oddly disconnected from the rest of me. I kept having to remind myself to breathe.

"I've got to make some calls," Mark said. "There's...not a community, exactly, but a network of people with power. The Eyeslasher murders have gotten them angry anyway; maybe they're angry enough to unite and fight back."

"There's a phone in the stage manager's booth," Iris said.

Reka grabbed his arm. "But you have to stay," she said, sounding a little broken. "I only told you so that you would stay. You can't go."

"Mother," he said, as if it cost him. "You really don't know that much about me."

She gaped at him.

"And don't attack Iris or Ellie while I'm busy," he added.

"See, I know *you*. If you try to get rid of inconvenient witnesses, I'll fight you. We'll fight for real. And then what'll become of the bloodline?" He tugged his arm out from under her hand, and she let him step clear of her, still with her shock.

"Ellie? What about you?" He looked at me, calm and beautiful in his borrowed clothes, and I saw again the bravery that had first made me love him.

The thought hit me like a hammer between the eyes. I could not love Mark. The idea was impossible, even if there wasn't a hidden war and a horrible disaster fast approaching. A harmless crush on a handsome loner classmate was one thing; hopeless yearning after someone who'd enchanted and lied to me something entirely different, and much more dangerous.

But still. "I'll go," I choked out.

Mark misunderstood my horrified expression. "Don't look like that," he said quickly. "We know what they're planning. We know where it has to take place: at the hook of the fish, near Napier. We can stop it, I promise." He hobbled toward the stage manager's booth, moving like an old man. Like his father. I flinched.

"You will really go with him?" Reka said, after a few minutes of silence, with Mark's careful mutterings the background track.

"Of course," I said, with as much scorn as I could muster. I'd volunteered for a war, and I wasn't a soldier. Last night's frantic struggle against the taiaha-wielding male had very quickly confirmed the difference between my dojang training and the realities of a real battle. I'd seen dead bodies now, and as much as I told myself that they'd hadn't been human, I wasn't even sure I *could* kill.

"It's not my war," she said. "And if Mark goes, I must remain, to be the last of my bloodline."

"And you'd quite like to live forever," Iris said with mock sympathy, obviously still smarting over Mark's implication that Reka had planned to dispose of her like an unwanted kitten.

Reka inspected the ends of her hair. I caught a glimpse of silver threads through the bright red before she began to braid it, her hands moving leisurely through the motions. I wondered, then, how long she had left. Mark had said they aged slowly in the mists, but she'd spent a lot of time in our world. "No, I think we should not go back. No living patu-paiarehe was born immortal. We should live in this world through our children."

"What a fantastic excuse for rape," Iris said sweetly.

"Robert loved me."

"But he didn't know what you were, did he? What kind of consent is that?"

Reka stood, gave Iris a mocking half-bow, and strode toward the greenroom door. She couldn't slam it—the door was padded against exactly that sort of accident—but she did manage a dull thud that echoed in the silent room. I looked at Mark's hunched figure in the booth, but he paid no attention to Reka's departure.

When I turned back to her, Iris was looking thoughtful.

"You can't go," I said, hating myself a little bit for saying it, however true. "You don't have any magic. I mean, it's bad enough for me."

She laughed, a creaking, painful sound. "Of course I can't," she said. "I'm not an *idiot*. But I'll buy your plane tickets."

"You don't have to."

She folded her hands neatly in front of her. "I can't see what you can, and I can't do spells, and I can't fight. I can help this way."

I made a face. "I feel weird about it."

She smacked the canvas, hard, and the dust haloed around her. "This is my land too!"

It was like a fist in the gut, the realization of what we truly stood to lose, while I quibbled politely over money. There was only one possible answer: "Yes," I said. "Thank you; you're right. Yes."

The male patupaiarehe's body was gone by the time Mark finished his phone calls, presumably by Reka's doing. I found myself grateful to her for that, if nothing else.

Iris packed our wet clothes into plastic bags to take with us, and conscientiously wrote a note for Carla, explaining that the costumes had been taken away for a photo shoot.

"You're a great liar," I said.

She smiled proudly.

Then we were outside, shivering in the early morning frost. There were no clocks in the theater, and no one's watch or cell phone had survived our watery journey. I looked at the sun to gauge its position, and nearly cried out. Wounded, the sun limped wearily across the sky, bleeding light from great cuts in his sides where Māui's weapon had struck.

The light was harsh in my eyes, and I quickly dragged my head down. Mark was watching me carefully as we picked our way through the nearly deserted parking lot.

"Sunlight's more dangerous in New Zealand," he said. "Highest skin cancer rate in the world."

"It's the hole in the ozone layer," I replied automatically, then paused. "Isn't it?"

He shrugged.

I looked up at the glowering sun. Māui's gifts were apparently double edged.

We crossed the road to the bus stop, where the display informed us that it was 8:30 a.m. No one spoke much, and I tried not to look at the sky.

Iris's bus lumbered around the corner. I looked at her, uncertain of what to do. Apologize for dragging her into this? Warn her to stay safe? No, that was silly—she was a sensible person, probably the most sensible I knew. Warnings from me would be insulting.

She wasn't paying any attention to me anyway, poking around in her ruined handbag while the bus disgorged its cargo of yawning students. She pulled out her wallet and handed it to me. It was a beautiful piece of leatherwork, a deep red with a tiny black flower stitched into one corner, only slightly water-stained. "I put the PIN for my cards in the coin pocket."

"I can't—" I began.

"You will," she said. "Don't even start. I never lose arguments. I'll call your room when I've got the tickets."

I hugged her, then, on impulse. She surprised me by yield-
ing, not at all stiffly, hands hovering lightly on my shoulders.
"Will you go ahead with *Dream?*" I asked.

She shrugged. "If I can find a replacement Titania who
isn't actually stealing human boys."

I laughed. "When I come back, you and I are going to be
friends."

"Aren't we already?" she asked uncertainly.

"Yeah, but we're going to stay friends."

She grinned. "Kevin will be so pleased. And then he'll be
scared."

"It will be very good for him," I said, and watched her
walk into the bus, straight-backed, chin raised, and brazenly
ignoring the driver's double take at her curious clothes.

Our own clothes got some comment as Mark and I trekked
over the university rugby fields and followed the creek down
Behn Road back to Mansfield. More by habit than anything
else, I led us over the garden fence and toward my bedroom
window, before I realized that school had started, and we
could just go through the door.

I walked in blithely, already calculating what to pack.

Mrs. Chappell stood in the middle of my room, soft pale
purple cardigan and pearls completely at odds with the blistering fury on her face.

My stomach went into free-fall.

She had clearly been through my room. The bottom bed

drawer was open, with the empty beer cans and full bottle of wine lined up on my desk in mute accusation. The mask looked even more beautiful beside them. It was the first time I had seen it with my eyes fully open.

It was calling to me, soft and sweet.

"Eleanor," Mrs. Chappell said, her voice like chips of ice. "Can you provide an explanation for these?"

"No," I said, over the singing in my head.

"No? How about one for your truancy yesterday? Your failure to turn up at our appointed meeting? Your absence last night—to the great concern of your roommates—and your reappearance this morning with *this* young man?" She gave Mark a sweeping up and down look.

"I'm a Mansfield day student," Mark offered helpfully. He fumbled with his bracelet, and then shook his head at me, frowning. Still out of juice, it seemed. Across the room the mask was gleaming whitely, though the pale winter sunlight from my window had not reached it.

"Indeed? Then Principal Kerrigan will certainly have something to say to *you*." She shook her head, blond bob brushing her shoulders. "Eleanor, I am extremely disappointed. Samia observes *hijab*, as you are well aware. Did you stop for even a second to think about what bringing men into this space might mean to her?"

The mask called again, and I gave way all at once. I brushed past Chappell, to her obvious consternation, and picked it up with my bare hands.

The first contact with Mark's bracelet had been a thunderclap inside my head. This was a great ringing of cathedral bells, the connection instantaneous and complete as the mask claimed me and surrendered itself to my care.

Like a shrilling buzz, discordant against that glorious tumult, Chappell spoke again. "Young lady, you are in *very serious* trouble! If you want to avoid suspension or expulsion, you need to start talking."

"I'm sorry," I said. "You're right, especially about Samia." I lifted the smooth, perfect face to cover my own and spoke through the pouting white lips. "But I need you to be quiet now."

There was no resistance at all. Mrs. Chappell went from glaring at me to gazing at my masked face in unfeigned adoration. The mask thrilled against my skin.

"You will remember that you found nothing in my room." She nodded, eager to please. I thought through the rest as carefully as I could with the mask caroling joy through my body. I didn't want her to get fired. "You will tell anyone who asks that the matter has been sorted out, and that I have gone back to Napier, saying there was a family illness. You'll remember these things, but you'll forget that we had this conversation. And when you leave you will be otherwise yourself."

She nodded again, still looking as if I was the only person in the world. "Go now," I said, and closed the door in her yearning face as she shuffled backward out of the room.

"What?" Mark asked breathily, then, "What did you do?"

I reluctantly lowered the mask. It protested briefly, then resumed its song in my hands, delighted to be awake again, delighted to be mine. "When I wear it, it makes me beautiful," I said. "If I want it to, it will make people love me. And then they'll do anything I say, just to make me happy."

Mark flinched. I turned the mask over and over in my hands, and felt the ghost of its smile against my mouth.

CHAPTER THIRTEEN

Not Given Lightly

I pulled out my biggest tracksuit for Mark and handed it to him, but he stood stiffly in the middle of the floor instead of taking the hint. I saw as if through his eyes the crumpled bedcovers, the piles of papers and texts. It wasn't as if I'd prepared for visitors.

"Sorry about the mess."

"It's okay," he said. "Our place is messy too."

I thought of his father's neatly ironed clothes and held my tongue.

"My place," Mark said. "I guess it's just my place now."

He sat down on the bed with a thump, pain pinching his face closed. I groped for words of comfort and solace, but the truth was I had no idea what to say. I had *thought* about my mother dying many times during the Cancer Year. But it hadn't happened.

Rather than risk saying the wrong thing, I said nothing at all. It seemed callous to kick him out so I could get dressed. My back kept protesting sudden motion, so I found clothes for the trip to Napier as carefully as possible. I was emptying out my tae kwon do gear bag, unused since February, when Iris called my desk phone. Mark started at the sound, and finally snuck out to the bathroom, clothes in hand.

"You're on the eleven a.m. flight," she said briskly. "Get a move on."

"You're a legend."

"I know," she said. "Let me know how it goes, with the nation-saving and all. And with Mark."

"With — what?"

"I repeat. I'm not an idiot." There was a beat, and when she spoke again she sounded wistful. "You were hugging each other. When you were sleeping."

That silenced me for a moment, as I felt warmth wash right through me. But: "He's a gorgeous, secretive patu-paiarehe boy who tells lies," I said. "And she's a gigantic, socially inept human girl with anger issues. The prospects aren't good."

"'The path of true love never did run smooth.'"

"That's *Shakespeare*, Iris, not real life. There's no happy ending here."

"Sure there is," she said. "Make it happen."

Taking advice from a woman who, since the age of eleven, had been pursuing someone who wasn't interested in sex was definitely a bad idea. I was tempted to follow it anyway.

"Oh," she said. "Kevin wasn't here when I got back. He left me a note, so I'm not really worried, but if you see him—"

There was a furious pounding at my window, rattling the glass in the frame.

"Don't worry," I said. "He's right here."

Kevin was wearing the green shirt stained with my blood and a thunderous expression, and he climbed through the window with no greeting at all for me.

"Are you okay?" I asked.

He glowered. "No. I woke up in Iris's bed, with wind whistling through the broken window in her living room, and your sliced-up clothes in the bathroom. What cut through your bra, Ellie?" He thrust out his hand, the sad scrap of blue cotton dangling from his fist. I retreated a step.

"I have next to no idea how I got there. But I think you do, Ellie, and I think you don't want me to know." He leaned in. "I am really, *really* not okay. What the hell happened?"

Mark took this opportune moment to walk in. He hesitated, closed the door firmly behind him, and said, "We don't have time."

"You," Kevin said dangerously. "You keep turning up, don't you?"

Mark said nothing, and I quailed at the thought of explanations. *Kevin, this is your cousin. Remember your great-uncle who ran away? Actually, he was kidnapped by Mark's mother, who also tried to kidnap you. Mark stopped her, so he really doesn't deserve that death glare you're giving him. Oh, and his father was murdered last night by inhuman magical beings determined to sink the North Island.*

No. It was impossible. I picked up the mask without really thinking about it, and it vibrated in my hand, eager to help me smooth over the situation. I could make Kevin forget everything, it suggested. I could keep him happy and calm and safe and still trusting me.

Just like Reka.

"Ellie," Kevin said, eerily calm. "What happened last night?"

I took a deep breath, and chose the other way. "I can't tell you yet," I said, and quailed as his face shut down in rage and betrayal.

Mark shot me an ironic look, probably remembering him telling me the same thing before I tried to beat the truth out of him. There was no magical binding to stop me telling all. Except... Kevin's power was still latent, still only potential. The patupaiarehe wouldn't hunt him. We could open his eyes, as mine had opened, but Mark was right. We didn't have time. And it was incredibly selfish, but I could risk myself so much more easily than I could drag Kevin with me.

"Give me a week," I said, over Mark's half-formed protest. Assuming we won, assuming I was still alive. "I swear, I'll tell you everything in one week."

Kevin's breath sucked through his teeth. "Are you *kidding* me?"

"Kevin, please," I said. "Please, please, trust me. I have *never* let you down, not once. I have never lied to you, or told your secrets—" that one hit home, and he flinched away. It hurt my heart, but I continued. "—and I need just a little more trust. Just a week's worth." The mask turned in my hands. "*Please*," I said. I could feel tears prickling at my eyes, and desperately blinked them back.

It might have been the tears that did it, or my tone; I could see him beginning to waver. I resisted the urge to beg, to go to my knees, to break and tell him everything. But I knew I couldn't. I would trade even this friendship to keep him safe.

"It's not drugs or anything?"

"Of course not!"

"But you're in some kind of trouble?"

I shook my head, and then nodded. "But it's nothing you can help with. I just have to go home for a while. Mark's coming with me."

"You barely know him!" He shot Mark a dubious look.

My grip tightened on the mask. "They're not all my secrets to tell, Kevin. And I have to catch the eleven a.m. flight to Napier."

"Okay," he said, after far too long, and gripped my shoulder, a little too tight. "Okay, one week."

My knees weakened with relief, and I felt tears stinging again. "Thank you," I said.

"Are you *sure* I can't do anything?" He was still angry, and fighting down hurt besides, that I was going to Mark, and not him, for help.

I cast around, looking for something to make him feel useful: "You could give us a lift to the airport?"

He rolled his eyes. "Sure. What's a little playing hooky from school just before exams?"

"Thank you. Really."

Mark nodded, earning another suspicious look. Kevin shook his head. "One week, Ellie. I've parked Theodore by the garden fence. I'll meet you there in twenty."

Despite his words, Kevin looked as if he was regretting the decision, hesitating by the open window. I went to brush my teeth, hoping that treating the deal as made would confirm it for him.

When I came back, Kevin had left, and Mark was standing by the window, looking bemused.

"He threatened me," he said.

"Threatened you how?"

"Well, if I do unspecified things to you, he plans to do specified things to me, none of which sound like much fun. Are all your friends this violent?"

"I'm sure that if he knew what you've done—" I began, not-quite apologetic.

"Don't worry about it. Uh. Did you know you were still holding the mask?"

I started and dropped it on my bed. It whined, hurt. "Mark? Is this thing alive?"

He peered at it, hands behind his back. "Not exactly." He scratched his chin, where reddish stubble glinted. "It likes you."

"It loves me," I corrected.

"Well, I don't think it loves me."

It didn't. When he spoke, a discordant buzzing throbbed through the bones behind my ears. It increased as he poked a cautious finger at the mask. My sister had given me a hideous black handbag for my birthday. I found it at the back of the wardrobe, wrapped the mask in a scarf and shoved it into the bag's depths. Unease was stirring in my stomach. "What I did to Chappell—was that bad?"

He shrugged. "I would have had to try it if you hadn't."

"That's not exactly reassuring."

He nodded distractedly and sat heavily on the bed. "I can't believe he's dead," he said. "I know everyone says that, but I really can't."

My heart squeezed for him. "I'm so sorry."

"You know the worst thing?" he asked. I sat beside him, legs pressed primly together, and made an encouraging noise, feeling worse than useless, and watched him push his hair back from his face. His knees were too bony. He should eat more.

"He couldn't be like other dads. He loved me, he was the best parent he could be, but he had no... On the worst days, he'd go down to the Square, and preach about what had happened to him. Reka did the same thing to stop him talking that she did to me, before she let him go. So he could only talk around it, and it hurts the more you try, but he'd do it for hours. Because he thought warning people was the right thing to do. And then he'd come home, and then he'd go catatonic. He'd sit at the table and shit himself. Or puke, or suddenly black out and fall. Or both. I was terrified that one day he'd do both and I wouldn't be home in time to drag my father's head out of his own vomit."

"It wasn't your fault."

"I know. I know that. It was her fault. I hate her." He plucked at the knees of his tracksuit.

"I don't blame you."

"Yeah? Would you blame me if I said I hated him too? Because sometimes I did—this sick man, out of his time, who had nineteen good years before he met my sociopathic mother. So, yeah, sometimes I hated him, because he made my life just that bit harder."

Pity swelled in my throat. I couldn't speak, only sit and listen.

"A couple of years ago, before Gribaldi came, I went up north, to talk to this guy. See if I could cure Dad, fix myself, find a better way to stop Reka from getting Kevin."

He fell silent. I wanted to ask what he meant by fixing himself, but his face was still mobile with some inner dialogue, and I was loath to interrupt. "That didn't go so well," he said finally. "Anyway, I came back early. I'd arranged for Dad to go into care for a week. I could have left him there for the last two days. But, I don't know, I missed him. So I took a taxi from the airport and picked him up again." He turned teary eyes to me. "He just kept talking, Ellie. He was preaching, and he didn't really see me. I was exhausted. I cooked dinner, and he ate it, and he went to bed. But he just talked through the wall, on and on, and all I could think was, he's been doing this all day and he's going to be sick. And I'm going to have to deal with it. Again."

"I was so tired. And then I thought, I just sort of *realized* that if he wasn't there in the morning, then I wouldn't have to deal with any of it. So I walked into his room with my pillow, and I put it over his face, and I pressed down."

I stifled my shock before he looked at me, but the blank expression I produced was just as telling. He smiled, taut with bitterness, and went on.

"He didn't fight me. He'd been thrashing around, but when I leaned against the pillow he went completely still." He plucked at his tracksuit again, long fingers restless. "And then I took the pillow off his face and went back to bed and he talked until four in the morning. Then he had a fit and pissed himself, and I got up and changed him and put him in my bed and I went to sleep on the bedroom floor."

"You're a good person," I said. It seemed so inadequate.

"You're not even half right. Even when Reka told me, it didn't hurt right away. The first thing I felt—the very first thing—was relief. I thought I could find a way to stop being a monster. But it's in me, indelibly. Body and soul."

He dropped his head, hair falling limply over his face. I stared at him.

"Well," I said, hearing the word crack the air, and knowing that I was going to say the rest of it now, that I couldn't stop. "That's pretty arrogant."

For a moment his expression was so full of affronted shock that the sadness was pressed out. I pushed harder. "Oh, right, sleep deprived and worn out you tried to kill your dad. For what, about five seconds? Yeah, you're Hitler. You're Pol Pot. Oh, wait! You can't be! Because they were human, and you're a *monster*."

"You don't—"

"What? Understand? You keep saying I don't know enough, I don't speak the right languages, I don't know the right stories, I don't look in the right places. And it's true. I've spent a day stunned by all the things I didn't even know I didn't know. But you can't tell me I don't know what it's like to be human. I *live* human."

"But I'm not," he said.

"I don't care. People kill people every day, for much stupider reasons than yours. If you'd actually gone through with it, then yeah, you could make a case. As it is, no, sorry. You don't measure up." I clutched his shoulders, feeling the bones solid under my hands. "The ones who did kill your dad, who want to drown three million people, *they're* monsters. It's what people do that matters. Okay? You're an arrogant, secretive, manipulative son of a bitch, but you're not a monster."

He seemed honestly confused. "What am I, then?"

I snorted. "Mixed up. A chimera. Like the rest of us." I shrugged. "You put the pillow down. You took it off. You're a good *enough* person. Okay?" I released his shoulders and wriggled back across the mattress.

Too late, I realized that he wouldn't see that backward motion as giving him space, but as a retreat. It was there, raw, in the way his fingers spread against his thighs.

"Oh, *hell*," I said, and kissed him.

Objectively, it wasn't a great kiss. I'd grabbed his chin at an awkward angle, so first our teeth bumped, and then my nose squashed into his. I could still taste the toothpaste in my mouth, but he hadn't brushed his teeth. And my back flared every time I did anything as complicated as raising my arms or turning to the side.

Subjectively, I was aware of all these things, and didn't give a damn.

Mark's lips were warm and smooth against mine, his fingers twisting under the tangled weight of my hair to stroke the back of my neck, careful not to touch my wounds. He made a sound that was part whimper, part sigh, and I pressed against him, the cotton jacket rough against my hands. His body was warm underneath it. I had my hands up under his shirt before I realized I was moving, had lowered him flat against my bed before I'd made any decision to hold him.

A thrill unrelated to any magic hummed between us.

"Whoa," I said, and pulled back to hover above him. Mark was looking up at me, lips parted. I reminded myself that his father had just been murdered. "Uh. Sorry if I—"

He got a better grip on the back of my head and tugged me down again. I decided less talking and more kissing was the order of the day, and lost myself in the taste of him and the feel of smooth skin flexing under my questing fingers.

Eventually, he tilted his head away and gave me a smile that expanded across his face like a fern unfurling.

"Um," I said, witty as ever.

"You're amazing," he replied, which was clearly another lie, but still something more coherent than I was managing.

The window rattled as someone pounded on it.

"Get a move on, Ellie!" Kevin yelled, clearly unimpressed on several levels.

"Shit," I hissed, and rolled off both Mark and the bed, waving Kevin away again. He rolled his eyes, but obeyed.

Mark was sitting up, looking at me carefully.

"Close your eyes," I said.

He obeyed, and I skinned out of the costume and into my cleanest pair of jeans. Half-clothed, I sucked in a breath when I saw the purple bruises neatly spaced up my right forearm. The patupaiarehe's taiaha had not been gentle. I tried to fasten a bra over the scratches on my back, but it just wasn't going to happen. I gave up and spared one moment for the fear that Mark would peek just when I was at my most unattractive—struggling painfully into my sweater with my face concealed and my stomach rolls wobbling hypnotically—but when I tugged the material down to cover my belly, his eyes were still closed and he hadn't bolted from the room.

"Open them," I panted. "Okay. Let's go."

CHAPTER FOURTEEN
Home, Land, and Sea

Kevin sped down the flat length of Memorial Drive, instructing us to look for police on the way. I reflected that between Mark and the mask, being pulled over wouldn't slow us down much, but neglected to explain that to Kevin. Instead I occupied the time by looking through Iris's wallet. The small family portrait in the ID pocket had survived the dunking: her father stood clasping one wrist with his other hand, wearing a severe dark suit, boxy at the shoulders; her mother sat on a low-backed chair, wearing a bright pink high-necked jacket. A much younger Iris sat on her mother's knee in a fluffy pink dress, beside an older boy I didn't recognize. His skin was darker than hers; Iris looked more like her father. I wondered what Iris's brother did, if he lived in the North Island.

I had to stare out the window, blinking fast.

At the airport, Kevin parked in the two-minute off-load zone, and insisted on getting my bag out of the trunk, oblivious to the glares of other drivers. Mark waited a tactful few paces away while we said our goodbyes.

"Thanks," I said, forcing the words out of a suddenly tight throat. "You know. For everything."

"You too," he said, and lightly touched my cheek. "It's weird. You look taller."

I touched the top of my head, appalled.

"Not actually taller," he amended. "But you've stopped hunching."

I felt my shoulders cave in. When my back protested I straightened again. He grinned. "Looks good, Ell."

Mark made a sharp noise, and took off toward the entrance.

I began to follow him, but Kevin caught my sleeve. His eyes were intent on mine. "I feel like a bad friend. I haven't been around for you much lately."

"You're the best friend," I said, and meant it.

"Are you and Mark Nolan together? Or is that part of the big secret?"

"Nope," I said, happy that I could be completely honest about *something*. "To tell the truth, I have no idea what I'm doing there." Mark was almost out of sight in the crowd, stalking toward the doors. "I better go."

"Okay. Whatever you're doing, be careful."

"I'll try," I said through a tight throat, and started moving, gear bag heavy in my numb-fingered grip as I jogged.

I realized why Mark had taken off so quickly when I saw who else was standing under the eaves of the sliding doors.

Reka wore dark, expensive sunglasses, but there was no disguising that erect carriage or the mass of shining hair, coiled and pinned about her delicate skull. She'd changed her clothes again — a black dress fell to flowing folds about her gleaming, booted ankles, a matching bolero jacket over her shoulders. Mourning colors, I thought, for a movie star's funeral.

Mark was speaking to her, his shoulders set and hostile. "—changed your mind?" I caught.

Her head tilted to look just over his shoulder. "Not quite," she said coolly. "I will not go with you."

"Fine by me."

"However, I have brought you two gifts. The first is the rest of the knowledge I gleaned. The attack will be tomorrow night. Be prepared."

Mark blinked. "Thank you," he said after a moment.

"And this is the second."

She reached down the neck of her dress, to draw out a small flax bag. It was hanging from her neck on a cord, and I was unpleasantly reminded of the bone carvings the patu-paiarehe had worn, on similar strings. The flax was newly made, still green, with the distinctive scent of sap rising from it. The cord shone gold-red in the light. Somewhere under that pile of glossy red hair was the bare patch of a missing strand.

"I told you, I don't want anything you have to offer."

"See it before you decide."

Mark hesitated, then took the bag, peering inside. I'd braced for something unusual, but the power hidden in the bag struck up through my heels and shuddered through my bones to the top of my skull. The mask stirred unhappily, and I patted the outside of the handbag to soothe it.

Reka smiled. "Do you accept my gift?"

"You shouldn't have done this," Mark whispered.

"That was my choice. Do you accept?"

He bowed his head. "I do." Pulling the bag closed, he slipped the cord over his head and tucked the bag into the tracksuit jacket. That vibrating rush vanished, with a feeling like the air after a thunderclap's final echo had gone.

"Well, then. I hope they may aid you. Come back safe with them." She hesitated, then held out her right hand for him to shake.

Mark took it, then reached for her left hand and grasped them both lightly. Very slowly, he bent down and pressed his nose against hers. She jerked, then sighed, relaxing into the *hongi*, sharing his breath, until he moved away again, ending the greeting. "Perhaps you don't know me as well as you thought you did," she suggested.

"Maybe not," he said. "I still can't forgive what you did."

"I have never asked for forgiveness."

This was way too awkward.

"I'll go inside," I suggested, and Reka started.

"Ah, yes. Eleanor Spencer. Guard my son."

The mirrored sunglasses were still tilted toward Mark. Evidently I was unworthy of direct eye contact. I had the immediate urge to tell Mark to go screw himself, but I nodded anyway.

"I want your word."

"You've got it," I snapped.

Some tension dissolved from her shoulders. People were passing us to go into the airport, paying us little attention. All the power of her presence was diluted into ordinary charisma, her beauty and clothing collecting second glances, but no awe.

"Goodbye," Mark said, and gripped her shoulder once on his way past. She stayed in the doorway, staring into the parking lot behind her expensive shades.

"What was that about?" I muttered.

"I'll tell you later. We better check in."

We picked up boarding passes and checked my bag without any hassle, and passed through the slow-moving security line. The mask in my handbag got a raised eyebrow from the man on scanner duty and I tensed up, but a visual inspection satisfied him that I wasn't carrying anything dangerous.

Hah.

The mask didn't care about the inspection; the security guard was no threat to it or to me. Throughout the check-in process, I was very aware of Mark's presence at my back, and had to prevent myself from oh-so-casually leaning back against him. One kiss was not enough. I was internally thrumming with the need for more.

But he didn't speak. Obviously, we couldn't discuss the really important things while surrounded by grumbling fellow passengers, but I was a little disappointed that we couldn't talk about something ordinary. I told myself that if he didn't feel like conversation, I wasn't going to push him.

Just wait, and want.

My stomach gurgled as we got to the departure lounge, and I eyed the small café off to the corner. "Do you want a sandwich or something?"

"Yes," he said, then: "Wait, no."

I rolled my eyes. "Which?"

"I better not eat anything," he said quietly.

I stared at him. He avoided my eyes. "I had better observe purity, as far as I can."

"What did she give you?" I demanded.

He glanced at the people around us. "Something tapu."

I reached for his hand, but he pulled away, giving me a look that pleaded for understanding. "Something really tapu," he repeated. "I shouldn't touch you. I mean, I shouldn't touch anyone."

My jaw tightened. "For how long?"

He looked away. "We'll talk about it when it's all over."

Wailing like a kid whose ice cream had fallen out of the cone after one taste was an attractive option, but would probably draw a lot of unwanted attention. "Fine," I said shortly, and went to buy myself an overpriced salad while he sat in a deserted corner of the departure lounge, staring at the planes leaping into the sky. I wasn't hungry for *lettuce*.

I finished the salad without speaking and went back to the small café to grab a chocolate bar. Waiting in line behind an elderly couple deciding between Belgium biscuits and custard squares, it occurred to me that if he'd had second thoughts about me, maintaining the sacred nature of whatever he was carrying would be a great, culturally untouchable excuse.

Or maybe, his dad had just been murdered and the body probably brutalized, and his mother was a psycho, and I should give the guy a break instead of being a paranoid bitch.

I put the chocolate bar back, half smiled at the woman behind the counter in apology, and slid my wallet into my bag. My fingers brushed the smooth, cool surface of the mask.

I could put it on. Mark would want me then. The mask could make him want me. The mask would give me anyone I wanted, because I was beautiful and it loved me.

A hand landed on my shoulder, and the buzzing in my head abruptly died.

"Excuse me?"

I jumped, dropping the mask back into the bag. I'd pulled it half out in my daze. A woman with frizzy orange hair was standing behind me, two caramel squares balanced on her tray. She wrinkled her tiny nose. "Are you all right?"

I was shivering. "I'm fine. I'm sorry. I just really hate flying."

She gave me a sympathetic smile. Beyond her, Mark was standing by the window, watching me anxiously.

"I'm sorry," I said again, and stood out of her way. My steps quickened as I moved toward Mark. He lifted his hand, then arrested the motion.

"What happened to you? You went completely still."

"The mask." I was shaking, and not only from fear. I knew it had been wrong, what I'd done to Chappell—but the adoration, the love, that had felt so good. And it was something I was never going to get without the mask's help.

He waved his hand near the bag. It shuddered. "Ow."

"Ow," I echoed. "What's wrong with it?"

A bored, pleasant voice announced our flight. Mark slung my pack over his shoulder. "It's just...very much yours," he said quietly. "I'll talk to the flight attendants and get us separate seats."

The mask thought that was a good idea. If I wasn't going to control the other magician, it wanted him far away from me. I followed Mark like a forlorn puppy, fingers tracing the outline of the mask through the shiny black leather, trying not to picture him looking at me with that same lost devotion.

It felt too good.

I spent the flight with a paper bag clutched in my fists, forcing myself not to use it. The Asian-featured man next to me eyed it with some alarm, and I gave him a sick smile that tried to be reassuring.

I couldn't very well explain that I never got travel sick and that the reason I was nauseated and sweaty was the view out the window. The land below me shifted and trembled. One minute, we were floating over the snow-dusted mountain range that formed the spine of the South Island. The next, I was seeing Māui's giant canoe beneath me instead, a vessel he'd hewn from a single log, the ancient, smoke-darkened wood evidence of a magic I couldn't begin to comprehend.

I could have avoided the whole sick-making ordeal by closing my eyes and turning away, but that struck me as somehow cowardly, and Mark had said I'd be able to control the vision eventually. I had some respite when we went over the strait that divided the two islands. But I stiffened as we reached the North Island, bumping my head against the weird side flaps of the headrest.

I'd known that Te Ika a Māui drifted through his uneasy slumber, while the children of the maiden of the dawn walked blithely on his back. After the canoe, I'd even prepared to see him.

But I hadn't realized the scale. I couldn't see the whole of Māui's fish, any more than I could see the whole island. Valleys and mountains were enormous slashes and humps in his skin, where the tools of Māui's brothers had torn at him. And as we came in to land at Napier, the worst of his wounds showed itself to me. All the green-drenched winter landscape vanished, the vineyards and patches of paddocks, and beaches as familiar as my own face in the mirror. Instead I saw the festering flesh of the great fish's belly and the massive bone hook, yellow with age, that was the steep curve of the bay.

I pressed the bag to my mouth and clenched my eyes shut against the wave of terror at the sheer immensity of our task. Huddled around myself, I didn't stir until the plane roared and bumped beneath me.

The man beside me tapped my arm. "We are here now," he said kindly, and pulled my handbag down from the luggage compartment. He had to go on tiptoe to do it, settling back on his heels with the bag cradled carefully in his hands. Guilt suddenly twisted in me. I wanted to tell him to go, to take the next flight back to Christchurch, where he might be safe.

But I couldn't warn them all.

Instead I took the bag, and smiled my thanks, and shuffled through the plane to the gate where Mark waited, hands stuffed in his pockets to prevent me from taking them.

Napier being what it was, I wasn't off the plane for more than ten minutes before I was hailed by a friend of my dead grandmother.

"Eleanor, dear! Hello!"

I ran a quick search through my memory to confirm that I had no idea who this round, purple-haired woman was, and pushed extra enthusiasm into my voice to make up for it. "Good morning! How are you?"

She flicked a quick glance to my left, where Mark was standing awkwardly. "Fine, dear. Just fine. Holidays, is it? Home to visit your school friends?"

I made a vaguely affirmative noise and looked around. "Are you meeting someone here?"

She patted her curls. "Oh no. Fred and I are off to Sydney for a fortnight with the lawn bowls team. Oops, looks like we're off!" The octogenarians were laboriously collecting small suitcases on wheels. She patted my arm. "Lovely seeing you, dear. Say hello to your mother from me. Hope she's enjoying her trip!" She bustled off.

"Who was that?" Mark asked.

I made sure she was out of earshot before I replied. "I have no idea."

"But she knew you."

"Well, yeah, this is my hometown. She was just one of those family friends."

Mark looked slightly stunned. "Oh. Do you have a big family?"

I knew it was mean, but I couldn't stop myself. "Just the usual," I said casually. "Two parents, four grandparents— three dead now—one sister in Australia. Some aunts and uncles and cousins. Nothing big."

"Oh."

"We had a dog, but he died. And about ten thousand guinea pigs, also dead." I glanced at him and stopped, carefully avoiding touching him. "You have family too, you know."

His mouth twisted bitterly. "My mother—"

"Not her. The Waldgraves. I mean, not that they're perfect or anything. Kevin's great, but his brothers are kind of assholes. His parents are okay, for High Country snobs." I paused. "Actually, his dad is named after your dad."

He looked stubborn. "I knew that."

"Okay."

"They're not—I couldn't tell them."

"Well, I'm telling Kevin everything when we get back. I promised." I shrugged. "Just something to think about. He really is great."

Mark looked thoughtful. "Do you, um, like him?"

"Like him? Smooches-like-him? Primary-school-want-to-get-married-behind-the-bike-sheds-at-morning-teatime like him?"

He smiled. "I wouldn't know about that either."

"Boy, you missed out. No. He's my mate."

He looked at me, then over my shoulder, blushing slightly, "Uh…"

To hell with it. "I like you, though," I said casually, clutching my handbag to stop my hands from shaking.

"Can we talk about it later?" he said quickly, staring over my shoulder.

I flinched at the rejection, and then, as the deep, pleasant voice came behind me, realized, once again, that the universe wasn't all about me.

"So this is the little woman!" the voice said, and I twisted to face someone I already knew I wasn't going to like.

He was a short, stocky man, not more than chin-height on me, with skin dark and smooth as oil, and thin, sharp eyebrows. His face was wrinkle-free, and his tight, short curls had no white hairs, but I had the impression of agelessness, not youth. He wasn't patupaiarehe, but now that I knew to look for it, there was a similar sense of something completely out of place, like a Chinese opera aria in the middle of a rugby match. A hot, rich smell stung my nostrils, unlike any cologne I'd ever smelled before.

"If you keep staring, my dear, your face might freeze that way." His voice, with its precise British accent, was so dry that it took me a moment to realize it was a threat, not a joke. He shifted his attention to Mark while I was trying to form a response. "Delighted to see *you*, naturally."

Mark's face was stone. "What are you doing here?"

The man splayed his fingers against his heart, looking shocked. "I live here, darling boy. Had you forgotten?"

Mark snarled, his eyes burning green.

Alarmed, I snatched the handbag open, but the little man seemed undismayed. "Oh, dear, shall we scuffle in the airport? Neutral territory, you know, terribly gauche." He paused. "Or you could introduce me to your little friend."

I was nearly a foot taller than him. "You can call me Ms. Spencer," I said, and thrust out my hand.

The fine arches of his brows lifted. "Clever girl," he murmured, and reached to grasp my hand in his. "You may call me Mr. Sand." He raised his eyebrows again when I met the painful grip without flinching.

"What are you doing here?" Mark repeated, but the intensity of his glare had calmed to ordinary human hatred.

Mr. Sand spread his hands. "I'm an envoy, dear Mark, regarding this council of war you've inspired. There's been a tiny little problem regarding venue. I made it clear that all were welcome to meet at my humble abode, but for some reason not everyone views that as a palatable solution."

Mark snorted. "They don't trust you. I'm shocked."

Sand's eyes glittered. "Careful, boy. If you were to accuse me of breaking guest-right, I would rightly take offense."

"In an airport?" Mark said, shaking back his sleeve. His bracelet jingled.

"Touché!" He looked Mark over. I didn't like the way he did it, like someone inspecting fresh apples in the supermarket produce department. "Goodness. What *have* you been up to? You're positively blooming."

Mark's mouth was a tight line. "What do you want me to do about the situation?"

"Tell them they can trust me," Sand said.

"No," Mark said flatly. "They can't. And shouldn't."

Sand looked mournful, an expression that looked as theatrically staged as everything else he'd done. "I had hoped you'd have come to your senses on that little contretemps. You knew what I was when you asked me to teach you."

Mark snorted, and Sand sighed. "We must confer in a *home*, Mark. Without the guarantee of guest-right, no one will come at all. And no one else lives here."

"I wonder why."

Sand bowed mockingly. "Still. What solution do you propose?"

I eyed my gear bag going around the baggage carousel again, looking lonely on the black rubber. "I live here," I said. "We can meet at my place."

Sand lifted an eyebrow at me. "Really. And what would

you know about the sacred obligation between guests and host?"

"I got an A+ for my essay on Ancient Greek Culture," I said, smiling sweetly. "Does that count?"

Sand waited a long, dangerous moment, then tipped his head back to expel a laugh like bubbles rising between his even white teeth. "Just so," he gurgled. "Ms. Spencer, I shall be delighted to accept your hospitality. The meeting is set for sundown. *Do* enjoy your day." He reached as if to take my hand again, but spun away when I stiffened. He leveled one more wide smile at Mark, and then sauntered away, a small, dapper man who lifted the hairs on the back of my neck, even in retreat. The hot smell faded as he disappeared through the wide doors.

Mark was staring at me.

"What?" I said, a great deal more insouciantly than I felt.

"You got an A+ out of Professor Gribaldi?"

I grinned at him. "It was an A-, actually. But don't tell our friend."

Mark cracked up. I watched him wheeze for a second, then strode over to retrieve my bag. Everything was still inside, though a note informed me that airport security had looked inside. I wondered what they'd thought of Mark's wet, stinking clothes.

"What was that about you asking him to teach you?" I asked.

"I'll tell you later."

He kept saying that. "Later will be soon," I said firmly, and led him out to find a taxi.

The taxi driver was a dark-complected gregarious man who wanted to chat about the Eyeslasher murders. "And one in Gore!" he said. "Why would anyone go to Gore?"

I managed a laugh. "How about we take the scenic route?" I suggested, and managed to divert him to the topic of Napier's many sights to be seen. The people walking around looked happy and healthy, and I was reminded how disproportionately white Christchurch was, compared to the North Island towns. I'd gotten used to it, over the last months.

The sea glittered as we drove along the waterfront, gorgeously contrasted against the oily green of the Norfolk Pines that edged Marine Parade. I caught a glimpse of the statue of Pania of the Reef. Pania, the legend went, had been a maiden of the sea, secretly wedded to a human man. Betrayed by him, she'd run back to the ocean depths. Their son was supposed to be the taniwha who guarded the bay.

Until yesterday, the most attention I'd paid to the story had been mocking the tourists who liked to pose by the bronze statue of a topless girl smiling out to sea. Now the story made my flesh creep. I'd swum in that ocean.

I mentioned this to Mark when we got out of the taxi. He shrugged. "Her son isn't there right now."

It hadn't been quite the response I'd been looking for. I'd wanted him to tell me that I was doing very well under the circumstances. "Is he dead?" I asked, lifting up the loose rock in the front garden to retrieve the key.

"I don't know. Not there. Some stories say he had children and died, or became a rock."

"Which is true?"

He laughed. "Will you hit me if I say that it depends?"

"Maybe," I muttered, and pushed open the front door, reaching automatically for the light switch. The electricity bill would clearly show our presence here, but after my truancy had been reported to my parents, driving up the bill was going to be the least of my worries.

The house felt weird—cold and far too empty. I tiptoed down the dusty hall to my parents' room, and deposited my bag there.

"I like your house," Mark said, following me. I blushed, suddenly uncomfortable about the old-fashioned bedspread and the piles of golf books and gardening manuals and medical texts heaped around its head. Mark was looking at everything with a weird hunger, and I was very aware that I was alone with him in my parents' room, two steps from the bed where they had slept for over twenty years of married mostly bliss.

"We shouldn't be in here," I said, and backed him out, closing the door firmly behind me.

He looked only slightly disappointed. "Where's your room?"

I pointed. "That one, and Magda's room is beside it. I shared it with her, until Nanny Spencer died. Bathroom there. Kitchen and living room and laundry that way." I shrugged. "It's nothing fancy. We only live on the Hill because my grandfather built here before it was fashionable."

"Where did your dog live?"

"In his kennel when Dad could make him, and on Magda's bed when he couldn't. So, Magda's bed."

"And the ten thousand guinea pigs?"

"Between guinea pig funerals, in the hutch."

"I never had a pet. Can I see?" He was already walking through the laundry, heading for the back door. I trailed in his wake, wondering how I'd lost control of the tour so quickly.

He flung the door open, heedless of the white paint flaking onto his palm, and stepped out into the muddy green expanse of the backyard. The weeds were flourishing in the vegetable patch, and the old clothesline squeaked and groaned as it slowly turned. The guinea pig hutch sat under one of the trees, much shabbier than I remembered, the chicken wire over the run sagging. "Oh," Mark breathed. "Oh, wow."

"It's not much in winter."

He pointed at my dad's roses in their proudly maintained mulch pits. "Those are not 'not much.'"

"Well, yeah, but they're not blooming."

"Is that tree a magnolia?"

"Yeah. You can still see what's left of the tree house."

"You hammered nails into a magnolia?"

"Blame Magda; I was only seven. But we hung the tire swing from the kowhai. No nails there."

Mark smiled at me. "And the view…"

The view, I felt, I couldn't fairly disparage. The lawn ran down the slope for a quarter of an acre, to the low wooden fence that separated us from the well-kept houses below. And down, and down, dappled in the harsh noon light like a tarnished mirror, lay the ocean, embraced in the sandy curve of the bay and the reef beyond the breakwater.

My sight flickered and doubled, but I pushed it away with a firm effort of will. For this moment, I wanted only the familiar sight of home. I sat on the back step and hugged my legs against the wind.

Mark sat beside me. Even on the narrow step, he left a hands-width of space between us, but I could feel him across the gap, prickling at my side. I stared at the lump under his jacket and wondered what his mother's gift had been.

But I couldn't ask that again.

Time to be brave about something else.

"Um, so, at the airport," I said, concentrating on tucking my arms firmly around my body. "Before Mr. Creep turned up, remember how I said I liked you?"

He nodded.

I was positive my face was glowing with the heat of my flushing cheeks. "Well, uh...I do. Just saying."

"I can't understand why," he said, looking uneasy.

"Oh, I have no idea either," I scoffed. "I mean, you're gorgeous, smart, mysterious, and when you make up your mind to talk, you have a lot of interesting things to say. What's to like?"

"Mysterious?"

"Chicks dig guys with a sense of mystique. It was in *Cosmopolitan*, so it must be true."

He gave me that shy smile. "I like you too."

My heart leaped, and I was reaching for him before I remembered. He leaned back warily, and I retreated, refolding my arms to resist the temptation.

"But it's complicated," he added. "I mean. With what I am."

Self-hatred was a serious turn-off, I decided, still dizzily turning over *I like you too*. He *liked* me. *He* liked me. He liked *me*. "You're not off the hook for enchanting me," I added. "That was not good. But I like you anyway."

"About that," Mark said, smile vanishing. He'd picked up a stone somewhere. Now he turned it over and over in his hands. "I should warn you about Mr. Sand."

I settled back.

"I came to him two years ago, three years after I'd left the mists. I could still travel under the earth then, so it was easy. I wanted him to teach me some magic, teach me how to protect Kevin."

"And he didn't?" I guessed.

He grimaced. "Oh, he did. He taught me everything I can do now."

"But you said Reka taught you."

"She did."

"Are you being confusing on purpose?" I demanded.

He weighed the stone in his palm, still looking at that instead of me. "Look. It's important that you understand that I'm still a monster. I still have the eyes, and I'll still live a long time, and the smell of cooked food makes me a little queasy, though I'm human enough to stomach it. Reka taught me how to walk the mists and make claws from my fingers, and charm people with flute-music or song. But I can't do that now. I can't use the patupaiarehe magic I was born to."

"Why not?"

"Because Sand ate it."

Shock curdled in my stomach.

"It's really not that different from what the patupaiarehe are doing. Just less messy. I...I showed him some of the things Reka showed me in exchange for his teaching me and making the bracelet. I thought I was getting the best of the bargain." He gestured at the kennel. "But I was stupid. While I slept like a dog in his yard, he gorged himself on the power I was born with."

"Like a vampire, but of magic?" I ventured.

"Pretty much. He calls himself an animavore." He shook his head. "He says he was old long before Greek got established as a language. He says he doesn't remember what he was called before that."

"He says?"

"He says he never lies, and I think that's true. But he's worse than Reka. He'll twist the truth around on itself, and hand you the knot, and laugh when you can't find where it begins."

"Poetic."

"Thank you." He flung the stone. It bounced off the guinea pig hutch, taking a small chunk of rotting timber with it. He made no apology. "We've got some breathing space. Want a lesson in the theory of magic?"

It was a neat bit of misdirection, but he was hiding behind his hair again. "You're not telling me something," I said flatly.

He brushed back his hair and glared at me. "Do you want to know the whole story?" he demanded. "Every little humiliation, every awful, petty task?"

I recoiled, cursing my impulsive tongue. "No. I'm sorry."

"Okay, then," he said, and held up a finger. "There are three kinds of...well, 'magicians' works. Three kinds of magicians. The first kind is born to magic. They're either supernatural creatures, or humans who are magic from birth. They're born with intrinsic power, and they learn how to use it as easily as you learned how to walk—it takes a little while, but it's instinct, and they'll always do it. That's rare these days, especially among humans." He held up a second finger. "Then there's people like you and Kevin, people with potential, either inherited or a genetic wildcard. That's more like...uh, learning to swim. You *might* figure out how to swim if you just jumped in, because you have everything you need to do it. But you're much more likely to learn how—and survive learning—if someone teaches you. And a lot of people get by without ever learning." He glanced at me.

"Got it so far," I assured him. His face was easing as he explained, and I watched the tension go out of his hands as he gestured.

"And the third category is everyone else," he said, holding up the third finger. "Almost anyone can learn to do spells, but if they don't have any power of their own, they need a power source, to see and to do. An object of power, or a tattoo, or a ceremony—something that charges them up. And they can't learn those spells by just messing away at them. It'd be like trying to put a computer together from the parts when they've never seen one before. They need an instructor, or at the very least a manual."

"So the patupaiarehe are...category one. But they're stealing extra power to tug at the fish."

"Yes."

I grimaced, and pursued another line of inquiry. "You said *almost* anyone can learn?"

"Some people can't even used stored power. I don't know why. It's like some connection is broken."

"Huh," I said, and thought about it. The world was much stranger than I had ever supposed.

"People will be on the way. I better let them know where to come. Can I use the phone?"

I stood too, disappointed that the moment seemed to be over. "Yeah, sure, I think it's still connected."

Someone thumped on the front door, and Mark startled, grabbing at his wrist.

"Ellie?" a familiar voice called. "Ellie, I know you're there."

"Shit," I said, and shook my head at Mark. "No, it's just the neighbor. You make your calls. I'll get rid of her."

He let go of his bracelet, tension easing, but I wasn't as confident as I sounded. Hinemoana Simpson was not the sort of person you could just get rid of.

Without letting myself think about it too much, I fetched the handbag holding the mask.

I summoned a smile before I pulled open the door, my cheeks aching under its manic force. "Hi!"

Hinemoana seemed unmoved.

I liked her a lot; she'd lived next door all my life, a

no-nonsense midwife who'd brought over casseroles and baking long after the rest of my parents' friends' donations to the Cancer Year had slowed to a trickle. But she had my parents' itinerary and the list of their hotel phone numbers in case of emergency, and she was absolutely the last person I'd wanted to notice I was back.

"Hello, Ellie. What are you doing here?"

"Home for a brief holiday," I said. "Just checking up on the place, you know."

"I've been doing that," she said. "Watering the plants, taking the mail. Your parents didn't mention you were visiting."

"They didn't? Well, I guess they're pretty busy in Vienna."

Her gaze didn't waver, but her generous mouth thinned. "Munich."

I tried to laugh. "Right. I get confused with all those German-speaking places. So how's it going?"

"I spoke to your mum yesterday, Ellie," she said, resting her fists on her hips. "You'd better tell me what's going on."

The mask hummed at me, and I heard her next question through the rising buzz of its eagerness to serve me.

"Do your parents really know you're here?"

I flinched, and that must have been answer enough.

"I know it's not school holidays, Ellie. David has another week to go at Boys' High. Your parents are spending a lot of money on that school. They're very proud that you got in."

"I know," I blurted. "I'm just... I'm just homesick."

This had the advantage of being true, but Hinemoana's eyes got even flintier. "Ellie," she said. "I saw the boy."

The mask hummed again, insistent.

"I'm calling your parents' hotel," she said. "You'd better come with me; you can't stay here with him."

What the hell was happening with Mark? Surely his bracelet had recharged; he could come and do his memory magic. Or had he taken me at my word, that I could handle it? I swung the handbag off my shoulder to clutch it in one hand, feeling the mask vibrate through the leather.

"I have to stay here," I said. "I have to do something, there's going to be a thing, I can't talk about it. Hinemoana, I'm really sorry but I can't—"

"Ellie, right now I think you'd better call me Ms. Simpson. Grab your stuff and tell your boyfriend to get out of the house. If he needs somewhere to stay—"

"You can't call my parents."

"Can and will." She was already turning away. There was no time to call Mark now.

I took a deep breath and opened the handbag. The mask nearly leapt into my hand, and its delight as I fitted it to my face was both thrilling and stomach-churning.

"Ms. Simpson," I said, and she turned around to stare at my new face. "Listen to me."

It was even worse than Mrs. Chapell, maybe because Hinemoana already liked me, when I wasn't being a disobedient liar. Her face went slack, all that intelligent vitality transformed to mindless devotion. "Yes?" she said, her voice eager. "Can I help you, Ellie? Tell me what to do."

"Don't tell my parents," I said. "Don't tell anyone; forget that you saw me. But remember these instructions. Remember that you shouldn't tell anyone I'm here." That ought to cover it.

I could feel Mark at my back now, too goddamn late.

The mask reminded me that I could make him love me, too. Forever and ever. All I had to do was turn around.

I shivered, and not entirely out of fear.

"Go now," I said, and Hinemoana turned on her heel and marched away. I watched her go back to her house and walk through the back door, never looking back.

I waited three long heartbeats, while the mask whispered in my head, and then gently pulled it free of my face.

"You did the right thing," Mark said.

"Don't talk to me about this," I said, without looking over my shoulder. "You gave me a migraine."

"If I'd had that mask, I wouldn't have had to. You didn't hurt her, Ellie. What we're doing is important. The hard decisions get easier."

"Yeah," I said, and only then noticed that I was stroking the mask. It was purring under the attention. I put it back in the bag and snapped it close. "That would be the problem. It already feels way too easy."

I looked at him then, but he was already moving away. I knew it wasn't fair to resent him for not being there to bewitch Hinemoana, so that I wouldn't have had to pull out the mask, and want all its promises to come true. I knew it wasn't fair, and I resented him anyway.

"I have to call some more people," he said.

"Yeah," I said, and decided not to think about how much the mask could do for me. "I should get ready for my guests. How many should I expect?"

Mark looked vague. "I don't know. Last night I called all

the magicians I know even a little and asked them to spread the word. Maybe...twenty?"

I calculated the likely cans in the pantry. Dad liked to shop for some forthcoming famine, and I could always go down to the supermarket with Iris's wallet. I was in so much trouble that it didn't really matter if anyone else saw me; Hinemoana had been the only one who could make the call.

"Twenty," I said. "No problem."

CHAPTER FIFTEEN

Unity

I leaned over Mark as he shrank into the dubious shelter of a corner of the laundry room. He looked torn between amusement and terror, and I had every intention of encouraging the correct response.

"You said twenty," I hissed. "I'm going to kill you slow."

"This many is *good*."

"It's good for fighting patupaiarehe! But how am I supposed to seat them? And I didn't make enough food!"

"They brought food," Mark protested. He slipped past me

and stopped in the doorway to the kitchen, pointing. "Ellie. Come on. Tell me it's not enough."

I glared at the kitchen table, fists on my hips.

There were plates of neat-cut sandwiches and bowls of salads. There were platters of roast kumara chips, and copper bowls of fragrant curries, and a plate of sweet roasted bananas. There were bottles of sherry, and apple juice, and ouzo, and Coke, and brandy, and something homemade in a green glass bottle that I didn't think even the ouzo-bringer was likely to drink.

Three Māori men in biker leathers had brought cheerful smiles, a pile of roast beef and potatoes, and a case of beer. A group of Fijian women in ruffled white dresses had brought grilled crayfish and vegetables simmered in spiced coconut milk. An older Pākehā man with a priest's dog collar sitting quietly above his dark blue sweater had handed me a trifle in a cut-glass bowl, apologizing that the custard was from a carton. A tiny Desi woman in a yellow blouse and sari had given me a vegetable curry so hot that my eyes had watered just from the smell. An oddly familiar skinny Māori boy with moko patterns newly tattooed on his cheeks had given me a measuring look and a bowl of raw oysters. A tall Asian man with an impressive flowing beard, trailed by an equally impressive black cat, had put an enormous Tupperware container of cooked rice in the fridge, and politely assured me that more would be supplied at my will.

The food had come, and come, and its givers also, and the few who hadn't brought anything had mumbled alarmed apologies when they saw the table, quietly slipping out to buy fruit and wine. By now there were more than fifty people milling in the backyard, trampling the grass between my father's roses. Mark didn't recognize more than half of them; the others were people who knew those magicians he *had* met. It seemed that most magicians didn't care much for community building, but I guessed that total isolation would be hard to pull off.

"This many is good," he repeated. "We're going to win, Ellie. Can't you feel the power gathered here?"

I could; it saturated the air and prickled against my skin. It didn't soothe my temper, but I had to admit—the numbers *were* reassuring.

There was a sudden hot smell that wrinkled my nose, and Mr. Sand wafted down the hall and past us into the laundry room.

"Hello, Ms. Spencer," he caroled. "I didn't bring refreshments; but then, I don't expect I'll dine."

He beamed at Mark and slipped through the back door before I could react.

"Right," I said, and started after him.

"You can't kick him out," Mark said sharply. "You already offered him guest-right."

I stopped. "I'm so stupid," I said, hearing it come out high and breathy. "What was I thinking?"

"No. It was really smart. You're about as close as it gets to neutral territory."

I sniffed past the lump in my throat. "I could use a hug."

"I can't. I'm sorry."

"I know. I'm just saying, I could really use one. I wish Kevin were here."

"Ms. Spencer," a drawling American voice said from the front door, and my jaw dropped at its familiarity.

"Professor," I said faintly.

La Gribaldi's many thin braids were coming down from their customary tightly-pinned crown. She flung them back over her shoulder. "The timing of all this is just appalling. Midterm exams are in a week, you know."

"It's not my fault," I said wildly. I was fumbling back through my memories, trying to find some hint that would anticipate her appearance here. A number of things Mark had said slid abruptly into place. I squinted at her. She looked exactly the same to my ordinary eyes: a contrast of bright skirts and dark skin, moving as if the world would make space around her. But with my new sight I could sense great power. And despite our obvious differences, a feeling of similarity between us. I wondered what her talents were.

"Of course not, Ms. Spencer," she said. "It wasn't an accusation." She plunked a black plastic bag on the table, where it clinked ominously. "Don't let anyone drink that until after we've come to an agreement. It's my best mead."

"Thank you," I said faintly.

"Don't thank me, young woman; don't you know anything? Mr. Nolan."

"Professor," he said. "Did you find them?"

She looked grim. "No. They're back in the mists. You're right; we'll have to meet them here. This way? Excellent. Then let's begin."

I waited until she was gone before I turned to Mark, waving my hands impotently.

"*She's*—"

"I said that!" he said quickly. "Or at least I meant to. We've been pretty busy."

"Well, wait, couldn't she help protect Kevin?"

He looked away. "She offered."

"And?"

"Her solution was to kill Reka." He wrapped his arms around himself. "She helped me research the spell I used, but she thought it would be safer the other way. And part of me knows she's right. But I couldn't do it. I hate Reka's guts most of the time, but I couldn't kill her."

I thought of my own mother, weak and vomiting and her hair coming out in great clumps, of the way she'd moved painfully through this hallway. I would have done anything to make her better and keep her safe, but I'd been helpless. And even if she'd been a terrible person, like Reka, if she'd kidnapped and raped and stolen—I nearly gagged on the thought. I was glad I hadn't had to make Mark's choice. Since he'd chosen what he had, I could at least make it easier on him.

"She's your mother," I said firmly. "No one could expect it of you."

He gave me a startled look from the corners of his deep green eyes, and then that slow smile unfurled across his face.

We went out to the gathered people, not touching.

The meeting began with a greeting from me as the host, assuring everyone they were safe here as my guests, which was apparently all I had to do. I was careful to deliver it exactly as Mark had told me. Some tension released as I finished the words, the magic in the air no longer tingling unpleasantly.

I was one of the few sitting on a chair—a lawn chair, in my case, unearthed from the garage. Mark leaned in the doorframe. The others stood, or leaned on the fence, or sat on the lawn, or perched in the remains of the tree house. They all looked human enough, but I wasn't taking any bets. There was, for example, a slight and very pale Pākehā girl whose incisors were a bit too long for comfort, and who I didn't want to think about too hard. And it was clearly a meeting of supernatural powers; small, round lights hung in nothingness, transforming the deepening murk into something that felt deceptively festival-like, and the air was early-summer warm.

Professor Gribaldi chaired the meeting, mostly by virtue of assuming that she would, though more than a few people looked disgruntled at that. This alliance was clearly a tenuous one. She called upon Mark to tell what he knew of the patupaiarehe plans. I'd thought that everyone had known that, but though several people nodded grimly, there was still a shocked whisper when he talked about the mass murder to come. I frowned when I noticed some of the guests eyeing the door. Or perhaps Mark, still standing within it as he spoke.

But La Gribaldi was as much in command of this gathering as she was of any classroom, and she didn't let the mutters grow.

Instead, she nodded at the tall Asian man, who was sitting

cross-legged under the kowhai tree. His black cat started from his lap when he rose, scampered a few alarmed steps away, and then sat down to wash her leg.

"It is clear that we must fight," he began, fingers folded into his sleeves. "First, because this land is or is now our home and pride demands we protect it. Second, because these children of the mist have harmed those with whom some of us were honored to share some bond, and honor requires that we revenge them. And thirdly, because they seek to alter the laws of the manner of life and death permitted them by the first Gods of this place, and duty suggests we must prevent it. Will anyone dispute with these principles, as I have here outlaid them?"

"Of course they won't," one of the Fijian ladies said indulgently, snipping off a thread with her teeth. She was sewing new buttons onto an old flannel shirt. "You keep going, man."

He smiled at her. "So then, we proceed to what must be done. Their strategy is twofold. First, they wish to tear the hook from the fish that is the land, and so induce his death throes. Second, at the moment this occurs, and Grandmother Death sinks deeper into her slumber to protect the dead, they wish to wrest immortality from her, by sending their representative through that dangerous passage." He held up two fingers. "Therefore, should not our strategy be twofold also? I advise that the bulk of us wait at the end of the hook to prevent their magic and destroy their army. But when they attack, let a small party—perhaps one man—journey to the underworld and kill their representative there so that even in triumph, they will not succeed, and we have this last satisfaction to comfort us." He bowed slightly, and sat again. The cat leaped into his lap and consented to stroking.

"That works," Professor Gribaldi said, nodding. "So who's going underground?"

"Who *can* go?" Sand murmured. "We're not all welcome, dear Smith. The entrance is all the way up north, and the journey to Cape Reinga is barred to the living, unless they know some cute little tricks." He looked around.

"Not exactly my department," the pale priest said, with some irony, and a tall, brown-skinned woman at the back folded her arms under her breasts and shook her head, frowning.

One of the bikers scratched his head. "We don't know a lot of the old stuff," he admitted. "City magic's more our line."

"I'll go," the skinny Māori boy said. "My grandfather taught me the way."

"You might not come back," one of the bikers said, with cautious respect.

The boy glared. "My grandfather taught me how," he repeated, and I realized why he'd seemed familiar. He'd been in the newspaper, standing proudly beside the murdered kaumātua in the family portrait that had illustrated one of the Eyeslasher stories. I felt a twinge of sympathy.

"It's a long journey," Mark said. "And dangerous, from the East Coast. But there's another, safer route through the mists."

Mr. Sand wriggled his fingers in the air. "All the heavens know I'm happy to let bygones be, dear boy," he began. "And it's easy enough to open the way to the mists, once you know the trick." He smirked at that, eyeing Mark insolently.

"But how can you propose it to be a *safer* route? Will you risk all on the chance of one of us journeying through them and coming out sane? You're the only patupaiarehe here, and you can't quite manage it yourself." He yawned behind his curled hand. "Well! Bygones."

Mark pulled the flax bag from under his shirt and tipped the contents into his palm. One of the little lights floating in the air rose to hover by his hand.

Reka had packed the bag with more of her hair. Nestled in the fine red fibers were two greenstones the same size, each smooth and slightly ovoid, polished to the same dark sheen. They were beautiful, totally unflawed, and probably worth a fortune. But my other sight saw them as more than just gemstones. Power radiated from them to thrum against my bones.

Everyone in the yard pulled away, then swayed closer, like trees in a gale.

"It's true that I don't have the power of the mists any-more," Mark said clearly. "But my mother lent me her eyes, and through them her power, and with them I can navigate through the mists to the underworld's entrance."

I remembered Reka's sunglasses; the way she had looked directly at neither of us. My blood rushed in my ears like the ocean. She'd plucked out her own eyes to give her son the best chance she could. She was still terrible; she was ruthless and remorseless and almost entirely indifferent to the suffer-ing of others. And she was the one who *liked* humans.

"If it doesn't work," the boy said, "if you can't get through, or go crazy…"

Mark nodded. "Then it'll be up to you."

"The backup to the backup, eh?" the boy said, and grinned. For a second I saw the same proud kid who'd stood barefoot beside his grandfather in the marae. Then the mirth was replaced with an expression of grim determination that he should have been way too young to produce.

I was suddenly, breathlessly, sad for him. He should have been stressing about an algebra test or mooning at his best friend's older sister. Not here, in my backyard, on the brink of a war.

But I knew, ashamed as it made me, that I wasn't going to be the one to turn him away.

The meeting formally broke up, and smaller groups formed to talk through battle plans and strategies. I tried to talk to Mark, but he evaded me to instead engage the Māori boy in intense discussion. Backups of backups, I deduced, and tried to fulfill my duties as host by mingling.

That didn't work very well. People were polite, and some were even friendly, but much of the discussion wasn't in English, and I couldn't understand a lot of what was. I still might have found it more interesting if I hadn't been so tired. Instead I gazed over the yard to the bright city and dark ocean while Professor Gribaldi and Mr. Sand argued about blood invocations and weather commands. Sand kept calling her Smith, which infuriated her so much he nearly won the argument. Perched in the magnolia tree, the Desi woman and the cat were staring intently at each other. Kneeling under the branches, one of the bikers unpacked the parts of a nasty-looking rifle from his black leather satchel and started to clean it.

He saw me staring and grinned. "For hunting rabbits, eh?"

I saw the patches on his jacket, swallowed hard, and gestured vaguely at the house. "I'd better put the food out."

He got up and waved to his mates. "I'll give you a hand. Hey, bros, help the lady, eh?"

In the end, they simply carried the laden kitchen table into the hall and out through the back door. The table was roughly three times wider than both doorways, and I didn't see the doors widen or the table shrink; just, somehow, it got through.

"Looks like a good feed," one of the bikers said. Try as I might, I wasn't able to tell them apart. When I tried to pick an identifying feature for one, it seemed to belong to another.

The food was universally fantastic. I tried the vegetable curry and thick slices of rēwana bread and managed to eat a bunch of grapes and nearly half a small circle of brie by myself. Mark eyed the table with longing, pressing his hand against his stomach, and then went back to his discussion with the boy with the moko. I wandered up to the pair, but they were speaking to each other in fast Māori and didn't stop when I paused beside them. Mark gave me a distracted nod; the skinny boy didn't look at me at all.

I took the hint and went back to try the mead.

No one had told me it was alcoholic.

Some time later, when things were pleasantly blurry, La Gribaldi came to me where I was sitting on the swing, swaying gently.

"This stuff is great!" I said enthusiastically. "It tastes like honey!"

She smiled. "It does indeed. Ms. Spencer, a moment's conversation. What do you see when you look at the moon?"

I looked at the sky. "The sad woman. Who can't get back down."

"Quite so. That's a strong story here. My father was Italian, and when we left Eritrea for Rome, he would sit outside and smoke and tell me stories: about his father's farm; about the war; about the gods. My favorite was the myth of Selene, who drives the chariot of the moon. She loved many men, but she loved beautiful Endymion best, and begged the father of the gods to give him immortality. This was granted, but Endymion sleeps eternally. Selene treasures him still, and rises every night she can, so that she might kiss him with the beams of her light.

"Now. Look."

I did. For a moment I saw it, the woman eagerly driving her silver chariot across the sky. The image wavered, and it was just the moon, a near-circle of white light; and then the anguished woman returned, clutching the tree on which she'd stubbed her toe.

"It changes," I said, astonished.

La Gribaldi laid her hand on my shoulder. I could feel the warmth radiating from her skin, like the heat stored in sun-baked earth. "Stories change us; they change the world. People are stories of themselves."

I squinted, my head spinning. "Like...history is written by the victors?"

She nodded, looking somber. "Or erased by them. Ms. Spencer, the stories we know are real things. Especially for people like ourselves. Remember that."

"I will," I said. "Did your mother tell you stories?"

"Of course. But I won't tell them to you now."

"Okay. Are you sure you don't want some mead?"

She shook her head and moved away again. I swung back and forth, listening to the priest and the Fijian ladies murmuring over the rosary. I hadn't heard it since Granny Spencer had died, but the familiar rhythm was soothing in my ears. From the bag in my bedroom, I could feel the mask humming along. It sounded lonely.

I woke later that night, sunk into the soft mattress of my parents' bed. La Gribaldi was standing, looking out at the moon. I must have made a sound, because she turned around.

"You're safe, Eleanor," she said, and I went back to sleep, lulled by the mead and the far-off whisper of the sea.

Chapter Sixteen

Why Does Love Do This To Me?

I'm going to have a hangover, I thought, a good ten seconds before the pain hit.

During those ten seconds, I managed to roll out of bed, stagger to the bathroom, and lift the toilet seat. The first spasm dropped me to my knees, and then I lost everything I'd eaten the day before. I hadn't felt this wretched since Kevin's birthday dinner in April, where we'd finished the long night of being polite to his parents and their friends by doing tequila shots in their enormous backyard. I spat and scowled into the spattered toilet bowl until I was sure that the nausea had abated.

There were food smells and cooking noises from the kitchen. I didn't really want witnesses to my humiliation, but I knew from experience that as bad as I felt, I was going to feel a lot worse if I didn't rehydrate.

I staggered in. "Kill me," I said before I remembered that this maybe wasn't a smart thing to say in front of a magician of unknown origins.

Professor Gribaldi looked up from the stove and forked another pancake onto the stack. "I warned you, Ms. Spencer. My best mead, I said."

"You didn't say it would do this," I protested, and turned on the tap. The water was so cold it pricked at my teeth, but I kept grimly slurping at it. "I'm the host. Is this even allowed to happen?"

"Hah! I can't harm you directly without breaking guest-right. No stabbing you while you sleep, for instance. But there's nothing against indirect harm, or you harming yourself by drinking too much too quickly."

"I didn't know," I protested weakly, although of course I'd worked it out when my head started spinning. But by then, it had just been so easy to keep drinking.

La Gribaldi ignored that and set the plate of pancakes down beside me. My stomach made an embarrassing noise.

"And in any case, it's not all bad. You have the memory of the taste, and you will have heard some truths while you drank. The pain's the price. Now eat." When I opened my mouth to protest she neatly poked a loaded forkful onto my tongue.

I lunged for the sink, but my body was a lot smarter than I was and was already chewing. "This is great," I said, when I could speak again.

She looked smug. "Whatever I make is made well."

My stomach quieted. My headache was suddenly less insistent. "Sit," she ordered, pushing the plate toward me. "Eat."

I did, with single-minded concentration, until my belly pressed against my jeans and I paused. "Where is everyone?"

"Down on the hook, preparing. I'm to take you there when you're ready."

"Should I bring the mask?"

She looked intently at me. "You have an affinity for items of power."

"Mark said that too."

"Bring it, then. But to use it to full effect, you must see your victim, and they must see you, and you must voice a command they can hear." She shook her head. "In battle, these conditions may be difficult to meet."

I frowned. "So what will I do? I'm not a street fighter."

"Mostly, you will be there, Ms. Spencer. You are our host, and you were born here. For a number of them, having you endorse our efforts increases their strength."

I didn't much like the idea of being a mascot. "Not you?"

"Blood and land isn't my way. I make things."

Like my little scrap of paper? MARK! BIBLE! DON'T FORGET! I'd made that in pain and only half-woken to my magic, and

I was suddenly curious to see what I could do now. Maybe I could learn to do what she did. "Is that why Sand calls you Smith?"

She was silent for a long time, stacking dishes in the sink and running water over them. The kitchen looked far too clean for a place that had hosted fifty-something people the night before.

"I'm not a Smith," she said at last. "I was the apprentice of the last Smith, before he died. But I never made my masterpiece for his appraisal." She wiped her hands on her skirt, leaving dark water marks on the scarlet fabric. "Did you know the English settlers imported Scandinavian couples to New Zealand? They came across two dark oceans to the strange land on the edge of the world. And when the couples got here, they found that the New Zealand townspeople would keep the women here while their men cleared the forests to the south. Dannevirke is named after them. Danish work. The women weren't quite hostages, but they weren't quite free, either. In the cold nights without their men, they told the old stories to one another." She snorted. "Don't look so confused, girl. They told the stories of one of my traditions, and it means I'm a little stronger here, that's all. Then again, everything's strong here, where Māui's hook sinks in, and worlds collide."

I thought of the pale people of the mist. "The patupaiarehe too?"

"Especially them."

I set my fork down. "Let's go," I said, and stood, no longer hungry.

La Gribaldi watched me, dark eyes smug.

"What—" I said, and then realized how easily I'd moved. I twisted and stretched, wide-eyed, and then thrust a hand up under my shirt to brush down my spine. My fingers moved easily across smooth skin. When I concentrated, I found five raised lines, barely noticeable, like scars from a wound that had been healed for years.

I began to stammer out my thanks, then thought better of it. "Those were fantastic pancakes," I said.

La Gribaldi nodded. "You'll need all your strength today," she said, and even that reminder couldn't make me less grateful to be moving without pain.

La Gribaldi's Ford Explorer was a monolith of polished black steel and gleaming, tinted windows. It welcomed me with a warm brush across my skin, purring like a friendly cat. I sat straight in the leather seats, hands crossed neatly in my lap to prevent them from stroking the dashboard, the mask grumbling jealously in its handbag.

La Gribaldi said a short word I didn't recognize, and the car leapt into motion, rolling smoothly down the hill. She hadn't put a key in the ignition, or her hands on the steering wheel. I flinched and she gave me an amused look.

"She won't crash, Ms. Spencer."

"It just feels wrong," I said weakly, as the Explorer swung neatly around a corner and headed for the coast.

At the south end of Hawkes Bay, jutting into the sea, was Cape Kidnappers. It was actually a little distance from Napier proper, closer to the small town of Havelock North. Small, craggy islands trailed off its edge in a wavering line out to sea and a few golden-headed gannets wheeled above the saddle of the cape, early-comers to the colony nesting season. The only way to get there was along the beach at low tide. As the Explorer headed down the shore, my double vision revealed once more the massive hook tearing at the flesh, under the deceptively calm water-kissed sand and green-topped white rock. When I swung my feet out of the car, I felt Māui's hook register my presence as I might note a stray eyelash on my cheek.

With the handbag under my arm, I wandered the beach, totally useless.

The council were taking advantage of the daylight and digging in to protect the hook. Driftwood fires burned, and every now and then someone would grab a slice of something from a plastic bag and throw it on a grill. No one seemed to be eating much, but the air was smoky with the scent of roasting meat.

Other than that, much of the activity was totally opaque to me. The woman in the bright yellow sari was carving wavy lines into the sand with a piece of driftwood, the muscles in her wiry arms standing out with the effort. The bikers had stripped to the waist and were smearing something reddish over their chests and faces. Past them, I saw Mark standing carefully upwind of the food smells, speaking intently to the boy with the moko again.

He hadn't spoken to me since the meeting, and had left without waking me. I thought about pretending that I hadn't been looking for him, and then I thought about the risks we were facing and whether I *really* wanted to waste my possibly last hours on earth in a snit, and went to say hello.

In the daylight, I could see the curves and lines of the boy's moko didn't sit on the skin, but were actually grooves cut into his flesh. It had been done in the old way, with chisels. He jerked his chin as I approached. "What's she doing here?"

I blinked. "I have to be here. I was born here."

"But you don't know anything," he said reasonably. "You can't fight."

"Listen, kiddo—"

Mark shook his head. "Ellie."

"Fine." I folded my arms and waited for them to go on.

They stood there for a moment, and then the boy said, not rudely, "This isn't your business."

"Because I'm a girl?" I demanded.

He rolled his eyes. "No."

"Matiu," Mark said calmly.

"Look," the boy said. "You don't know anything, understand? You're like my two-year-old brother. Always asking stupid questions and wanting to do stuff he's too young for and breaking things by accident. You're just going to get yourself killed."

Mark sighed. "Ellie, can I talk to you for a second?" he said, and shifted me away while I was still trying to come up with a response. I moved with bad grace, glaring at Matiu. He looked unperturbed.

"How old is he, anyway?" I muttered. "Twelve?"

"Fourteen. He's right, you know. I mean, not that you shouldn't be here, but that it's going to be dangerous. And you can't listen to us—that's secret knowledge. You're not entitled to it."

"Oh, come on, it's all magic, isn't it?"

Mark halted, still upwind of the bonfires. "Matiu is discussing the knowledge of his people. He gets to decide who hears it, not you."

His voice was quiet, but it stopped me in my tracks.

"The way I look...I know I'm not, but I pass as completely Pākehā," he said. "My dad doesn't." He winced. "Didn't. In the sixties, when he first came back and I visited him for the first time...you should have heard the things they said about the crazy brown guy, Ellie. Don't think it's all gone now, just because the signs on public buildings are in Māori as well as English."

I bit my lip on my immediate response, which had been *I don't really think of you as Māori*, and instead felt self-disgust rise in my throat. "I'm sorry," I said after a moment, hoping he could hear the sincerity in my voice. "Can you tell Matiu I'm sorry?"

He nodded. "What did you want to see me for?"

I hesitated, but there was no helping it. "I just wanted to say hi. I know you're not avoiding me or anything, but this is all scary and I only—"

"I am."

I squinted at him. "What?"

His mouth was tight. "I am avoiding you."

"...oh."

"You don't—I want to touch you, Ellie. I want to kiss you, all the time. I want to talk to you for hours, and...I don't know." He scowled at the ocean. "Watch bad TV with you.

Sit beside you in Classics and scribble on your notebook. Whatever normal people do. I just…I wanted you to know that."

I eyed him carefully, trying to think over my own excitement. The words were exactly what I wanted to hear, but the resigned, bitter tone didn't fit. "So why avoid me?"

He grimaced, and glanced over his shoulder at Matiu. "Look, I've gotta go. I'll talk to you later."

"Sure," I said, and watched him walk away. I turned, meaning to find Professor Gribaldi, and stopped when I saw the dark, stocky shape moving toward me.

"That was a brief conversation," Mr. Sand noted, stepping out of the clouds of smoke.

"Eavesdropping?" I asked, scowling.

Crisp and cool in his white linen suit, he deflected my question with an airy wave. "I notice that you didn't speak of *me*. I'm deeply wounded."

"I *wish*."

He laughed, a thin, nasty sound like metal scraping. "You little partisan."

I set my legs and let my arms rest ready. "Little?"

"Oh, dear girl, I'm not looking at what you see in the mirror. Although I wonder what you *do* see in the mirror." He lifted an eyebrow but I declined to answer, glancing down the beach and wondering how to get him away. I had no intention of turning my back on him.

He extended his hand suddenly, and I stepped back to clear kicking range before I realized that he wasn't holding a weapon, but a glass bottle full of sparkling water. "Have a drink."

I took the bottle. It'd make a good weapon.

"It will be a full moon tonight. Not my kind of time, Ms. Spencer. I danced with your grandmother once, on a night with no moon at all. There was a pretty woman." He paused. "Tasty too. Did you know yours was *inherited* potential?"

I went dizzy with rage, shifting my weight as my focus narrowed to the bridge of his nose. He'd preyed on my Granny Spencer, who had stopped seeing ghosts. "You son of a bitch."

"Oh, don't. A fight would be terribly dreary for me and deeply humiliating for you." He waved at the hook of the bay, and the bonfires. "Besides. You really don't want to experience what happens to someone who breaks the bond between guest and host." He grinned. "Just one blow, and you'd be mine, and everyone here would give you to me."

I lowered the bottle, fighting back the fury. "You ate my grandmother's power. Like you ate Mark's."

"No, not like Mark's. I didn't eat your grandmother's power before she passed the potential on. Good husbandry on my part, and only wise. Your father didn't manifest the power, of course, nor your sister, but *you* certainly did. Mark was an entirely different matter." He looked at me. "You think I'm a monster."

"You're going to tell me I'm wrong?"

"No. But tell me, darling, what dark deeds would *you* perform to ward off starvation?"

I started at the question. He smirked as if he'd expected no answer, and seated himself on the damp sand as neatly as a cat folding itself up for a nap.

"My dear girl, when the days of magic faded and the age of

iron began, I could no longer dine on the power that had once saturated the air and trembled underfoot with every step. I did try to do without. It left these islands a little later than in most places. But hunger is an incredible force, you know. One can survive nearly forty days without food, while your body eats itself. It devours the fat reserves, feeds on all the large muscles. Finally, desperately, the heart." He twitched his fingers impatiently, the first unpolished gesture I'd seen him make. "So it was for me. Metaphorically."

"Boo-hoo."

"Would you condemn a woman who steals bread for her starving children?"

My throat was dry. I took a swallow of the water. "There's plenty of bread in the world."

"There's still some magic too, but most of it is sadly attached to beings and things reluctant to lose it. And only one animavore left, reduced to explaining himself to callow children. I don't usually *kill* people, of course. Fights are terribly risky, especially with those who know what they're doing. I prefer…bargains. Should you ever need something from me, rest assured I'll be eager to trade." His smile was sharp.

I thought of my grandmother, who had once seen ghosts, and lost the power after her son was born. "Bargains, and people who can't fight back," I said.

"Indeed. It's only sensible, isn't it?"

I took another long pull of the water to give myself time to think. "Does Mark know? That you need it to live?"

"Oh, yes." He grinned horribly. "If Mark were me, he'd make my choices."

"You're wrong."

"I'm afraid he's not as noble as you think him, dear girl. When he asked me to eat his power, I was happy to oblige."

My heart stammered. "You're lying."

"No. I don't do that."

"He said you stole it. He said he showed you patupaiarehe tricks, in exchange for—he said you *took* his power."

He laughed. "Oh, that's delightful! A truly tragic tale. The truth, Ms. Spencer, is that he wanted to stop being what he is, and he asked me to help him do that. He was wise enough to specify without killing him, or it would have been *much* easier. But he didn't want to be powerless either—some nonsense about a kinsman in trouble. No, he wanted knowledge in exchange."

I'm a monster, Mark had said, sitting on the end of my bed, vulnerable and sad.

"So—with his full participation—I ate the power he was born to, and I bound up certain useful bits and pieces into that charming bit of tat. And in fulfillment of our bargain, I placed on him a rather tricky and very ancient curse of transference and transformation. I rather suspect he wasn't expecting that, but that was hardly my affair. I did what he asked for."

"But he's still patupaiarehe," I pointed out. "You didn't fulfill your bargain."

"Oh, but I did. I created the circumstances he needs to achieve humanity. He will stay patupaiarehe until the day he dies. That is, unless someone confesses their heartfelt, drippy, squishy love for him. Then, poof! The curse kicks in. He'll be a real boy. And the poor devoted lover, on the instant, won't be human anymore."

"What?" I whispered.

"Darling girl, it's a tale as old as time! But they can't ever seem to get the ending right. The Beast becomes human and rides off on his merry way. But Beauty, beautiful no more, howls and hurries through the enchanted castle, her claws clattering on the hard stone floors." He waved his hand. "'And they all lived happily ever after.' Oh *dear*. I really cannot abide lies."

"You twist the truth," I said. My head was pounding.

"You seem such a nice girl," he confided, reaching to pat my arm, smiling when I shied away. "I thought I would warn you."

"You twist it into knots."

"I certainly do, my sweet. But I never lie." He looked over my shoulder. "Do I, dearest Mark?"

I whirled. Mark's eyes met mine through the smoky air, their vibrant green dulled. But if there was guilt there, or even sorrow, I couldn't see it.

"No," he said. "You don't lie."

CHAPTER SEVENTEEN
The Day I Went Under

I discovered Mark had been holding back on our wild flight through the Gardens. He was impressively speedy as he raced after me.

But he'd been fasting for over a day, and my legs were as long as his, and as it turned out, I was faster.

I pounded down the beach, ignoring the sand weighing down my sneakers and the weird buzzing in my mind. The handbag thumped against my ribs as I pumped my arms, and I ignored that too, scrambling up the rock path at the sharp curve of the beach, climbing for the cape. The birds shrieked and scolded as we climbed, almost loud enough to muffle the refrain of *stupid stupid stupid* that reverberated in my head.

Mark cried "Ellie!" and "It's not safe!" but I was their dumb mascot because this place was my home. I knew where the rough-cut steps went shallow at the top, and I shortened my step, still at the full speed Mark couldn't match.

Behind me, there was a thump, and a breathy curse word. You could hurt yourself badly, falling on the steps. I smiled, and only then noticed that I'd run that tricky stretch still holding the damn water bottle. I flung it to the side and ran faster, up the long-grassed curve of the hill. The prickling sensation that had urged me to *run, run, run* faded as soon as the bottle left my hand, but I'd settled into my stride.

I was well up the slope, moving fast, when I fell.

I didn't trip. The ground bucked and twisted under me and my feet tangled, so quickly I could do nothing but fling my arms around the handbag to cushion it. I landed hard on my back and lay there, trying to breathe, trying to make the black spots in my eyes go away. I was not going to cry.

I was *not* going to cry.

Mark panted up and crouched a few steps away from me, just barely in my field of vision. He'd cut his lip, on the other side from where I'd split it, only three nights before.

"Fuck off," I said, after a few silent minutes where he didn't seem to have gotten the hint.

"I just want to talk."

"You were trying to *trap* me." He'd betrayed me so many times; how had I thought it possible that some of it was genuine?

"No!"

"Oh, screw you." I stood up. "Strike that; I'm glad I didn't. You said you liked me! Bad TV, talking for hours!"

"I do!" he cried.

"Liar! I believed you. I thought—" My voice cracked. "I am so *stupid*. Have you been laughing at me this whole time? Dumb, fat Ellie, thinking someone like you could ever—"

"No!" he said, face stark with horror. "Oh, no, Ellie, no! I meant to *tell* you. Warn you. I just couldn't find the right time."

"Well, that's original."

"I heard Sand telling you. He knew I was there. I thought, well, she can't love me now. She'll be safe." He looked at me. "I want you to be safe, Ellie."

"Too late!" I snarled. "And since when do you get to choose that for me?"

"I was going to tell you about the curse," he insisted. "But I didn't think you were in any danger."

I laughed, high and mocking. "Are you kidding me, or just yourself? I pushed you down on my bed and stuck my tongue down your throat!"

He flushed. "I thought maybe that was—you know. Just... attraction. Sex."

"Oh, *please*! You think I'm that shallow?"

"I think you're amazing," he said, and my last words stuck in my throat. "And I really do like you. I know I shouldn't, but the thing is—"

"The thing is, you told yourself 'she won't say she loves me,' all the time secretly hoping I would. Didn't you?"

"I hope not," he whispered.

I flattened my anger over the hurt welling up under my rib cage.

"You knew what I was," he said, raking his hair back from his face, eyes wild with the will to make me believe. "You knew that my face is a lie, just pretending to be human. And you still wanted me, you could touch me, you could see what I am, the only one who knew and wanted me all the same, and you said I wasn't a—" his chest hitched. "Not a monster. I was going to tell you, and then I thought, well, I'm probably going to die in the underworld, so why can't I have this until then? I'm the stupid one; not you. I'm so sorry."

I studied his face. He was so beautiful. So obviously repentant. "I remember. I said you were a *good enough* person."

He nodded, hope flaring in his face.

"I was wrong," I said. "I was so wrong about you. You are every *inch* your mother's son."

Watching Mark cry made me feel mean and bitchy instead of righteously avenged, so after a few moments of the awful choked noises coming from behind his cupped hands, I opened the handbag to check on the mask.

It was fine.

It also had a number of suggestions for what I could do to Mark. Perhaps he should lick the dirt from my shoes. Or dance off the edge of the cliff. Or eat his own fingers. He'd do anything, if I only I put it on and made him love me.

No, I told it, aching, and stuffed it back into the bag.

Mark was staring at me, tears smeared over his high cheek-bones.

"I wasn't *going* to use it," I said before I remembered I didn't have to defend myself to him.

"Shut up," he said.

"*What* did you just—"

"Shhhh!" He was looking past me, head tilted as if he was listening, eyes wide and terrified.

With a jolt I realized just how far we'd run from the beach. We were high on the slope, the rest of our people hidden behind the swell of the hillside and the curve of the cliff. I couldn't hear them singing.

It's not safe, he'd said.

I'd thought he was talking about running on wet rock. Now I registered the gray wetness in the air. A sea mist had come in, and I didn't need to ask if it was natural. It tingled unpleasantly against my bare face. In seconds it was so thick I could only make out Mark by my memory of where he was. I caught a strain of aching flute music, high and discordant.

A light rain began to fall.

"Oh, no," I whispered. The patupaiarehe weren't waiting for the night. They were trading the power the night gave them for the chance of taking the beach defenders unprepared.

I stood up as quietly as I could, sliding into a defensive position with Mark at my back.

"We're surrounded," he said softly. "They'll find us in a moment."

I peered through the murk, hoping to see the attack before

it came, trying to find someone to kick. Three dozen patu-paiarehe, and I'd barely survived a fight with one. *Just one*, I thought, *just let me take down one.* My parents were going to come home to bury their daughter. *Oh, Mum, I'm so sorry.*

Mark hit me with the charm while my back was turned.

One last betrayal, I thought, wondering how I could even be surprised. My legs stiffened and I toppled. Mark's arms were around my waist to ease my fall, lowering me flat. He hadn't touched me at all since we'd kissed on the end of my bed, his skin warm under my palms.

I couldn't feel his hands now. The spell was taking me under, transforming me into something still and quiet. I didn't have a shred of anything to resist it. Even the mask was numb, taken as unawares as I was.

It was the pebble charm, which turned flesh to stone.

I watched Mark yank it free of his bracelet and balance the small gray stone in the hollow of my collarbone, fingers resting for a fluttering moment on my throat. Motionless as the rock I was becoming, I waited to die.

But instead of pressing down, he tugged the flax bag out from under his shirt, hooked his free hand into the neckband of my sweater and shoved the bag under it. His mother's eyes lay between my breasts, alive and horrible, and unhappy to be near me.

He balanced over me on all fours and whispered into my ear. "If you can, get these to Matiu. Tell him to go."

I could no longer speak, but my eyes must have asked the question.

"I'm sorry," he said. "It'll wear off after I'm dead."

And then he was running into the fog, bright hair gleaming. The patupaiarehe shouted when they saw him, and he shouted something back, but whether it was "Come and get me!" or "I love you," I couldn't tell. Stone crept into my mind until I could feel nothing at all.

Grateful, I slept.

Lying on the cold hillside, my mind woke before my body did. There was one terrifying moment of being rock, and being aware I was rock, before the last of the charm faded and I could move.

I jerked up, the skin on my hands fading from dark gray to splotchy pink. Reka's legacy banged against my chest.

I wasted no time in finding out if my legs could hold me, and scrambled down the slope on my hands and knees, pleading under my breath to a God I didn't believe in. Somewhere, I knew the hope was useless. If it hadn't happened, I wouldn't have woken up.

Mark lay a little further down the hill, a motionless, crumpled heap of blood and rags.

My head rang with the suddenness of the silence. For that stretched moment I couldn't hear the cries of the birds or the yells of the people fighting on the beach below. My vision narrowed to Mark and the bright smears of red that had been his face.

I stood up. One part of me noted that I was remarkably steady as I sauntered down to sit beside him. I'd torn the knees of my jeans as I'd crawled, and blood seeped through one of the holes. It didn't hurt. That was the weird thing. Nothing hurt at all.

He'd flung up his arms, trying to protect his head. The charm bracelet was gone.

"You should have learned to fight," I said vaguely, and bent to stroke a gore-soaked strand of hair. "I could have taught you." In the movies, you could close the eyelids of a dead man by passing one hand over his face. I had to pinch the skin of his right eyelid and tug, and even then it wouldn't close all the way over the emptied eye socket.

It looked like a picture taken by some jaded war photographer, or a special effect in a slasher film. It was too stark and awful to be real. This crumpled thing couldn't be brave Mark, of the bright smile and dark green eyes and unbearable burdens that he'd somehow managed to bear.

"You lied to me," I said suddenly, and poked his shoulder. "On *numerous* occasions. Asshole." Anger was good. If I could just stay angry...

The bag under my shirt swung heavily forward at the movement and I remembered what he'd told me to do. "I have to get these to Matiu," I told Mark. "I'll come back after that. Straight after."

My throat was starting to close up, but I took deep breaths and forced myself to my feet, hunching over the empty ache in my chest. The mask was whispering something, but I made a black handbag in my mind, and locked its voice away in there along with everything else that hurt too much to think about.

A nimbus of sunset-pink light danced along the edge of

the cliff, then an explosion of violet sparks burst into the air farther out to sea. When I got to the edge and peered down, I couldn't see much of the fog-shrouded beach. The fires had been put out, but the mist swirled or lit up in strange colors, showing me flashes of hectic activity. I saw the bikers crouching by a pile of crumbling driftwood, reloading their guns, and Professor Gribaldi swinging a hammer with a head as big as my thigh, and the tall Māori woman chanting, her voice clear and mournful over the din. I couldn't see Matiu anywhere. Maybe he was dead. Maybe I was dead, and this was what happened after.

The flashing mists revealed bodies on the beach, and many of them were the white and naked patupaiarehe. It looked like we were winning, but I didn't know exactly what the patupaiarehe needed to do on the beach, or if they could do it in the middle of a battle. Matiu was right. I didn't know anything.

The familiar hot smell wrinkled my nose, so that I knew who was behind me before I turned.

"Hello," I said. "Mark's dead."

The words were too flat, too wrong. I tried to breathe them back in, but they were already set free.

Mr. Sand floated six inches off the ground, staring at my chest, where Reka's eyes hung. It was the least lascivious thing I'd ever seen. "I know."

I touched the bag under my sweater. "I have to give these to Matiu. He knows the way."

"You could give them to me," Sand said. "I could give them to Matiu."

Something tugged at the corner of my mind. "Could," not

"would," and the mask and Reka's eyes were both shrilling warnings at me. And what was he doing up here, and not down on the beach with the rest of the defenders? But he couldn't hurt me. I was the host.

I said the last part out loud without meaning to, and he shook his head, smiling slightly. "I can't strike you, or poison you, or slit your throat," he said. "Nor may I steal from you, more's the pity. But I can relocate you, and remove the advantage you give to those who rely on such things. Who knows? When this is done, I might even ask them to fetch you for me. You won't be sane, of course, but it would be a pity to let your potential go to waste." He sighed. "You should have kept running, you silly girl."

Far too slowly, I reached for the screaming mask. He caught my wrist before I could undo the handbag's clasps and I stopped, every muscle rigid.

"Don't," I said, high and angry, like a child. "You're on our side."

"Oh, *darling*," he said, and patted my cheek. "You are so funny. I'd have kept you if I could, I promise, you and poor little Mark. But bread for the starving, you know. There'll be lots of bread today! Plenty of dead magicians, with their power floating free." He shivered, with all the lust that hadn't been there when he'd stared at my chest. "But the real dealmaker was the death of the fish. They don't want *his* power. And after that, I should be really...*spectacular*."

My head buzzed. He leaned forward and passed his palm in the air over Reka's eyes. They blazed, glowing green through my sweater. He tilted his head at something behind me. "There we are."

I could feel the entrance open at my back, cold and wet and utterly alien.

"In you go, dear," he said, and threw me, falling, into the mists.

The psychic impact of entering the mists was peculiarly useful; it was so painful that I couldn't stay shocked and stoic anymore. I felt emotion return in a blazing rush, and cried out, sobbing a little at the clenching pain.

Excellent: I was lost in a bizarre world inhabited by homicidal fairies, and just standing in it felt like stuffing my skull with steel wool, but at least I had gut-churning anguish to keep me entertained.

Mark had betrayed me, and now he was dead, and I didn't know which grieved me more. But Mr. Sand had betrayed both of us, and he was very much alive.

"I'm going to kill him," I said, and clung to the sound of my voice, hanging dead and flat in the wet air.

It was a goal. Goals were good. This one only required I find my way to the entrance to the underworld, intercept and defeat whatever patupaiarehe were on their way there before they could get to the Goddess of Death, find my way home, and kill a very powerful and ancient magician.

And I would have to do it by feel, because I could see nothing except myself. My surroundings, if there were any, were concealed in the shifting gray of the fog. I put my foot out to take the first step and felt nothing under it.

"Oh, *hell*," I said, and burst into tears. They dripped down my cheeks, some comfort that I, at least, was real.

There was a clinging, tearing pain like a dog bite, right over my heart. I reached up instinctively to beat away what attacked me, and touched the bag that held Reka's eyes.

They greeted the touch with a pain that flared up my spine, pooled at the base of my skull like lava, then abruptly disappeared. Knowledge arrived in my head: the power represented by Reka's eyes could keep me alive here for a very long time.

But I wouldn't stay sane for anywhere near that long.

"Inventory," I said, trying to control my panic. It helped to talk. "Two stone eyeballs. Two sneakers, damp and disgusting. One pair of jeans, ditto. One sweater. One handbag, evidence of Magda's complete lack of taste." I stopped. I'd forgotten the mask. How had I forgotten the mask?

I knew as soon I fumbled the flax bag open and tipped Reka's eyes into the white bowl of the mask's back. They hated each other, and both howled at me. But I was scared, and desperate with it.

Reka's eyes could guide me, but they hated me. The mask loved me, but couldn't guide me. I had a mask with no eyes, eyes with no face, and a knack for making things.

I braced the mask against my bleeding knee and fought to shove each greenstone into an empty eye socket.

They struggled against me, then each other. The green orbs forced back against my fingers until I thought I would break my hands pressing them in. The mask slid on my jeans, somehow never collecting any of the mud that spattered them to smear its surface. The mask definitely wasn't porcelain—porcelain would have shattered under our triple assault.

I shouted something, high and wild, and pressed with the palms of both hands. The eyes went in with the sickening grind of stone on bone, and stayed there.

I closed my own muddy blue eyes in my own plain, broad face and lifted the mask. It shifted and clung as I placed it against my skin, as if it meant to sink into me. When I lowered my hands, it stayed in place.

"Show me the way," I said, half-plea, half-command, and opened my eyes.

It was black—dusty black, not the mists' gray. I thought that the mask had maimed me, that Reka's eyes were punishing my presumption with blindness, and screamed.

Then the spotlight came on, cold white on the stage's black wooden boards.

The panic subsided as my eyes adjusted. I was sitting in the Ngaio Marsh Theater, knees cramped against the seat in front. I could hear the rustling of the audience around me as they opened packets and rearranged coats. The performance was just about to begin.

You bring your own mythology with you, Mark had said. I settled back, handbag tucked behind my feet.

A small young woman dressed in gold with skin the color of old porcelain stepped into the spotlight, and the audience hushed expectantly. Pushing shining black curtains of hair away from her perfect face, Iris Tsang raised her head. She was looking directly at me.

"Enter, from the audience," she commanded.

I could feel the focus of the audience shift to me, huge and cramped in the too-small seat. I tried to shrink back.

"Enter, Ellie," Iris said, looking harassed.

I stood up. The audience was audible on every side, but I saw and touched no one as I clambered down the rows. The orchestra pit was raised level with the last row of seats. I walked across it and stepped up onto the stage.

Iris smiled and tapped her palms lightly together. Her gold dress glinted in the light.

"I've gone mad," I told her. "The mists make people crazy. And I'm lost."

She shook her head, already fading into the dark. "You're finding your way."

Then she left me there, all alone with the curious watchers just out of sight.

"Hi, Ellie," Carrie said, stepping into the circle of light. "Teach me how to fight." She moved with far more competence than the real Carrie, and her first strike glanced off my cheekbone.

"Hey!" I said, and the second grazed my ribs. I hissed with the pain and circled back and away, feinting to the right.

"I am not so low that my nails cannot reach unto your eyes," she snarled, and leapt, thrusting clawed hands toward my face.

Behind her, Iris flung her arm around Carrie's throat and yanked back. "That's not your line," she said reproachfully, as Carrie sank down to slink around her on feet that resembled paws. "Why didn't you ask for help, Ellie?"

"I didn't know you were there."

"I was here all the time. You were seeing someone else."

"Don't come crying to me," Blake said, lowering himself from the fly floor. The rope he clung to ran up into the dark cavern of the stage roof, much vaster than the Ngaio's fly floor tower. The stage lights were the stars clothing Rangi, the sky father.

Blake's face was made up of patches, two brown buttons gleaming above a red satin nose. He turned lazy cartwheels around me, tapping out the syllables of his speech with hands and feet. "Se-xy El-lie Spen-cer."

"You're not real," I said. "None of this is real. I'm using my own experiences to make sense of the mists, that's all."

He spun on his heels and pointed at the back wall of the stage. "Real enough, Ellie. Look!"

The painted backdrop was the same as in the real theater—the arch painted in two halves, and the dense mass of ancient forest that sprawled over the rest of the canvas.

Something glinted among the trees. I peered closer. A silver-haired woman was running smoothly down a fern-lined track, moonlight gleaming on her pale skin, on her dark, polished club. A long way up the track was a small, withered tree with burn-black branches hunching over a deep hole.

Encircling her left wrist was a familiar charm bracelet.

"Long road," Blake observed.

I shouted and reached for Mark's murderer. I meant to pluck her from the picture and twist her tiny body, but when I stretched out my hands, they were already stained with blood. Blake caught my wrists.

"It's your fault, Pandora," he said. "You failed. And even if you knew what to do, she's too far ahead—you'll never catch up."

"Iris," I cried. "Help me!"

The house lights flared and Blake stumbled back into the shadows. Iris beamed from the lighting box.

I leaned back into someone tall and solid. "Don't forget you saved *me*, Ell," Kevin whispered in my ear. "You loved me enough to hold on." He gripped my shoulders. "And look. There's a shortcut."

The orchestra pit lowered with a sickening rumble. The movement reverberated through my skull, as if something was shifting there. I stared into the depths where no light shone.

"Give the old lady my regards," Kevin said.

I spread my bloody hands like wings, and leaped.

I landed hard, tough grass tearing at the soles of my bare feet. The mask was a mask again, the green eyes pressing cool against my closed eyelids, before it began to slide off my face. I fumbled to catch it one-handed and held it uncertainly. I'd somehow left the handbag behind.

Also, apparently, my clothes.

I hugged my bare torso and surveyed my surroundings. I was high on a cape, much like the one I'd left, but covered in scrub. Far below, a white, sandy beach stretched straight back to the horizon. It looked like any beach in winter, windblown and spare, but I saw also the long tail of the massive fish, and shuddered. On the cape a spring bubbled nearby, and at its very tip something wavered in my uncanny vision: sometimes it was a lighthouse; and sometimes an ancient pohutukawa tree; and sometimes a grotto with steam drifting from its craggy mouth. Flickering images suggested other entrances, but those three were clear and strong.

It was dusk here. How much time had I lost in the mists?

There was a steady procession of people, as naked as I was, making their way up the slope, lamenting and wailing as they walked toward the spring, calm and purposeful after they had bathed in it and drunk from the water. They moved to the tree—no, lighthouse—no, grotto—wavered, and were gone. If their journeys continued from there, I couldn't see them.

"I made it," I breathed. I had come safely through the mists to Cape Reinga, Cape Underworld, the leaping-off place of the spirit.

I gripped the mask loosely, and entered the crush of bodies, heading for the stream.

"Hey, girl!" said the man beside me.

I shrieked and leaped back into kicking distance, my free hand raising in a block.

He flashed me a white grin, taking no offense, and I took in his ochre-smeared chest and the tattoos writhing down his impressive shoulders and arms. I hadn't recognized him without his biker leathers.

"I'm sorry," I said. It was so inadequate, but it was all I could say. I didn't know his name. Even now, I couldn't tell which of the three he was.

"Me too, eh." He glanced at the eyes in the mask I carried and suddenly straightened. "What are you doing here with those? We thought that Mark was going."

I cringed. "He died. I tried to find Matiu but—" A sudden hope washed over me. "But *you* could go!"

He stepped away from the proffered mask as if it was some venomous creature, eyes fierce in his weathered face. "You kidding me? You want to send me down there, dead and remembering forever? I'm not coming back, girl! I'm one of hers now."

"I shouldn't be here! I don't know what to do! It's not meant to be me!"

"Well, it's not going to be me," he said definitely, and gave me a long look as we reached the stream. "Don't drink the water."

I thought of the waters of Lethe, the river in Hades that made the dead forget the living. Was it something like that? "Why not?"

"Jesus. You really don't know anything. Here." He strode into the water, then wrapped his massive arms around my waist and lifted me across.

I nodded my thanks, a little stiffly, and started walking.

"Hey!" he called, and I turned. His hands were cupped together in front of his chest, dark water tricking from the gaps in his fingers. "You're *not* meant to be here. But you're all they've got. Don't screw up, eh? And good luck." He dipped his head and drank before I could thank him.

The thing at the end of the cape solidified as I approached. It was a tree most often now, and I wasted a thought on whether it had chosen that form or I had. The woman before me climbed into the twisted branches and leapt gladly toward the setting sun.

But I knew that wasn't my route. Between the exposed roots, sprawled like the legs of a sleeping woman, was a dark hole that stretched away into nothingness.

I took a deep breath and let it out slowly, cradling the mask in my arms. I could turn around right now; count on the people I'd left behind to defeat the patupaiarehe. This was the backup plan. There was no point in going if all the monsters were dead. I'd fail for nothing.

I curled my bare toes in the sandy soil and waited, a little curiously, to see if courage or fear would win.

The ground buckled under my feet. I threw myself backward, clutching at the matted grass with my free hand to keep myself from being flung into the air. In my double vision, the tail of the fish was twisting wildly. The air was filled with a high-pitched keening.

"Oh no," I panted. "Oh no, oh no. Those *bastards*!"

I couldn't stand on the writhing earth. Flat on my belly, clutching the mask awkwardly, I hauled myself to the entrance to the underworld, grass and sand scratching at my bare skin. I was hissing through my teeth, a low litany of curse words. They'd killed Mark, and my guests, and now they were going to kill my home.

But not unpunished.

I had neither courage nor fear left, only a violent urge to deprive them of their blood-won victory. "Hine-nui-te-pō," I whispered, hanging half into the hole. "I'm coming." Then I kicked with my powerful legs, and for the third time, fell.

CHAPTER EIGHTEEN
Won't Give In

There was bare, wet rock underfoot, and the air smelled musty and dead. I waited a minute for my eyes to adjust to the blackness, then realized they wouldn't. There was no light at all. Grimly, I fitted the mask against my face.

It hummed its content and sank easily into my skin again. Reka's eyes cooperated more grudgingly, showing me the wide limestone tunnel as if it were lit by the moon—all deep shadows and rocky forms. There was no opening above me, and the only direction was forward.

I ran, revenge black and twisting in my heart.

The earth didn't shake here. It wasn't as formlessly terrifying as the mist—humans could walk here, it seemed, even living ones. I wondered if it was real for a moment, then dismissed the question. It was real enough to hurt my feet as I ran, real enough to score my shoulders and thighs as I banged against toothy stalactites dripping water and the stalagmites thrusting upward. They were the largest I'd ever seen.

A sharp piece of flint slashed the sole of my left foot, and I thought of Iris limping, bloodied. Mystical adventures seemed to involve a lot of minor aches and pains that didn't make it into the stories. I wondered if Orpheus had ever stubbed his toe on the way to rescue Eurydice. Lopsided, I ran on, leaving my blood smeared on the pale rock floor.

My breath was coming in pants, nearly sobs. The patupaiarehe were going to live out the remainder of their long, pointless lives, and then they were going to die, and stay dead. I had the hardening ambition to help some of them get there a little sooner. Maybe Reka could help me, once I gave her back her eyes.

But first, I had to stop the fair-haired woman from completing her work. Find her, before she got to Hine-nui-te-pō, and crawled between the legs of the sleeping guardian to bring her people the immortality they craved.

Lie in ambush, the mask suggested. Let her get one look at the mask, and then she will be ours. Tell her to beat her own brains out. Or we could order this goddess to kill her for us.

I stumbled to a halt. The mask could work its magic on the will of Hine-nui-te-pō?

Certainly, it replied, full of confidence. It was very old, and very strong, especially with these mist-born eyes. And it loved me. Everyone should love me. All the gods should love me and order the world to my desires. Did I want the pale boy back? I could have that too, if this guardian of the dead were mine.

Of course, she would have to love me forever. I couldn't let one like that ever go free.

I braced against the worn cave side, trembling. The mask shivered anxiously. Had it offended?

"We'll stop the patupaiarehe," I whispered, and it subsided, satisfied, as I began to run again.

The tunnel widened gradually, until even Reka's moonsight could not show me the ceiling. I heard the slow sighing of the wind, like massive exhalations, echo through the caves. The final cavern was cathedral-huge, and finished in a massive dark shadow leaning against the back wall—rocks, I guessed, piled three stories high.

I swallowed defeat, bitter in my dry mouth, and faltered to a slow walk. The rock fall barred my way, and even the mask couldn't order it open.

The shadow moved. Wind gusted over me as Hine-nui-te-pō exhaled.

My own breath stuck in my throat.

She was sleeping against the wall, her knees tucked firmly against her chest. Her black hair fell over her shoulders and coiled on the cavern floor in thick strands, gleaming like kelp. Her skin was the dark brown of sooty tōtara wood, her fingernails and toenails iridescent with the pink sheen of mussel shells. She was the largest living thing I'd ever seen, and so beautiful it made me ache.

Stones scattered behind me as the patupaiarehe woman leapt from her hiding place.

I wasn't the only one who had considered ambush.

She was unarmed and as naked as I was, but her bony elbow came up in a hammering blow to my diaphragm. My lungs emptied, and I barely got a hand down to break my fall. The pain in my shoulder told me I'd sprained it as I rolled. A dainty foot crashed down where my face had been.

Make her stop, the mask said frantically. But I had no breath to shout orders, and only enough momentum to roll, and roll again, heedless of my bare flesh scraping on stone. I tumbled into something warm and unyielding, and could retreat no further. I was going to die at the feet of a goddess. A useless, desperate fury filled me as the patupaiarehe woman raised her clawed hand.

It wasn't much of a shout; only a sputtering, wordless wheeze as I forced my rage into voice.

But it was enough.

Hine-nui-te-pō, guardian of the dead, once Hine-titama, the maiden of the dawn, first woman born of woman, and the mother of humanity, opened her greenstone-dark eyes and roared.

The sheer force of her voice tossed me up and halfway across the cave. The mask ripped clear from my face as I fell, a house-height or more from the floor. Inconveniently, I recovered my breath just in time to scream.

She held up a massive hand and the wind of her will caught

me, setting me none-too-gently on my bleeding feet. The mask clattered to the ground a few steps away, but there was no question of my diving for it. The goddess was speaking.

"Woman," she said, through a mouth filled with sharp obsidian teeth. "Why do you disturb me?"

It wasn't English. I wasn't sure it was Māori either, or any language ever spoken by human voices. But I understood it. This was the beginning tongue that created what it communicated, the language of conception.

I was incapable of response.

But the patupaiarehe was better prepared. Her voice was as beautiful as the rest of her and all the power of her people's music was behind it.

I listened, dazed by the somnolent rhythm of the silver-haired woman's chant. I didn't understand the words, but I could easily guess at the meaning. She was pleading her case, pointing out the great wrongs done her people by Māui, the diminishment of her race with the coming of humans to the cloud-covered islands. Was it not unjust that they should pay for Māui's crime? Was it not right that Hine-nui-te-pō release the patupaiarehe from their grievous mortality?

The goddess's eyes glazed as the woman's voice went on, smooth eyelids drooping over her enormous eyes. Her knees relaxed, legs as long as tree trunks spreading in her slumber. There was another cave between her thighs, filled with a second set of obsidian teeth.

The patupaiarehe woman sang her lullaby, and walked easily toward that toothy opening.

In the backwash of that seduction, my own eyelids

fluttered. I folded gently onto the floor, stretching my arms in the prelude to sleep.

The fingertips of one hand touched the mask.

The fog in my brain cleared at once, and was immediately followed by an awareness of just how much I hurt. I felt like one huge, raw bruise as I yanked the mask onto my face and sat up.

Help me, I pleaded and the mask, exultant, poured power into me like a waterfall into a paper cup. My skin wasn't enough to hold it all, I thought dimly, and waited to tear under the force of it. But I expanded instead, to the limits of myself and beyond, until I trembled on the brink of losing everything I was in the glory of that flow. It was Reka's eyes that stabbed me, strong and fierce, with the knowledge of my task and the will to perform it.

It had taken seconds. Still singing, the patupaiarehe was just ducking her head to crawl between the thighs of Hine-nui-te-pō.

"Hey," I said, my voice cracked and small.

The woman whirled, her hair flaring around her like Christmas tinsel, her mouth open to unleash some withering curse.

"Love me," I told her, and felt the stony strength of her will crumble like a clump of dry dirt. "Stop singing."

Her dissolution was terrible to watch, the more so because I knew she hated me. Her eyes alive with silent adoration, she sank to her knees, clawed hands lolling against the walls of the goddess's thighs.

The last echo of the lullaby faded. Hine-nui-te-pō opened

her eyes to stare, horrified, at the woman between her legs. Lips twisting over those nightmarish teeth, she smashed her knees together three times.

The patupaiarehe must have died in the first crushing blow. By the third, all of her beauty and power were stinking red and purple smears.

She had looked at me while she died. Loved me, and I'd used that love to bring her death.

Legs pulled tight against her chest, Hine-nui-te-pō took a deep breath.

Now, the mask decided. Tell the goddess she loved me before the winds came again. Make her love me forever. Hardly a violation, to save myself.

I clawed the mask off and flung it at the ground.

Bile swelling in my throat, I crouched, hiding my face in my hands, and spoke between my fingers, gabbling without consideration of the words. "I can't. I can't do it, not even for this. Aren't you sick of lies and betrayals? I am. I'm so *tired*."

There was silence while I waited to die, then: "Yes," said Hine-nui-te-pō. "I am very tired of lies."

I uncurled slowly, because I was sore, not because I was being cautious. There wasn't any point. Even if I could bring myself to put it on again, the mask lay meters away. The goddess was looking at me. It was hard to read complex emotions on a face so dizzyingly large, but I thought she seemed curious.

"Hello," I said, and discovered that even in the awe of this moment, there was room for embarrassment at my own inanity.

"They still tell my story," she said, sounding satisfied.

"Yes. My friend—Mark Nolan. Mark told me. But they tell all the Māui stories."

Her straight eyebrows drew together in anger. "Māui's story! Māui the thief, Māui the rapist, Māui that men call hero!" She shifted her legs and I caught a glimpse of the great teeth grinding against each other as she moved. "This is *my* story."

"Yes. I'm sorry."

"Now you will tell me yours," she declared, and settled back against the rocky wall of the cave. "Where are you from?"

I was so exhausted that I would have preferred to have gone to sleep and never woken up, but goddesses didn't have to bow to the whims of mortal girls. I started at the beginning, from bumping into Mark at the gates, to preventing the silver-haired patupaiarehe from crawling into the goddess. "And then you woke up," I concluded, and rotated my shoulders. Every muscle was aching. Rolling on the stone floor had given me scratches to replaces the ones La Gribaldi had healed.

Hine-nui-te-pō smiled, which was probably supposed to look friendlier than it did. "So, you aided me. I will not be obliged to you. What do you want?"

"Nothing," I said, surprised. "I wanted to stop the patu-paiarehe winning everything, that's all." I felt my face twist. "They sank the North Island. I wanted them to pay." I hadn't expected that it would leave me feeling so empty.

She looked at me blankly. "But Te Ika a Māui is not yet dead."

I staggered to my feet. "What?"

She gestured downward, grimacing. "This one—you

forced her hand. She made her attempt too soon. He wakes, he writhes—but he has not died."

"Can you stop them?" I said. "On the surface, can you stop them? I want that!"

"I will not enter the world of the living," she said flatly, and I felt it like a kick to the gut. "But it is his death dive that will destroy your people, and he is half-dead already. If it is your wish, I can take Te Ika a Māui faster, now. His body will remain surface-bound, hooked to the sea and sky. Your people will live."

"Yes!" I said. "Please!"

"You are certain?"

"Of course!"

She looked at me for a long moment, her eyes unreadable, then she raised her hand and twisted it. Something spun itself out of the air and wove around her fingers; something that smelled sharply of salt and sweetly of green things after rain, something replete with the sound of dolphins squeaking and the melodic song of the tui bird, something that remembered tall, flightless moa stalking through the dense bush and the huge hawks that had eaten them, and the taniwha in the rivers and the patupaiarehe ghosting through the forests and along the shore. Māui's fish had lain under the tortured sun for eons in unimaginable agony, and had still given endlessly of himself to the tiny, chattering creatures that clambered over his surface and dug for shellfish at his edges and crawled through his caverns to watch glowworms spreading tiny galaxies over underground lakes.

He came to the goddess gladly, and Hine-nui-te-pō waited

until the last of his spirit was gathered in her hand, glowing like a dark moon. Then she twisted her fingers, and he vanished, pain ended.

I was crying, huge drops dripping down my face to splatter on my stomach and thighs.

"It is done," she said, and sighed. "I must care for my children. There are many waiting. Go, and take your other face with you."

I picked up the mask, and it trembled in my hands like a dog frightened of a beating. I knew then that it had been overconfident in its power. It was strong and old, but it was nothing to Hine-nui-te-pō. I could never have made her love me and I had been right in more than one way to reject the possibility. "How do I get back?" I asked hesitantly.

"My obligation is paid. Make your own path from here," she said, and closed her eyes.

I waited in case she had any less cryptic advice, but she was silent and sleeping. Still, I stayed. The wind of her breath gusted evenly for long minutes, until, aching, I crept out of the cave of the guardian of the dead.

The network of tunnels were gone as if they had never been. I stood instead beneath a dim sky in which no sun or moon shone, at the bottom of the high bank beside a gray river. White herons stalked in the shallows, mincing through the mud on their skinny legs.

I could hear singing over the hill, too ordinary to be

patupaiarehe song. Hunger gnawed at me, and I turned to climb up the slope.

Mark was sitting on a rock. "Hey, Spencer," he said.

His face was restored, grave and beautiful. But underneath the high cheekbones and clean, straight hair, I saw the gore-smeared skull patupaiarehe clubs had broken.

"This isn't fair," I whispered. How much pain could anyone bear? "What are you doing here?"

"Bird watching."

Well, it had been a stupid question anyway. "This isn't even real," I said.

His shoulders lifted. "Yes and no. I'm really here. It's really me."

I bit my lip, hands twisting.

He waved at the hill. "I was trying to psych myself up for my first meal. But now I'm glad I've got a chance to say sorry."

"First meal? Is this some sort of Persephone deal?"

He laughed. "There are some interesting parallels. You should read up on this stuff."

"I will."

He cocked his head. "In books."

"Smartass," I said, and let the tears come. He wrapped his arm around my shoulders and held on while I shook into him, kissing my wet cheekbones and the corners of my eyes. It felt so good to touch him again, after so long. He *felt* real. I wasn't even embarrassed about my nudity. What did it matter now?

"I'm so sorry, Ellie," he said, when I recovered enough to pull away a little and look into his face. "Please believe me. I meant to tell you. Right after this all went down, if I survived."

"I believe you," I said absently. "I think I knew you weren't lying about that. But I was in danger of loving you, and you knew it. I bet that was tempting."

Something was nagging at me under the grief; something someone had told me about stories. I chased the memory until I held it firmly, a new but growing hope.

In my mead-happy daze Professor Gribaldi had said that the stories in your head changed the world. Mark had said that too, or something like it, sitting on the banks of the Avon. And he was really here.

"Stories I believe," I muttered. "Not Persephone. Orpheus."

Mark was still holding my bruised shoulders. "Can you forgive me?"

I gently disengaged from his grip. "Not yet."

He flinched.

"We'll talk about it later," I said, and turned around, clenching my eyes shut.

His voice was startled. "Ellie?"

"Don't talk to me," I ordered. "Don't touch me. Don't make a *sound*. Just follow."

I thought turning my back on him had been difficult, but the first step was harder still.

I walked for a long time. The sky never got darker or lighter, and I could hear, always, the singing rise above the banks of the river. But I never saw any of the other dead, and strain as I could, I never heard Mark's breathing or the echo of his steps. After a while my stomach stopped cramping, leaving me with a vicious headache and bouts of dizziness. The thirst was worse, and as I followed the river path I caught myself looking at the water far too often. Just one mouthful of that gray water would have made such a difference.

But if my stories would help, the ones I had heard and read and loved until they became part of me, then I had to follow the rules. Don't eat. Don't drink. Don't step off the path.

Never look behind.

The river narrowed to a stream, and then a creek, lined with lichen-covered rocks with ferns in every crevice, and trees that tangled their long roots in knotty clusters. I had to go slower, picking my way awkwardly with my one free hand. The mask noted that it would be easier if I put it on. I ignored it, and squeezed my eyes shut every time I stumbled, in case I fell facing the wrong way.

The creek narrowed to a trickle that disappeared altogether, and I stood on one side of a small clearing in the dense bush.

On the clearing's other side were two gates standing next to each other, not quite touching. There were no walls to hold them in place—only the trees crowding around them. It was as if they had grown there.

I swore viciously, and stalked across the grove to inspect them.

One was constructed from heavy planks of dark wood, with eaves hewn from tree trunks. The gateposts and eaves were covered in intricate carvings, the wood decorated with taniwha and *tupuna*, with eyes of paua shell and teeth of bone. The other gate was made of limestone, with the eaves in a sharp point over the two massive blocks of stone held upright by white Corinthian pillars crowned with agapanthus wreaths.

There were two gates in one of the stories I knew: gates of horn and ivory, for dreams false and true. If I'd seen those gates, I would have known which path to take. But this was something else, some other choice.

"I don't even know what I'm choosing," I said, and felt my voice break in the silence. "How can I choose one or the other?" I dug my nails against my thigh, striving not to turn and ask Mark's advice. "The story is supposed to be *mine*. I should know this!"

But my stories weren't singular. I had been born in a land where many had brought stories, and I had chosen others on my own. And then there was Mark. I stood there and trembled, staring at the gates until tears sprang to my eyes and smudged my view.

In that blurry vision, the dark gap between them stood out in sharp relief.

"Oh," I said, astounded. "Of course. It's about chimeras. Chimeras and balance."

Was that an intake of breath behind me? I couldn't tell over the thrumming of blood in my ears, but I held to it as if it had been shouted approval. I forced down one last, fierce urge to look behind, and stepped forward, to walk between the gates.

The gap was tight. I canted my shoulders to get them through, unwilling to turn completely to one side or the other in case it was taken as a choice. Stone scraped at my right hip on one side and splinters stabbed the left. It seemed the gates weren't just gates, but enormous buildings; the walls went on and on as I forced myself deeper into the alley. The light faded. I felt an immovable pressure on the top of my head, and obediently bent, then crouched, then crawled, finally squeezing myself through on my naked belly, mask tucked under my pinned arm.

Why did I have to be so *big*?

The walls squeezed inward in a heart-stopping contraction. I gasped, on the edge of panic, and tried to wriggle a little faster. They squeezed again, so hard I felt as if my bones were cracking. I didn't have the air for a scream, only a pathetic whimper that suddenly infuriated me with its helplessness.

"Stupid!" I hissed, and reared upward, ducking my head. My shoulders pounded into the ceiling. Pain flared as my skin tore, but I felt something shift and tried again. The wall definitely recoiled under the blow, and I swung back an elbow strike that skinned half the back of my arm, but made the wall flinch even further away. "Stupid metaphors," I grunted between blows, settling into a rhythm as the walls expanded. "I'm not too big. This is too small!"

I cleared enough space to take a stance and caught my breath. There was dim light now; enough to see the blood that oozed from my scraped body; enough to see the ceiling dip threateningly. "Oh no," I said sweetly. "I know what to do." I twisted into a high kick, and snapped my tensed foot at the ceiling.

It shattered, as delicate as blown glass, shards spinning away into a void. The light failed and the ground dropped away. I was falling again; falling bodiless and blind.

I landed with a thump on something cold and hard, and was scrabbling for balance long seconds before I knew where I'd ended up.

I was sitting on the roof of my parents' house, precariously perched on the central ridge, with my back to the bay. The sun was setting over the hills, shafts of pale yellow light slanting up through the clouds. I was still naked, still sore, still freezing, but for a moment I hunched and shuddered with sheer relief that the horrible journey was over.

I held the mask in one hand and clutched the ridgepole with the other, grinning fiercely. The stainless steel slid under me as I turned to look behind, filled with desperate hope.

Mark wasn't there.

Neither was much of Napier.

Horror froze my throat as I saw the altered skyline; buildings half-collapsed; roofs crumpled obscenely to expose the chaos of their contents. Of the houses on the hill, mine seemed to be the only one untouched. A red rescue helicopter buzzed like a hornet, but the city itself was horribly silent. Only when I strained could I hear the urgent shouts. The shape of the bay had twisted beyond recognition, acres of new, wet land glinting gunmetal gray in the dying light. It looked like the carcass of some massive beast, but even when I squinted, I couldn't see the shape of the great fish.

Hine-nui-te-pō had taken his spirit. Te Ika a Māui was just an island now, and the earthquakes that came after this day would only be earthquakes.

It probably didn't make a lot of difference to the dead.

And I'd failed to bring Mark home.

Numb grief welled up, seeping through my veins and leaking out of my eyes as I sat, calm and desolate. I was too frozen for sobs, too tired for anger.

"Hello, Ms. Spencer," a silky voice put in beside me. "You seem to have misplaced your attire."

I screamed and launched myself at Mr. Sand, the mask clattering down the roof. Whatever kept him midair failed under my added weight. We fell more than floated to the ground, his thick body jerking as I landed on top of him.

"Kill you," I snarled, and went for his throat. His mouth opened and closed on imprecations he couldn't voice, slender fingers clawing at my strong wrists. It was probably the stupidest thing I'd ever done. I was sure he could have killed me with a word. But with my fingers locked around his neck, I wasn't going to let him get the words out.

He was *smiling*.

A huge hand settled on my shoulder and I screamed again, whipping my elbow back.

"Hey, girl!" one of the bikers said, easily deflecting the blow. His remaining brother, or lover, or whatever, stood beside him. Behind their leather-clad bulk, La Gribaldi rested blood-smeared fists on her hips, a dog leash dangling incongruously from her hand.

"She's unstable," Sand wheezed.

I banged his head against the earth.

The biker reached around me, prying my fingers loose, but it took both of them to lift me away. I got one good kick aimed at Sand's chin, but his reflexes snapped in to block it.

He stood slowly, ostentatiously wiping my blood off his immaculate white jacket. "Guest-right has been broken," he said, his voice calm and even again. He wasn't even breathing hard. "I'll take her now."

"He threw me into the mists!" I shouted.

"Oh, darling, naive Ms. Spencer," he purred. "I certainly did. But I didn't directly hurt you or yours—clearly, since you returned to us in all your naked splendor—and *you* just hurt me."

"Breaking guest-right is a great affront, and the penalty dire," Professor Gribaldi said calmly, and Sand smiled his bright, terrible smile. "But someone told the patu-paiarehe when and where to strike. Treachery, also, has consequences."

He went very still. "You accuse me?"

She planted her feet. "I do."

"And your proof?"

She shrugged. "Oh, proof. A story told to a girl betrayed. A drink enchanted to make her want to run, leaving those behind bereft of her birthright strength. A boy running after her with our best hope around his neck, sent to die unde-fended. I suspect I could find some proof if I tried." She lifted the leather leash and stretched it between her dark hands. "Relinquish your claim on Ms. Spencer and I won't try too hard."

He snarled at the leash. "You wouldn't *dare*."

"Would I not? The first Smith made a chain of seven hundred gold rings. I am not him, and this is not that, but diminished as I am, I can yet dare a leash to hold a dog!" She snapped the leather again.

His expression soured.

"Get out, man," the bikers rumbled together, and their power passed through their grip on me like a current, building with every circuit.

Sand took a deep breath, eyes glittering like black glass, and I felt his own stolen power surge. He hadn't had a chance to eat the fish's magic, but it seemed he'd dined well all the same. I held my breath, certain he'd attack.

But I'd forgotten. He'd lived a very long life, and not by picking fights he wasn't certain of winning. Bargains and scavenging on the weak, that was Mr. Sand.

"I forgive the affront of Eleanor Spencer to my rights of guesthood," he said, waving his fingers negligently. "And I do believe it's about time to leave these dreary little islands."

Professor Gribaldi inclined her head. The four of us watched him turn and walk away, a dangerous little man much older than human history.

"Hm," the Professor said after a long minute. "You can have this back, Ms. Spencer."

I stared at the leash she put in my hand. "Isn't it yours?"

"And when would I have had time to make it? I found it in the kennel."

I blurted, "You drove him off with my dead dog's leash?"

319

She nodded, and I finally lost it completely. I sank onto the soft soil, laughing until my gut ached.

Washed and dressed and bandaged, with a belly full of left-overs, I felt something closer to sane.

It had been a cold shower, and there was no electricity to make miraculous pancakes. The phone was dead, and most of the city was in blackout, but the emergency kit under the laundry sink provided candles and a battery radio. I listened long enough to get an idea of the casualties, and switched it off.

"Blaming yourself would be counterproductive," Professor Gribaldi observed.

The quake had run the length of the island, in patterns that baffled seismologists, striking at the beginning of rush hour. The Mt. Victoria Tunnel in Wellington had collapsed on the motorists trapped within. The outside lanes of the Auckland Harbour Bridge had tumbled into the ocean. No one knew anything, but estimates were running as high as thirty thousand dead.

It was a lot better than three million. Still, if I'd been faster, if I'd known more, if I hadn't drunk the water he'd given me—I shook my head, hard. "I know who to blame. I…Is Matiu okay?"

"Not a scratch," she said approvingly. "There's a boy with a future."

The bikers glanced at each other and stood up. "We've got to go," one said. "Find out if the *whānau*'s all right."

I stood too, reminded by this mention of family. "I saw your—the other one of you. On the way."

The one I thought was taller nodded. "He told us."

Every time I thought I had given up the capacity to be surprised, I surprised myself. I turned "How?" into "Oh," and squinted at the two men. The taller one had a nose that spread a little broader and long eyelashes that rivaled Kevin's. The shorter had slightly darker skin and three black moles in a triangle on his cheek. I couldn't tell whether I had changed or they had, but I dropped my eyes when the shorter one met them.

I walked them to the front door, limping on my bandaged feet. "Goodbye. Thank you."

They hugged me in turn, smelling of leather and sweat and salt. I stayed by the open door, listening to the stuttering roar of their cycles dwindle, wishing them unbroken roads and a safe journey.

So I was there when Reka came walking out of the night, still in her black dress and dark glasses, with a cane to guide her over the raw ground until she reached the smooth path that led to the front gate.

I stepped back over the threshold, ready to slam the door and call for La Gribaldi, but she held up her hand. "I mean you no harm," she said. "You have what belongs to me. I want them back."

"Right," I said, remembering, and fumbled at the mask. The greenstone eyes came out easily, eager to return to their owner, and the mask shuddered with relief when they were gone. I held them out to her, then felt like an idiot when she didn't move.

"Hold out your hands," I requested, and carefully placed the eyes in the cup of her palms. She closed her fingers and breathed deeply, but her face stayed remote and calm.

I wanted to ask how she'd come here without them, but there were three good reasons not to: it was probably an inappropriate question, I knew she wouldn't tell me the answer, and there was something more important I had to say.

"Mark died," I said, wishing I had the energy to soften it. "I'm sorry."

She didn't visibly react, still holding the eyes. I didn't know what I'd expected her to do with them, but obviously just shoving them into her eye sockets after my grubby hands had been all over them was out. "Eleanor Spencer...can you see the ocean from here?"

"Uh. No. From the backyard, I can." Of all the weird conversations I had had this long and weary day, this was unquestionably the weirdest. Had she even heard me?

"Go, then, and look to the sea," she said, then hesitated. "Did any of my people survive?"

"I don't know," I said. I was hoping none of them had, but I wasn't going to be that honest when she had her eyes back and I was injured and exhausted. A nasty possibility occurred to me, hard on the heels of that thought. "You gave Kevin up! You can't have him to make more."

"Not him, no," she said absently.

My fist clenched, but my sore muscles protested even that

small motion. The mask was quiet in my hand. "If you touch *anyone*—"

Her teeth glinted. "I have no intention of doing so. For now. Goodbye, Eleanor. Look to the sea."

"Fine," I said shortly. I was tense with waiting for the next catastrophe, but, true to her word, she walked away. When she was out of sight, I shut and locked the door.

I startled when I turned; La Gribaldi was waiting a few steps behind me, massive hammer in her hand. "So that's her."

"Yes."

"Hm," she said, and leaned the hammer against the wall. "Do you think you're up to assisting the Civil Defence Service? People like us can be very useful in times of crisis."

Awful as I felt, there had to be people feeling much worse. "Yes. Just a minute." I walked through the house, turning over Reka's last words. La Gribaldi followed me silently as I threw the back door open and stepped into the yard.

"Okay," I said, mostly to myself. "I'm looking."

My vision abruptly expanded, as if the ocean view was rushing up on me. I swallowed back the vertigo and saw with that part of me that was growing more familiar with use.

There was *something* in the bay, beyond the reef; a long, sinuous shadow gliding through the water. For a moment, moonlight glinted off something that could have been a scale.

"It's a taniwha," I said, wondering why my hands were trembling. Then my brain caught up with my body and I sat down hard on the step. "*Mark?*"

"Ah," La Gribaldi said, sounding surprised and pleased. "Well. I'll start putting together food packages." She squeezed my shoulder, and went back to the kitchen.

I stared past the ruined city and watched him swim through the moon's silver path over the uneasy sea.

Then I got up, and went out into the world, to do what I could.

EPILOGUE—MAYBE TOMORROW

"And you promise you're okay?"

I clutched my new cell phone between shoulder and ear as I sorted my old clothes into piles. "I'm fine, Kevin. I'm doing much better than most people. The main roads are clear, and food's getting through."

"I only ask for the sake of my social life. You're not much of a friend, but you'll do until someone better comes along. So you're really okay?"

I rolled my eyes. "If you don't stop asking me that, I'm

going to figure out a way to punch you over the phone line. You remind me of Mum and Dad."

"Have you heard when they're getting back?"

"Not sure. The airstrip here isn't open to passenger flights. They're flying into Christchurch in a week and driving up. Magda might get here a bit earlier."

"How pissed are they? About you running away from Mansfield and everything?"

I sighed. "Let's just say Magda's looking forward to being the good daughter for the rest of the century."

"Well, you've achieved legendary status here. The last time we had a runaway was Jeremy Chalmers, and he only got as far as Ranfurly."

I groaned. "So now I'm notorious?"

"You're *respected*," he amended. "I would tell everyone that I helped you, just to get the street cred. But I really want the Rutherford Scholarship, and I don't think aiding and abetting counts as good service to the school community." There was some urgent whispering on the other end of the line, and Kevin's voice came back bemused. "Iris says, remember happy endings."

I grinned. "Tell her I miss her too."

"Have you two been talking behind my back?"

I laughed at the indignation in his voice. "Yeah, you'll want to get used to that. Look, Kevin...about the week you gave me to tell you what's been going on."

"It's okay," he said immediately. "Whenever you're ready."

"No, I mean...Iris is going to tell you all about it tomorrow. And you'll really wish she hadn't. But try to keep an open mind, and I'll demonstrate some of the more unbeliev-able bits if my parents ever let me out of their sight again."

"Cryptic," he noted.

"You have no idea. Good luck for opening night. Break two legs." The show would go on. All the profits were going to the quake survivors' benefit.

"Wish you could be here. Love you, Ellie."

"Love you too."

I hung up, and realized that the mask had woken up again, humming at me from its hiding place in the back of the ward-robe. I was going to have to construct a better hiding place than a couple of old blankets; something that would protect the mask from the people who might be very happy to take possession of it, and something that would protect me from the mask. It was a living thing. I couldn't just destroy it.

But as long as I could feel it promising love and endless devotion, it was a very dangerous temptation.

I told it go back to sleep with all the firmness I could mus-ter, and walked into the living room. Hinemoana Simpson was arranging the new donated mattresses on the floor, try-ing to find a way to fit in our three new arrivals.

"I'm going for a walk," I said. I felt guilty every time I saw her, a reminder of what principles I'd compromised. True to my orders, she hadn't called my parents, even after the quake; I'd had to do that myself, choking on the shame.

She nodded, but it was her own nod: a judicious agreement, not a forced compliance. "Good idea. Clear your head."

"How's David?"

"Getting better," she said briefly, and I withdrew without asking more. Her son might never walk again. But when she wasn't at the field hospital, she was here, organizing volunteers and working, every minute, against the destruction that had nearly crushed the city.

Nearly, but not quite.

The last week had taught me a lot about courage. It was time to be brave—brave enough for this final thing. I snagged an apple from the pile on the kitchen table, and set off for the sea.

On most other days, a teenage girl with as many bruises as I had walking past two police officers might have gotten a second look as they wondered where I'd received them. A week after the worst natural disaster in New Zealand's human history, I got a distracted glance and a curt warning to stick to the middle of the street. Unstable buildings still crumbled irregularly, the sound of masonry hitting asphalt enough to start me out of my dreams, sick and shivering on the living room floor.

I'd picked a beautiful day for this meeting. The air was drenched in the Napier winter light that saturated everything with bright color—the white and yellow chunks of painted stone, the orange police tape, the enormous blue sky. Plastic bags and scraps of paper blew about. Every now and then there was something more horrible—photographs, torn pieces of clothing. I might have tried to ignore them once, but now I looked steadily at everything I saw, scratching absently at the needle mark in the crook of my arm. The nurse taking my blood donation hadn't had much time to be gentle.

I took my time wandering down Marine Parade, eating the apple and watching my feet as I negotiated the broken road. I was rehearsing questions and explanations in my head, hoping that I'd get a chance to use any of them.

The bronze statue of Pania of the Reef had fallen off her stone plinth when the quake hit. Someone had lifted her back on, with a black-lettered note scribbled on the back of a supermarket flier: "WARNING: Pania is wobbly!" The ornament in her hair had snapped off and the formerly flowing locks were dented, but she gave the same head-tilted smile to the ocean. I touched her polished hand for luck and for courage, and walked out into the bay.

The newly raised land was strewn with fish carcasses and white patches of salt. I pinched my nose shut, already regretting the apple. The tide was coming in. As I approached the sea, so slowly that it was almost imperceptible from moment to moment, mist began to gather. I waited until it hovered thickly before me, squared my shoulders, and walked into the heart of the fog.

It was the first time I'd met Mark since his transformation.

He sprawled in the shallows, his head planted on the wet sand, watching my approach with opalescent eyes. His scales were a glossy green, undimmed by algae or chipped by time. He didn't have the enormous bulk of his grandfather. *Only as long as a bus*, I thought. Well, clearly that was all right then.

"Hi," he said, through jagged teeth. His voice was the same.

All of my carefully prepared speeches vanished. "Hi,

yourself." I impulsively leaned in to touch his neck, as thick as my torso. He shivered under my hand, a sinuous writhe that shook water free in a clean-smelling spray. I let my hand drop away. "I'm sorry I didn't come here earlier. I've been volunteering at the Civil Defence center at my old primary school. You know their motto?"

"Nope."

"'Lay Well Thy Foundation.'"

"Ironic," he said cautiously.

I shrugged. "I don't know. The school's still there. All of the kids made it."

"Do you—I mean—"

"A lot of people lost everything," I said. "A lot of people died." My cousin Reeve had died in Whangarei, crushed under the roof of his apartment building. Two of my old high school classmates had been killed driving home from hockey practice, and another was clinging to life with the fingernails of her remaining hand. I remembered them, and I grieved, and in the really bad times, the grief was needles in my throat.

The needles were stabbing me now, making my voice hoarse. "I don't think there are many people who didn't lose someone."

"I'm sorry," Mark said, very simply, and I let myself cry for a while, wrapping my arms around myself and wishing they were his.

When I was done and wiping at my swollen eyes with my damp sleeve, he heaved himself a little further onto the sand, tail whipping up clouds of sand as he rose. "I need to tell you again. I'm so sorry I deceived you."

I looked up into the alien face, trying to read emotion from the enormous features. "It doesn't—well, it does matter. But I don't really care right now. Are you okay about… everything?" I gestured at the length of him.

He didn't pretend not to understand. "I hated you," he said. "When I opened my eyes and realized I was breathing underwater, that I was a monster again, I couldn't stand it. I had followed you the whole way, never saying a word, with my hands clamped together so I wouldn't steady you when you stumbled. I stared at the back of your head for hours when all I had to do was reach out and touch your hair. And I came back to this. At least I'd *looked* human before."

I let out a shaky breath. "I'm noticing a lot of past tense."

His lips split to display the jagged array of teeth. After a second, I identified the gesture as a smile. "I kept remembering how you kept going. The muscles jump in your back when you climb over rocks, did you know? It was hard to hate you then.

"And when I worked out that the curse had been broken, and I *still* wasn't human, it was just funny. I laughed so hard I scared a school of tuna away."

My heart clenched. "What?"

"Tuna. Big-ass fish, sharp teeth, very tasty."

"No! The curse! It's broken?"

"Sure," he said. "It was meant to last until death, and I died. Does Sand know I'm back yet? I bet he'll be pissed."

"Shut up," I said, and planted my fists on my hips, staring up into his glorious eyes. "Sand's gone. I love you."

I tensed against the transformation that never came. Mark blinked at me, lipless mouth hanging open over those horrifying teeth.

"I love you too, Ellie," he said, and something quivered under my breastbone, light and beautiful as a butterfly's wings: the immense, ordinary magic of hope.

"Oh, good," I said, and scrubbed at my wet cheeks. "After I'd gone to all that trouble, it'd be a shame if—"

"Shut up, Spencer."

I floundered into the cold water and leaned into his wet body. The scales were softer than they looked, slick and cool against my hands. "This is such a mess."

His laugh rippled right through him. "I think Reka's a step ahead of us."

I jerked back from him. "She's still *here*?"

"No, she's gone back. But she asked grandfather to visit, so that he can teach me how to take a human shape."

I let out my breath in an incredulous laugh and slid down his side to sit in the water, hissing as the cold salt water washed against my raw patches. Mark twisted his neck to watch me, and I felt the easy glide of his muscles against my back. He was stronger than me now. And still beautiful.

He hesitated. "She's matchmaking, you realize. She can't take Kevin, and she knows she'll have to fight to take anyone else. Maybe she'll settle for grandchildren."

"*Grandchildren?* I'm seventeen!"

"Her view, not mine." he said. "Anyway, the change takes a long time to learn."

I exhaled. "Well, I can't exactly pose on a window-seat and wait for you. If my parents don't make me stay in Napier and Mansfield doesn't expel me, I'm thinking about doing Classics at Canterbury. Iris wants to direct *A Winter's Tale* for February Orientation." I paused. "And La Gribaldi wants to give me some extracurricular tuition. She said I did a good job. Can I trust her?"

He tilted his head. "You could do a lot worse. 'You did a good job,' is Gribaldi-speak for, 'You saved the day.'"

"No," I said flatly. "Hine-nui-te-pō did that."

Mark flicked the end of his tail. It tapered into delicate membranes that flashed greens and yellows through the sand. "What was she like?"

My memories of the guardian of the dead were mostly mist by now. I'd been shocked and injured, and the mask had been whispering in my head. And I wasn't sure if humans were supposed to remember the gods too clearly. But I remembered the fury of her breath, the anger in her eyes, the glad rush of Te-Ika-a-Māui to her embrace. I didn't know if her guardianship extended to me, but if it did, I might see her again, one hopefully far-off day. It wasn't an unwelcome thought. "She was beautiful. Beautiful, and scary, and strong."

"Sounds like this girl I know," he said, and didn't even have the courtesy to pretend my mock-punch hurt.

I rubbed my cheek against his neck. "Summer will be here in six months, and I'll be home for Christmas. Lots of long, bright days. Barbecues. Walks on the beach."

There was guarded hope in his voice. "So I guess we'll see what happens?"

"I guess we will." I leaned against his cool weight and, smiling, closed my eyes.

I was thinking about happy endings.

Afterword

Māori mythology and cosmology are infinitely richer and more complex than could be presented in this novel. The Polynesian peoples who settled New Zealand (also called Aotearoa, or Aotea) brought with them the faith, myths, and family legends of their origin lands. Over time, some of the original stories altered to accommodate New Zealand's unique ecology, landscape, and culture, and some entirely new stories were created. Old, adapted, and new stories were handed down through artwork and oral storytelling for centuries, and some were eventually recorded by the new technology of writing brought by the European settlers, generally accompanied by translations and publicized to a mostly European audience. Especially in their earliest written recordings, these stories were often substantially altered in their translation for an English-reading audience, while being presented as "genuine" Māori legends.

Guardian of the Dead is obviously not a "genuine" Māori legend, but because those original stories were adapted and the adaptations went unnoted for an uninformed audience, I think it's important to point out where I have stuck to the translations and traditions I had available, and where I have, to the best of my knowledge, altered or extrapolated. (I also took some liberties with history and geography: most notably, Mansfield College does not exist, and there are no stone steps up the cliffs at Te-Kauae-o-Māui/Cape Kidnappers.) When Mark tells the legends of Papa-tuanuku, Rangi-nui, and their children, the deeds of Māui, the story of Hine-nui-te-pō, and the story of Pania of the Reef, he is telling stories based on those popular translations. When Ellie goes through the library stacks looking for information on patupaiarehe, she finds a lot of what I did researching for this novel. However, Mark, Reka, and Mark's grandfather, while representing real mythological creatures, are themselves invented, and I have wandered a little from the popular portrayals of patupaiarehe and taniwha.

The legendary patupaiarehe (or *tūrehu* or *tiramāka*, or other names, depending on the region the story comes from) are sometimes depicted as dangerous kidnappers or otherworldly and threatening figures. They are also said to be attractive tricksters, or a shy and beautiful people who make excellent spouses for humans provided certain requirements are met. For consistency of narrative, I have gone with the scarier versions, but the other stories exist. That the patupaiarehe have eyes of *pounamu* (greenstone) is my invention, and while they are often depicted as beautiful and persuasive, as far as I know, the idea that they can be magically so is another stretch on my part, although the power of the spoken or chanted word is emphasized in Māori culture. Eyes, and the head in general, are *tapu* (sacred) in the Māori tradition. Food is *noa*, or unsacred. To despoil the head or eyes, especially by associating them with food, is an act of grotesque disrespect for the previous owner, and eating portions of the head was considered a consumption of the knowledge and *mana* (power) of the dead.

Although considered by many people to be purely mythological, taniwha are also said to be tangible physical and spiritual presences. Whether you believe this or not, taniwha have a real impact on New Zealand life; in 2002, for example, road works in the Waikato region were halted while transit authorities consulted with local Māori over the location of several taniwha near the route. In the stories, some taniwha can take many shapes to look like floating logs or driftwood, whales, eels, giant tuatara, or toothy water-serpents, and some taniwha are formerly dead humans, returned to protect their people and land. As far as I'm aware, the possibility of those taniwha taking their former human shape is my own twist on the tale, although other Māori monsters (such as the giant lizard-like *ngārara*) have demonstrated that ability. My descriptions of Mark and his grandfather are based on the more serpent-like taniwha depictions, especially bone and marae post carvings, which often show taniwha with sinuous curves and inset eyes of paua shell.

If you're interested in reading more about Māori mythology and cosmology, I especially recommend: *Traditional Māori Stories: He Kōrero Māori* (introduced and translated by Margaret Orbell) and *The Illustrated Encyclopedia of Māori Myth and Legend*, also edited by Orbell; the *Reed Book of Māori Mythology* by A.W. Reed and Ross Calman; and *Wahine Toa: Women of Māori Myth* by Patricia Grace and Robin Kahukiwa. If you'd like to read more young adult fiction that draws on Māori mythology as inspiration for contemporary stories, Witi Ihimaera's *The Whale Rider* and Joanna Orwin's *The Guardian of the Land* are fantastic. Gaelyn Gordon's *Stonelight* and the sequel *Mindfire* are contemporary fantasy adventures that show the patupaiarehe in a much more positive light. Dylan Horrocks's graphic novel *Hicksville* features Te Ika a Māui (very much alive) and is just generally wonderful. If you can get your hands on it, I also recommend the excellent television horror/drama series *Mataku*, where contemporary New Zealanders encounter the Māori supernatural — much of it is based on stories maintained in the oral tradition rather than those recorded in writing.

Finally, I caution the reader against drawing parallels between the mythological constructs depicted here and contemporary Māori society. This novel is greatly indebted to Māori mythology and draws on some points of traditional Māori social and religious custom: it touches only very lightly on the diverse cultures, politics, and history of modern Māori life, and that only as seen through the eyes of a seventeen-year-old Pākehā woman, who is very far from being a reliable narrator.

Glossary

New Zealand has three official languages: English, Māori, and New Zealand Sign Language. Māori is a language for study as a first or second language at many schools and tertiary institutions, but a number of Māori words are commonly understood, and are not unusual for even non-speakers (like Ellie) to use in everyday circumstances.

If you want to learn more about the language, I recommend Kōrero Māori (http://www.korero.maori.nz/) as an excellent starting point.

Haka: Traditional group dance, performed by men, women or mixed groups, accompanied by chanted words. Many schools and institutions have their own official *haka;* the most well-known internationally is probably the one most often performed by the New Zealand rugby team before international matches.

Hongi: A greeting where the noses are pressed against each other, signifying respect and welcome with the sharing of breath.

Iwi: A Māori people, analogous to a tribe, usually made up of various *hapu*, or sub-tribes. Each iwi claims ancestry to one of the original *waka* (canoes) that carried the first settlers.

Kapa haka: A performance displaying traditional Māori performance skills, including *haka*, *poi* dancing, and several styles of singing. *Kapa haka* groups comprise individuals linked in some way (for instance, by iwi or institution) and exist in many high schools.

Kaumātua: A respected elder, chosen by the people, with great status, wisdom, and expertise in at least one area of traditional knowledge, such as genealogy or oratory.

Kia ora: Literally "be healthy," this is a fairly informal greeting, the equivalent of "Hi."

Koru: Literally, an unfurling new fern frond. *Koru* patterns, important in Māori and Māori-influenced art, echo this curved shape.

Marae: A meeting place, central to community life and identity. Various protocols and instances of tapu surround the proper use of the marae complex.

Mere: A short, teardrop-shaped club, carved from bone, wood, or stone. Mere made from greenstone are especially valuable.

Moko: Moko are traditional tattoos, most often applied to the face, thighs, and buttocks (men) and chin and lips (women), by a tattoo machine or in the traditional *tā moko* method, which involves slicing the skin in patterns and rubbing pigment into the cuts. They can convey ancestry, status, and the completion of rites of passage. Non-Māori traditionally cannot wear or apply moko; "tribal" styles that are aesthetically influenced by tā moko are actually *kiri tuhi* ("skin art") designs.

Ngāi Tahu: (Also *Kai Tahu.*) The principal South Island iwi.

Pākehā: Usually refers to New Zealanders of predominantly white European ancestry. Also sometimes used to refer to non-Māori of any ethnicity.

Taiaha: A long club, about five feet long, with a blunt clubbing end and a pointed stabbing end.

Taonga: A treasured thing, tangible or intangible, culturally or personally significant. The Māori language is a taonga, for example, as are pieces of land, or physical heirlooms like dogskin cloaks.

Tapu: The concept of *tapu* applies to especially sacred and protected things, places, knowledge, or people. Tapu means a "restriction" has been placed and this can be permanent or temporary. Breaking tapu (often by touching or approaching) can carry serious spiritual consequences. Today tapu is most often observed in circumstances of sickness, death, and burial, and areas of land or people can become "restricted" as a consequence, keeping others safe from harm.

Tupuna: (Also *tipuna*.) Ancestors.

Whānau: Family, including extended family. Several whānau often make up hapu, which make up iwi.

Acknowledgements

I am indebted to many, many people, not all of whom I can mention, but all of whom I remember.

First, I owe a great deal to the storytellers who made and handed down the myths I make use of in this story. I was fortunate to have Lauana Thomas, Olive Roundhill, and Dr. Jane McRae lend their cultural expertise and advice on various portions of the manuscript; any remaining errors are mine.

My thanks to Holly Black, Libba Bray, Delia Sherman, Dawn Metcalf, Becca Fitzpatrick, and Stephanie Burgis for encouragement and inspiration, and to the Tenners for sharing those debut author jitters with so much style and fun.

I'm grateful for my first readers: Tui, Jeff, Willow, Carla, Betty, Rachel, Gina, Terry, Jameson, and my mother, Mary. They caught innumerable problems and wielded the clue-stick with enthusiasm. Special thanks to Robyn for always reading, over and over (and over!) again.

I have an amazing editing team, who have made me look so much smarter than I really am: Alvina Ling, Connie Hsu, and Melanie Sanders at Little, Brown, and Eva Mills, Susannah Chambers, and Nicola McCloy at Allen and Unwin. I'm lucky to have my most excellent agent, Barry Goldblatt, and his English counterpart, the wonderful Nancy Miles.

Finally, my thanks to the University of Canterbury and its Drama Society, for five great years and oh so much material.

Reading Group Guide

1   Mark asks Ellie early in the novel, "Do you know what you are? What you could be?" (page 16). Who is Ellie at the beginning of this book? Who has she become by the end?

2   Ellie grew up in the North Island of New Zealand and attends school in the South Island. What does she think are the important differences between the islands?

3   Professor Gribaldi thinks that New Zealand students don't work as hard as American Advanced Placement students, while Ellie thinks that working too hard could be dangerous. What are some differences between the New Zealand and American educational systems? Why might those differences exist?

4   Ellie buys a mask at an outdoor market. What attracts her to this seemingly simple object? How does she discover its power? How does it help her save her homeland?

5   Who are the *patupaiarehe*? What do they want? What role do they play in the Eyeslasher murders?

6   Discuss Mark's complicated relationship with his parents. How does he look after them? How do they look after him? Are there similarities between Mark's relationship with his parents and Ellie's relationship with hers? If so, what are they?

7   Mark calls himself "all in-between" and "a chimera" (page 148). What does he mean by that? What is the bargain he makes with Mr. Sand? How does he try to betray Ellie?

8   Who is the guardian of the dead? Why can't Ellie lie to her?

9   "Stories change us; they change the world," says Professor Gribaldi. "People are stories of themselves" (page 267). How do stories shape the way Ellie sees her world? How do they shape the way you see yours?

Don't miss

THE
SHATTERING

The thrilling new novel from
Karen Healey

Coming in September 2011

Turn the page for a sneak peek.

CHAPTER ONE

Keri

⚡

THE FIRST TIME I BROKE MY ARM, I WAS READY
for it.

I was seven years old, and Janna van der Zaag and I were
playing in her backyard. Janna's backyard was a fantastic place
for kids — a big dollhouse and a lot of bush out back for playing hide-and-seek in and a brand-new zip line her dad had
made, sloping from a tall platform built into the sturdiest
tree down to a brace attached to the next sturdiest.

Janna had been using the zip line for days, and she flew
down with style, blond hair like a banner, the T-bar gripped

tightly in her hands. I climbed the ladder and clung there as she ran the T-bar back up to me on its long rope. The zip line hadn't seemed so high up from the ground.

What if I fell off and broke my arm? I thought. And I mean I really thought. I pictured it in my mind, working out the way it could happen and what I should do if it did. I decided that a bone would go *crunch* or *crack*, and I would sit up and cradle my arm and yell, "Janna, get your mum!" and then go to the doctor in the family's big blue van that fit all the van der Zaag kids for Sunday Mass.

Then I opened my eyes, grabbed the T-bar, and took off flying all the way down the wire, screaming laughter at the rush of flight. My landing was perfect, and I ran the T-bar back up to Janna for her turn, heart jumping with joy and terror.

My body was so free.

On the fourth time down the line, my palms were too sweaty. They slipped, I fell, my left arm went *crack*, and I yelled, "Janna, get your mum!" before her big blue eyes could even fill with tears.

Everyone praised me for being so brave, but I had still been scared. I had only known what to do if the worst happened.

After that, it just seemed a good idea to be prepared. I hung a go-bag on my door in case of a fire or an earthquake and put a mini first-aid kit in my backpack, and I rehearsed possible disasters in my head, over and over, until I was sure I knew how to react.

I knew it sounded a little bit crazy, and I stopped telling anyone about it when Hemi Koroheke called me creepy and, with smug emphasis, neurotic, which was our Year Eight Word of the Day.

But I did it anyway. I had plans for what eulogy to give if both my parents were hit by a car, how to escape or attract help if I were kidnapped, and how to survive if I were lost in the bush. It wasn't as if I thought all these things were likely to happen. But I knew they could, and if they did, I wanted to be ready.

In the end, it didn't do me any good. Because I didn't have a plan for what to do if my older brother put Dad's shotgun in his mouth and pulled the trigger with his toes.

My mistake.

I found Jake — I mean, I found the body — but I don't remember that. A couple of weeks later I couldn't find my favorite pair of jeans, and Mum said she threw them out because of the blood, and I suddenly remembered the feeling of something heavy in my lap. I might have imagined it — I don't know. But I think it was real, that memory of wet weight across my thighs.

That's it, though.

Jake killed himself and he didn't leave a note, and I lost bits of my memory and my favorite pair of jeans. I'll never get a pair like those again — they don't make that style anymore. They were scuffed in all the right places and cut to fit my short legs and big bum, and they were comfortable and a choice faded dark blue that looked good with everything.

That's not a metaphor. I loved those jeans.

I loved my brother more. Jake was my favorite person — my best friend, my first supporter, the last one to get angry with me when I said something that was just too sarcastic. At nineteen, he was two years older than me, but we weren't one of those sibling pairs who hated each other as kids and then hit adolescence and got along. We'd always been that close. My first word was *Chay*.

There had been no warning. He didn't give away his possessions or say things like "It'll all be over soon." His girlfriend, Sandra-Claire, swore up and down that he didn't act depressed or fight with her, and even though she is a heinous bleached and bony bitch who told me that if I kept cutting my hair short everyone would think I was a lesbian (and she didn't say *lesbian*), I believed that Jake hadn't done any of that stuff, because I knew he would have told me first.

I knew what to do if someone you love showed signs of suicide, because we'd studied it in Health. It's a myth that people who talk about it aren't going to do it; 74 percent of suicides give a warning sign of some kind, and if Jake had ever mentioned it, I would have had a plan. A plan for what to say, how to tell Mum and Dad, what to do if he did it and failed, what to do if he did it and succeeded, what to do if he did it and succeeded and I found the body. But he didn't and I didn't, and it happened anyway. It made no sense at all.

It was a lot easier to think about how irrational Jake's killing himself was than to think about how my insides had been ripped out.

Because Jake's death was a suicide, we nearly didn't get to hold a proper *tangi*, in case all the celebration and ceremony for the dead encouraged other kids to copy him. But I think Nanny Hinekura put her foot down, and all the family on Dad's side turned up at the *marae* farther down the coast. It was three days of people crowding around us and talking about Jake. All the stories: how he'd bagged his first deer; how he'd gotten his first swimming medal by crashing into the end of the pool; how one Christmas he'd played Play-Station for twenty-one hours against any cousin who'd take him on, and he'd fallen asleep in front of the TV, thumbs still twitching. I liked the stories a lot better than the formal speeches, which were mostly in Māori. I'm all for valuing our cultural heritage and that, and I'd taken Māori for two years to make Nanny Hinekura happy, but it turned out I was just no good at languages.

Jake was much better. He would have translated for me.

The mourners cried and laughed and talked—so much noise, everyone saying "Jake, Jake, Jake," echoing the way my heart beat out his name. When everyone slept, on the mattresses spread out under the high carved rafters of the *wharenui* roof, I could feel the thick emotion leeching out of them, sticking to my skin like steam. I was surrounded by love, but it felt like I was smothered by it. I'd been at tangi before and watched grieving families take comfort. But I couldn't. Not with Jake in the closed coffin beside us instead of sitting with me, adding his own stories to this mix.

I gripped Mum's hand, very pale in mine, and didn't let go.

Once we went back to Summerton, I didn't go to school for the last bit of the year—there was no point with the Christmas holidays coming so soon, and I got compassionate consideration on all my final assessments anyway. Mum cleaned the house as if she would die if she didn't, and Dad had to go back to work. I walked a lot, trying to avoid people who would say useless, comforting things, like "Well, I'm sure he's in a better place."

I couldn't believe any of that crap. The room he'd died in had been blessed and a farewell *karakia* chanted, but Jake wasn't going to take the long trip to Cape Reinga to find the home of Dad's ancestors. He wasn't in heaven with some white-bearded God. He wasn't hanging around, keeping an eye on me. And he sure couldn't do all three, which was what Nanny Hinekura seemed to believe. Those were just stories, things people made up to make the world nicer. How did they know? Where was the proof?

No, Jake was dead. He wasn't in a better place. Everything left of him was in the ground, where it would rot.

Two weeks after the burial, I was in Summerton's only department store, trying to find a replacement pair of jeans. Janna van der Zaag walked up to me and said, "If you want to find out who murdered your brother, follow me."

So I did.

Janna was cute and short when she was seven. Now she was tall and skinny and gorgeous in a perky blond-and-milky-complexion way, which was probably one of the reasons why she put on eye makeup like she was painting the house and dyed her hair every two weeks (right now it was shiny purple-black) and wore black velvet blazers and plaid skirts.

The other reason was that she was in a band.

She looked right at home in the alley between Lauer's Department Store and Mimi's Muffins, leaning up against the redbrick wall behind the trash-filled Dumpster, wanting to talk to me about murder.

"Hi, Stardust," I said. "I thought you only came out at night, with the other vampires." Ever since primary school, everyone had called Janna Stardust: van der Zaag → Zigzag →Ziggy Stardust → Stardust. So it's not actually a cool nickname, but she acts like it is.

Normally this is the sort of thing that gets me a reputation for being a bitch, but Janna didn't seem to care that I'd just called her a bloodsucking creature of the night. She probably thought it was a compliment.

"Do you believe me?" she said. "About the murder?"

I looked at my fingernails, all bitten down to raw nubs. "Not yet. But it makes sense."

She nodded. "No note, right? No warning?"

My interest sharpened. "Right."

"I knew it. Exactly the same thing happened to Schuyler."

I very nearly said, "Who's Schuyler?" but then my brain got in the way. Schuyler was Janna's older brother. He'd killed himself ten years ago by hanging himself in the garage. It happened about three weeks after I broke my arm on the zip line.

"Someone murdered your brother?" I said instead, and Janna nodded again, tugging at her collar with black-painted fingernails. Hers weren't bitten at all.

"And yours."

I leaned my head to one side. "Huh."

"You're weirdly calm about this," she said.

"I'll cry later," I told her. She rolled her eyes, so she might have thought I was being sarcastic, but I was telling the truth. I felt like a girl-shaped open sore, walking through a world made up of salt and lemon juice. But there was a limit to how much anyone could cry in public, and I'd reached that limit at the tangi, tears rolling down my face while the aunties clustered around me.

I refocused. "If you think they were murdered, shouldn't you go to the police?"

She laughed. "In this town? I don't know who the murderer is, but he'd know I'd been talking in about ten minutes. Twenty, tops." She made a gesture at her throat. "And then I might 'suicide.'"

She had a point, even if she was being typically melodramatic about it. It didn't take long for gossip to get around Summerton.

"I want you to meet someone," she said.

"Who?"

"This guy I know. He gets here from Auckland tomorrow."

I choked on a laugh. "Wait, he's a tourist?"

"Sione's a good guy!" she said, really defensively, as if being a tourist and being a good guy were normally mutually exclusive. As far as I could tell, they were. Summerton is a tourist town. People got worried a while ago when an earthquake destroyed the famous limestone Steps to Heaven, which stood just off the coast, but the tourists keep coming every summer, and the money keeps rolling in. In fact, there are more tourists now than ever before. Other towns on the coast have lost young people to the cities and old people to retirement. Thanks to the tourists, Summerton's still going strong.

But no one actually likes the tourists, though people like Janna are happy to party with them. In my experience, most of the tourists are rich snobs, and the ones our age are only interested in surfing, snogging people of the opposite gender (mostly other tourists), and leaving puddles of vomit drying on the streets for me to dodge when I did my paper route.

"He lost someone, too," Janna said.

"Has he looked under the couch?" I asked.

Janna gave me a look that said I wasn't following the script and then proved she had a sense of humor by giggling. But she looked guilty afterward. "Are you doing okay?" she asked, and her voice was soft and kind.

Up until then, I had been just about enjoying the conversation. Sure, Jake had been a big part of it, like every other conversation I'd had for the past few weeks. But Janna hadn't bothered to keep her voice low and her gestures gentle, or even, right up to that point, ask me how I was.

"How do you think I feel?" I said.

"How I felt," she said. "How Sione feels."

I rocked back on my heels and considered it.

"We'll meet tomorrow at the Kahawai to show you something," she said. "Eight PM. Okay?"

"Okay."

"Well," she said, and made a sort of uncertain gesture. "And...I can't believe I didn't start by telling you that I'm really sorry. Because I am."

"It's okay. We're not exactly friends."

"Well, we used to be. And Jake was always nice to me."

Jake was always nice to everyone. I took a deep, deep breath against the hurt and the tears. "See you tomorrow."

Other people might have tried to hug me, but Janna just nodded and walked away, the thick soles of her red platform shoes making no sound on the asphalt. I sniffled for a while, then took more deep breaths of leftover-food stink. How could anyone wear black velvet in this weather? She must have been sweating like a pig under all that makeup.

I wondered if she was pulling some kind of joke. I didn't really know much about her now, and people change a lot from when they were seven. We didn't play pretend anymore; I played rugby, and she played bass. Not that you couldn't do both, but we didn't. We were in the same English class (I was okay; she sucked), and we knew each other enough to say "Hi" and "Good game" and "Good gig."

That was about it.

But I was pretty sure she wouldn't do this to me, not after Schuyler. Her intense face had said she believed every word coming out of her mouth. So she was delusional or had been fooled by this Sione guy—or she was right. Jake had been murdered.

I scrubbed my eyes with my T-shirt hem. I didn't have what I'd come for, but I didn't want to go back to Lauer's and buy inferior jeans from Candace Green or let anyone in Summerton see me and think, *That poor Keri, she's been crying again.*

I had to get through the holidays. The holidays and then one more year of school and the holidays again. Then I could get out of here. Go to uni in Dunedin, or head to London for a working holiday, or anything to get away from Summerton and the room I couldn't go into and the memory of Jake laughing all over town and heavy and wet in my lap.

I rode home with the sun on my back, warm through my T-shirt. It rains a lot on the West Coast—outsiders joke that it should be called the Wet Coast—but Summerton has the kind of summers you read about in books. Long, warm, dry days, perfect for swimming or lazing around with a book or doing a bit of a hike in the green and shady bush. But maybe not so good for biking along Iron Road, up the hill, past the fancy hotels and time-share apartments, to the places where real people actually lived. There was sweat pooling unpleasantly at the base of my spine.

I coasted down the concrete driveway, leaned the bike against the garage, and slammed my way into the kitchen. I needed a shower, a cold drink, and some quiet to think about what Janna had said.

Mum was waiting for me, still in her clean white blouse and black trousers, but her sleek, blond hair was falling out of its French knot, and her eyes had that red pinched look.

"Where have you been?" she snapped.

"I went to buy jeans."

"You didn't tell me you were going out!"

"You were at work."

"You could have dropped in. You have to tell me when you go places, Keri!"

"No, I don't," I said, and she reached across the kitchen island and slapped me. I stared at her for a moment, then slapped her back.

"Oh, *God*," she said, and spun away to lean over the counter.

"I won't do it, Mum," I said. "Not ever." *Damn Jake anyway*, I thought, and then felt guilty for the rage. My hand was stinging, and pain and anger and guilt went around and around in my brain. Grief was so exhausting.